Chasing Chaos

a novel

*For the Crosses,
I hope you enjoy getting
to know Daphne.*

Katie Rose

KATIE ROSE GUEST PRYAL

7/19/2016

velvet morning
press

Published by Velvet Morning Press

ISBN-13: 978-0692621004
ISBN-10: 0692621008

Cover design by Ellen Meyer and Vicki Lesage
Author photo by Chris Guest Adigun

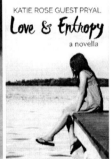

For Michael, Adrian and Edward

Prologue

Daphne ran through the emergency entrance of Cedars-Sinai hospital, once again wondering if someone she loved was going to be alive when she got there. She dashed through the sliding glass doors, through the metal detectors, past the guards.

Moments later, she arrived on the surgical floor. A nurse informed her that the surgery could take a while. Hours even. It could take hours before she knew whether she'd caused the death of someone close to her.

Whether tonight she'd set in motion the dangerous actions that had put two people in the hospital and one person in an operating room fighting for life.

She couldn't stand herself. Self-blame nearly suffocated her.

After minutes or hours—Daphne couldn't tell—the surgical nurse emerged from the wide double doors.

Daphne glanced at her watch. That couldn't be right. She had only been waiting thirty minutes. Thirty minutes that had felt eternal, but thirty minutes nonetheless.

Daphne fixed her eyes on the nurse's face as she reached behind her head to untie her mask. And then another person caught Daphne's attention. Another person passed through the doors, wearing darker scrubs and a floral surgical cap. The way this new woman carried herself, Daphne could tell she was the surgeon.

Daphne could infer what it meant when the surgeon came out after thirty minutes of surgery. Someone had died.

No one else was in the waiting room but Daphne.

They were sorry to inform her. They did all they could. The damage was too severe, especially to the cervical spine and skull.

The surgeon asked Daphne if she had information about next of kin.

"Next of kin?" Daphne asked.

They needed to notify the family. They thought Daphne might have contact information. But there's no rush, the surgeon said. If they have to wait till morning to make the call, that's OK.

Daphne tried to imagine waiting until morning to hear about a loved one who had been dead all night.

Dead, and no one knowing except the woman who had caused it to happen.

April 2005

One

Daphne eased from the bed, her slim limbs barely casting shadows across the floor of the man's studio apartment. The spring sunrise shone through the security metalwork bolted to the bedroom windows. His walls were white, spare. On the floor, here and there, leaned framed images waiting to be hung.

Daphne located her panties—plain, black—and her dress—long, blue. She held her sandals so she could move quietly. A rustle sounded from the bed. She turned. The man propped his head on his hand, his elbow on the mattress, eyeing her. She stood straighter, facing him.

"Leaving so soon?" he asked.

"I have a meeting."

"On a Sunday?"

"I told you I'm a freelancer."

"Can I see you again?"

"Sure." Her bag sat on the man's kitchen counter, where she'd left it the night before. She passed over her business cards tucked in their pocket. She pulled out a notebook instead. She wrote a name, Akane, and a phone number one digit off from her own. She tore the page from the notebook and handed it to him.

He leaned back and held the paper in both hands, reading

it, cradling it, a young Jim Hawkins with his treasure map. If only he knew it held false coordinates.

Daphne dropped her sandals to the floor and slipped them on.

"Bye, Akane," the man said.

His name was John. If she could help it, she would never see him again.

She smiled at him as she lifted her bag over her shoulder.

Once the door shut behind her, Daphne released a deep sigh.

Although Los Angeles as a city was large, Brentwood, her neighborhood, and the film industry, her industry, could both be quite small. Giving a fake name to a man might seem risky. But she'd done it many times without trouble.

She'd only had one close brush. She'd been buying groceries at a market on San Vicente. She and one of these men like John, a man named Andrew, had reached for the same carton of eggs. She'd recognized Andrew immediately, of course. Daphne never forgot a face. But she'd kept moving placidly, placing an egg carton in her basket and turning toward the cheese.

"Wait—are you Akane?" Andrew asked, stumbling over the pronunciation of the name.

She gave him a skeptical look, one that a woman gives to a guy who is using a cheap line.

"No, wait," Andrew said, as she backed away. "We've met. I'm sure of it."

"We haven't met," Daphne said, keeping her voice as crisp as the morning air outside.

Daphne could see Andrew's frustration as he began to doubt himself. She felt bad for him. "My name is not Akane. If it wouldn't be creepy I'd show you my driver's license."

"But, like, six weeks ago, at Mija's—"

Daphne shook her head, putting pity in her eyes. "There are a lot of Asian women in Los Angeles," she said and left him standing alone by the yogurt.

❦

She skipped down the steps leading away from John's apartment, making her early morning escape. It wasn't that she never wanted to see John again in particular. Last night wasn't about John at all. He'd just had a role to play.

Lately, she'd felt restless. She'd felt restless with her current scripts (she always worked on two at a time) and with her boyfriend, Dan. She knew she could just dump Dan. But she also knew that dumping him would hurt him, and she didn't want to hurt him. He was a nice person, despite his flaws. Dan was another freelance screenwriter like she was. In fact, he was the reason she'd had the courage to go freelance in the first place and leave behind studio life. She would always be grateful to him.

She climbed into her car and drove the short distance back to her condo on Montana.

She was happy to be out of the studios. The studios created monsters, men with gigantic egos who thought they could do anything, to anyone, and get away with it. She'd seen it happen.

She pulled into the garage under her condo and shut the garage door behind her. She'd bought the condo after her first freelance scripts sold big a few years ago. She'd had enough money for a down payment and got a great mortgage rate on the rest, a monthly amount she could pay alone even though she had two bedrooms and two parking spaces. The building still showed its early 1970s genetics, but Daphne didn't mind. That was LA—a hodgepodge of classy and derelict and disco. And she loved it.

From her home she could walk to all the shops and restaurants on San Vicente and Montana. As much as she loved to drive, she loved to walk on cool mornings with her laptop in her leather satchel and sit in a small corner where she could watch people and write.

Somehow, after everything that had happened five years ago, and everything that had happened since, she'd found, if not happiness, at least peace.

She thought of Dan as she climbed her stairs. This was the

fourth time she'd cheated on him, finding an anonymous man to spend the night with and then leave behind. Each time, she'd sought to bury her restlessness in a stranger's bed. She wasn't *in* love with Dan, no, but she cared deeply for him, and she loved having someone to share ideas with, someone to cook dinner for.

And, she suspected, he wasn't always faithful to her either.

She entered her apartment and firmly locked the door behind her. After what had happened to Greta and her five years ago, she was meticulous with locks. Back then they'd been girls. That December five years ago, Greta had been twenty-two and Daphne twenty-three, both of them only a year out of college. But that crisis made them grow up fast. Greta, her college roommate, best friend, and sister in spirit— had almost died because of Daphne's carelessness.

No. Because of Daphne's curse.

She set her keys on the midcentury sideboard that stood in the foyer. In fact, all of the furniture in her apartment, with a few exceptions, was from the midcentury era. The furniture was easy to find at estate sales and at the thrift stores that stood near higher-end neighborhoods like her own. It was amazing what people would throw away. The sideboard, for instance, she'd picked up for free in front of a house in Laurel Canyon. The homeowners had set it out with the trash. She'd stood next to it until Greta had come with her pick-up truck to help her bring it home.

Sure, the top surface had needed refinishing in a bad way, but she'd done that in her second parking space one Saturday. Now, everyone who walked into her apartment remarked on it.

Even her large sofa was midcentury. Greta had picked out the sofa back when they'd been roommates. When Daphne had moved into this place, the only furniture in the living room was the sofa, a glaring reminder of what she'd done to Greta. Over the months and years, she'd acquired everything else to match it.

Greta had taught her all about midcentury furniture. Greta liked its simplicity. The straight legs. The large, functional drawers. Greta was—or had been, since she'd softened a bit over the years—all about function.

At the thought of Greta, Daphne checked her watch. She was meeting her friend for brunch before noon and needed to get ready.

She slipped off her sandals, adding to the pile of shoes next to the door. She set her bag on the sofa, which was upholstered in brilliant orange vinyl (an inevitable conversation starter). Then she walked behind the island into the kitchen and set a pot of coffee to brew.

She started pulling off her clothes as she entered her bedroom. She threw her dress on her bed and kicked her underwear to the dirty clothes pile in the corner. Daphne had always been a slob, though these days she tried to restrain her mess to her bedroom.

In the shower, she thought again of John. She'd encountered him the night before at Nick's, a club in Santa Monica. Earlier in the evening, Daphne had met some old friends from Sony there, and they'd sat in the courtyard around a fire pit under the small palm trees. The other women had ended the night early because they had to be on set at six in the morning. As they left, Daphne once again knew she'd made the right choice leaving her job. Daphne had decided to stay at the club. Her restlessness had been eating at her for a couple of weeks. Last night it had her fully in its grip.

She'd headed toward the bar. As she approached, two men stood up and ceded their barstools to her. She sat on one stool and motioned to one of the men—John—to sit down next to her again. The other man surrendered the contest, wandering off in search of easier prey.

John was handsome in a perfunctory way. Tall, well built. Brown hair and eyes, nothing out of the ordinary. Late twenties, like she was.

Perfect.

"I'm new in town," John said. "You?"

"I've lived here for years."

"You don't look old enough to have lived here for years."

Men often thought Daphne looked young. They also often underestimated her. She used both of these mistakes to her advantage.

"Nevertheless," she said.

"Did you go to college here or something?"

"I didn't."

"What do you do?" he asked.

"I freelance."

He smiled ruefully, as though he were beginning to understand the lay of things. "Would you like to know what I do?"

"We could talk about work, if you really wanted to."

"Or we could not talk about work."

Daphne smiled and pulled her valet ticket from her purse. "Let's get our cars."

She didn't want to know about him. About any of them. It was easier that way.

John drove a Toyota Camry, the everyman's car, and that made her happy. He was even easier to forget with his anonymous automobile to match his ordinary features.

She followed him to an apartment building north of Brentwood. It was nice enough, but not too nice, and he waited for her by the exterior door, holding it open for her, leading her down the hall to his apartment. The studio was large enough for a bed and a small sitting area, but not for a table. She supposed he ate at the bar extending from the kitchen counter, dividing the narrow cooking area from the rest of the space.

"Do you want a drink?" he asked.

"Do you have beer?"

He opened the fridge and gazed inside for a moment, as though contemplating his selections. He pulled out two different beers and offered her a choice.

"Wow. I'd love the Allagash," she said.

He popped the lids on both bottles and took the one she didn't choose.

"Cheers," he said, tipping his bottle's neck toward her. She tapped it with her own, then drained half the beer. She set it on the counter next to her bag. Then she kicked off her sandals. She held out her hand, peering up at him.

Dan always told her she had Disney Princess eyes.

"That's why I can't help but do what you tell me to," Dan

said to her. "No man can say no to Ariel. To Belle. To Princess Daphne."

ೂ∘ಌ

Daphne stepped from the shower, dried off and dressed. The restlessness had settled by the time she pulled on her skinny jeans and the Nirvana T-shirt she'd bought at an In Utero Tour concert shortly before Kurt had killed himself. She only hand-washed the thing and then only rarely. She grabbed a pair of ankle booties from her closet.

She loved that these were the clothes she got to wear to work. She loved that she got to dress like this to go to a place like Rivet, the restaurant where she had her weekly brunch with Greta. Daphne still liked to dress up, of course, and her wardrobe was still rambunctious, but sometimes she just wanted to dress comfortably, even invisibly. Well, as invisibly as she could, given that she attracted attention wherever she went. Sometimes she wished she would start to age, to lose the starlet glow. Even in Los Angeles, where everyone was beautiful, Daphne seemed to stand out. She realized now that standing out was part of her curse.

She tucked her boots under her arm and poured herself some coffee in a to-go mug, screwing the lid on tight. She didn't want to spill on her T-shirt.

She grabbed her bag—it contained the items she brought with her everywhere: her notebook, composition style; her laptop, MacBook Pro with charger cable; pen-case, made in Japan; fountain pens and extra ink, made in Germany; wallet, keys, lipstick, cell phone and other smaller necessities. Greta called it Daphne's Neurotic Bag. Now that Daphne no longer had an office, her office was her bag. It was her whole life, really. So yeah, she was a little neurotic about it.

She sat in the chair next to the sideboard and zipped on her booties, then stood. It was time to go meet Greta.

Two

At eleven a.m. on Sunday, Daphne was already waiting at a table on Rivet's covered patio when Greta Donovan arrived, her gaze steady as she strode over to where Daphne reclined in a chair. Greta was very tall for a woman, over six-one. She had broad shoulders, narrow hips and long legs—she only wore men's jeans—and in college she'd been terribly awkward. Her red curls had been a frizzy halo and her wardrobe cartoonishly ill-fitting. Early in their friendship, she'd asked Daphne to help her, and with Daphne's advice, Greta had bloomed. Greta's features would never be considered conventionally pretty; her nose was too large and her chin too square.

Daphne sat at a corner two-top, a private table that gave her a view of the entire patio, of the long bar that lined the stucco exterior wall of the restaurant, and of the patrons who were sneaking glances at other tables and wondering who else had chosen this exclusive restaurant for brunch today. Reservations at Rivet could only be made by those whose names were on a very particular list. The interior was outfitted in dark woods and leather. The exterior patio was done in Parisian style, with wicker and white linen.

As Greta made her way toward Daphne, Greta's eyes never wandered over the crowd.

The table where Daphne sat was Greta's table. It was the table where she and Greta ate brunch every Sunday, no matter what. Greta took a seat next to Daphne and pulled off her leather jacket—it had been a cool April—revealing her customary black tank top. She didn't need the jacket underneath the gas heaters that dotted the patio.

Daphne's eyes caught on Greta's scar, extending from the armhole of Greta's shirt and across her shoulder in a crisp white line. The scar was the final remnant of reconstructive shoulder surgery required when Greta's shoulder couldn't quite heal itself after she was attacked five years ago.

When she was attacked five years ago at the apartment she and Daphne had shared.

When she had almost died from a vicious blow to the back of her head.

When her attacker had left her bleeding out on their well-worn kitchen floor.

The dislocated shoulder had been the least of their worries, then.

Greta's red-gold hair had grown long, no longer the short, curly bob she'd always worn when they were younger, in college and after, when she'd first moved to Los Angeles six years ago.

"I've discovered the benefits of ponytails," she'd told Daphne a few months before, explaining the longer hairstyle.

But Daphne smiled, seeing that today Greta wore her hair down, with only the front pulled back in a bare metal clip, the rest of her curls hanging nearly to her shoulder blades. Her hair was beautiful. Greta was beautiful, if unconventionally, and it seemed that Greta finally believed it.

They lounged together, in jeans and casual tops, in a place where all others wore designer clothes and sat at conspicuous tables to see and be seen. Daphne reflected on her lingering feelings of guilt over their shared past. It was true that she and Greta had made it. They'd escaped their families. They'd escaped everything they'd left behind in North Carolina and found themselves here, where they finally felt like they belonged, and they were here together. Still together, despite everything.

But Daphne knew there were some things she could never have. Sometimes Daphne joked with Greta about being a bad luck charm, but Greta always told her to stuff it. The words made Greta angry because she knew Daphne still blamed herself for the attack. Greta also said there was no such thing as luck.

But Daphne knew the truth. She was bad luck. She knew she could only date guys like Dan because nothing worse could happen to them than what they could do to themselves. And the good guys? They didn't even know her real name.

If Daphne wasn't completely happy, she'd be OK. Few people were completely happy.

"You look sleepy," Greta said, direct as always.

"I've only had one cup of coffee."

"That's not why."

"Let's get some coffee first, and then we can talk about it."

Greta nodded.

A server appeared, a woman. Female servers were one of the many changes Greta had instituted since she became partial owner of Rivet. *No more rampant sexism*, she'd said.

"Ms. Donovan," the server said to Greta. "Ms. Saito." Daphne recalled the young woman's name. Carrie. She was a recent hire, just out of film school at UCLA.

"Hey, Carrie," Greta said. "I just want a BLT and fries."

"Me too," Daphne said, stifling a laugh. Around them, patrons ate such delicacies as steak smothered in poached eggs, hollandaise and lump crab meat, and frisée salads covered in all sorts of things like "lardons"—basically French bacon. She'd had the quiche, and it was delicious. But she and Greta were simple girls. Burgers. BLTs. Their taste in food was one of the reasons they were friends.

"And could you please bring a whole carafe of coffee and leave it on the table?" Greta asked.

Daphne sighed with contentment. Truly, Greta was the best.

The server turned to leave. "Carrie," Daphne said, calling her back. "Working on anything interesting?"

When Carrie met Daphne's eyes, Daphne was surprised to

see a familiar ambition there. The same ambition drove Daphne herself. Carrie was one of only two non-white servers at Rivet—and the only black woman. Rivet was a place where you could serve a BLT to a former senior production assistant at Sony-turned successful freelance screenwriter—to Daphne—and maybe get a leg up. Rivet was one of the film industry's golden gates. Daphne knew this well. She'd once come here regularly on the arm of its former owner, hoping for a leg up herself.

She'd never gotten one.

When Daphne had explained Rivet's role in the film industry to Greta, Greta had taken over hiring.

"I'm working on a few things," Carrie said.

Daphne handed Carrie her card. Daphne's cards didn't have Sony printed on them any more. Now they just provided Daphne's name and email address. Carrie took it and tucked it in her pocket without looking at it.

"You free tomorrow morning for coffee?" Daphne asked.

"My shift ends pretty late tonight," Carrie said.

"How about lunchtime?"

Carrie nodded. "That'll work."

"You know Uptown Coffee on San Vicente, near Montana?"

"Sure."

"I'll be there starting early. Come when you get hungry." Daphne nodded at the pocket holding her card. "Send me an email if you need to change plans."

"They let you work at Uptown Coffee?"

Daphne laughed. "I buy a lot of coffee."

Carrie tried to hide her skeptical expression. "I'll be back with your drinks." She headed off purposefully.

"I would say that was nice of you," Greta said, "except you don't do things like that just to be nice."

"I like her."

Greta nodded, waiting for the complete explanation.

"She reminds me of me."

Daphne knew how much of herself she'd nearly lost to be where she was today. She didn't want another woman to have to make the kind of choices she'd made. Not when she could give her the path that anyone should have, no matter where she came from or what she looked like.

No matter what she'd suffered.

So she would have coffee with Carrie tomorrow, and if Carrie's ideas were promising, she would introduce Carrie to her agent. She could do that much for the girl.

"I have news," Greta said. "Timmy asked me to marry him."

"Again with the marriage proposal?" Daphne laughed.

"It's been a while," Greta said. "He used to ask every time we did payroll. Lately he's been keeping it to once a quarter, when we do the taxes for Pac Lighting and Rivet."

In addition to being partial owners of Rivet, Greta and her boyfriend, Timmy, owned an event production company, Pacific Production Lighting. They produced live events at the convention center and hotel ballrooms, and also helped provide gear for theaters, music video productions and smaller film productions.

"When it gets really late at night and the numbers run together, he proposes," Greta said.

"What'd he use this time?" Daphne asked.

Greta held up her fisted hand, thumb pressed tight against her fingers, ready to throw a worthy punch. "A ring."

Daphne paused, examining the shining thing on Greta's finger. Timmy had never used a ring before. Over the past few years he'd proposed with a spoon (saying she'd never go hungry), a new moving light for their company (because Greta shined so brightly), and a bottle of George Dickel Number Twelve (Greta's favorite). But never a ring.

"I said yes," Greta said. "I was thinking we'd get married this afternoon downtown. His uncle can be the witness, since he's already in the building, and you, if you're free."

Timmy's uncle Brian was a Los Angeles city councilman.

"You said yes?"

"Will you come? Maybe around four o'clock? They stop doing weddings at five on Sundays."

"You're not getting married at City Hall."

"Timmy doesn't mind."

"Of course Timmy doesn't mind!" Daphne snorted. "You

said yes! He'd do it at the water treatment plant if it meant you'd finally be married."

"Don't be rude."

"Let me handle it, please. I want you to have a proper wedding."

"If you're talking about a church, I'm moving the time to noon and disinviting you."

"No, I'm not talking about a church, just—" Daphne thought quickly, "just give me until the end of the day to come up with an idea."

"I don't want to wait forever."

"What counts as forever, Greta?" Daphne asked, exasperated.

"Wednesday. You have till Wednesday."

"Wednesday evening."

"Deal."

"But if I only have till Wednesday, then I get to plan everything. Food. Music. Even the invite list."

Greta frowned.

"I totally get carte blanche on the invite list."

Greta glared at her.

"What if Sandy and I make the list together?"

"That is not an improvement."

"Carte blanche. We don't have time to run it by you. We need to get the invites to everyone today."

Greta nodded, considering. "That is true."

"Of course it's true! We only have four days."

"Agreed. You may have carte blanche on the invite list."

Daphne heaved a sigh. "I'm happy for you."

"I know." Greta smiled, her green eyes twinkling a bit. Greta always found humor in Daphne's exasperation.

Carrie returned with the coffee carafe and two mugs, and Daphne gave her a grateful look.

As she sipped from her mug, holding it with both hands to absorb warmth, Daphne looked around Rivet. Few things had changed since she first began coming here six years ago, back when it was owned by her then-boss. Now it was owned by her friends, and now her friends were getting married.

Things might be OK now, but they weren't OK back

then. Daphne felt another wave of guilt.

Guilt because Greta had trusted someone she shouldn't have, all for Daphne. Guilt because Daphne had tried to use people to get what she needed out of Hollywood, and years ago she had tried to use the wrong person—and Greta had gone along with it for Daphne's sake. The shitty thing was, Daphne had indeed needed that help to get ahead.

Because of Daphne, Greta nearly died.

Because of Greta, Daphne owned a condo in Brentwood and could meet Carrie for lunch at Uptown Coffee where they let her work all damn day and never considered kicking her out. They loved having Daphne work there. And she was only twenty-eight years old. A wunderkind by anyone's standards.

And now Greta and Timmy—the man Daphne had tried to drive away from Greta because of her own petty jealousy— were getting married.

All of Daphne's remembered pain came back in a flash, a flash of the light off the ring on Greta's finger.

For an instant, Daphne wanted to run from the table. How could Greta still call Daphne a friend? How could any of this new life of Daphne's be true? She feared she would wake from a dream, and it would be five years ago. Greta would be in the hospital, and that pool of blood would still be on their apartment floor.

"I need to pee," Daphne said, standing. "I'll be right back." She needed a moment to herself, to convince herself not to run. This was an argument she'd been having with herself for years.

Sometimes she thought she stuck around only because she didn't have anywhere to run to.

෴

Five minutes later, Daphne sat down again. To Greta, she still appeared troubled. Greta had an idea of what Daphne might be thinking about.

"How's Dan?" Greta asked, deliberately interrupting Daphne's thoughts.

Greta had noticed when Daphne's thoughts started

drifting. Greta had been concerned that her agreeing to marry Timmy would affect Daphne in negative ways, but she wasn't sure what those ways might be. So she'd observed her friend to ascertain what she might be thinking. She'd meant it when she'd said she knew Daphne was happy for her. Daphne's petty jealousy of Timmy had died a long time ago. No. She was afraid Daphne might be feeling something far more insidious than mere jealousy.

Even though many years had passed, Greta knew her friend still felt an irrational sense of guilt over Greta's attack, as though Daphne had wielded the weapon herself. And no matter how much Greta tried to convince Daphne she was wrong, Daphne would not believe her. Daphne thought Greta had been targeted because of their proximity to one another.

Daphne could not see reason where Greta was concerned. And Daphne still suffered for it.

So if Daphne wanted to plan a ridiculous wedding-type event for Greta and Timmy, then Greta would let her. It was a small gift Greta could give her. Even if Greta really would have been fine with the water treatment plant. After all, the one in Playa had great views of the ocean.

"Dan's fine," Daphne said. "But I cheated on him again last night."

"I'm so sorry." Greta placed her hand on Daphne's.

Daphne would know what she was expressing sympathy for. Daphne clearly felt guilty for committing an act that was the equivalent of lying. And this wasn't the first time she'd done it.

"Thank you."

Greta waved at Carrie, who came over to the table. "Can we get a pitcher of the sangria please?"

Carrie grinned. "Sure."

Daphne gave Greta a wobbly smile. "I do have somewhere to go this afternoon."

"I deduced as much. But we have time." For the first time in a long while, Greta was worried about Daphne.

"Oh Greta. What if I'm not meant to be happy?"

"The part of that sentence that makes no sense is the middle part."

"You don't believe in 'meant to be'."

"Correct. There's no such thing as fate." Greta gestured around them, at the crowded patio—or as crowded as Rivet was ever allowed to be, given how exclusive it was and how much space they kept between the tables for the sake of privacy—and she saw the many faces that were likely on grocery store entertainment magazines, and, these days, on entertainment websites.

Daphne might belong at a place like Rivet, with her physical beauty and professional success.

But Greta? Greta had defied what anyone would have said she was meant to be in Los Angeles. She was a woman with sub-par beauty who had simply moved as far away from the radioactive decay of her family as she could without boarding a plane. Six years ago, Daphne had invited her in, and Greta had come. The fact that a monster had lurked among them hadn't been Daphne's fault, and Greta didn't blame her. Even Timmy didn't blame her.

Only Daphne still felt guilty about that now.

Greta didn't believe that hearts did much more than circulate necessary fluids in the human body, but she also knew that hers broke for Daphne.

"I'm sure you've considered that Dan isn't the right fit for you," Greta said.

"We do fit in many ways. I like working with him. We have great conversations. We even have great sex."

Carrie appeared with the sangria pitcher and two tall glasses. She poured. Her smile revealed that she'd heard at least the tail end of Daphne's words. Greta and Daphne grinned back.

They picked up their glasses, and Daphne took a big sip. Greta watched Daphne smile and lick her lips in an exaggerated motion.

"You should stop doing that," Greta said. "There are two prime-timers over there who might try to talk to us."

"Oh, crap. Where?"

"Table eleven."

Rivet's regulars knew Greta was one of the owners. They knew she could ban them from the restaurant forever. And they wondered why the tall, funny-looking girl in the tank top and jeans was in charge. She was secure enough now to find their speculation amusing.

Daphne, for her part, had always seemed to know how to handle anything men threw her way. That was why the self-doubt Daphne now manifested was causing Greta serious concern.

"Greta, do you think there's something wrong with me?" Daphne asked.

"No."

"Then why do I always seem to destroy things?"

"I don't think you *always* do anything," Greta said. "No human is that consistent."

Daphne snorted. "Stop trying to make me feel better. I'm being serious."

"I know you are. I'm sorry." Greta took another sip of sangria. "I think it's possible that you feel—despite all evidence to the contrary—that you don't deserve certain things." Greta eyed the prime-timers again, who still stared at her table, but who, as usual, mostly stared at Daphne. "It's possible you believe you deserve to be punished for a wrong—multiple wrongs—that weren't yours to begin with."

"I thought you always said social sciences were bunkum," Daphne said with a laugh.

"I didn't say that. I said that science not based on replicable empirical observation was bunkum." She gave Daphne a devious smile. "But I've been observing you for years."

Carrie arrived with many plates on one arm, an impressive feat of balance. She placed the food in front of Greta and Daphne with the professional care expected of all Rivet's servers. "Can I offer you anything else?" she asked, and they shook their heads. She left them to their meal.

"If Dan hasn't captured your attention by now, he never will," Greta said. "And if you're punishing yourself because of his failing to do so, that's illogical." She ate a fry.

"He's a good person."

"Irrelevant."

Daphne dropped her face into her hands. "I know."

"Did you at least have fun last night?" Greta asked.

"The guy seemed nice enough. Not really my type, but somebody's, for sure." She cocked her head, as though imagining a person in front of her. "Surprisingly well-defined muscles once his clothes came off."

"That's good. At least we're having guilty brunch over good sex. Otherwise this," Greta gestured at the spread of food and drink, "would be a serious waste."

They laughed, and the prime-time guys were transfixed. Greta felt sorry for them. Daphne's beauty had always been, and, Greta suspected, would always be, transcendent.

"So you're getting married," Daphne said.

"It won't change anything."

"Only you would say that." Daphne shook her head.

"Nothing is going to change," Greta insisted. *Why should it?* she thought. She'd been with Timmy for more than five years.

"Greta, everything is going to change. You'll see."

"Timmy would kill you for saying that. It sounds like you're trying to talk me out of it."

Timmy had grown to love Daphne over the years, despite everything that had happened before. But it wouldn't take much to make him suspicious.

"You deserve to know," Daphne said. "For people like you and me—forever means something different to us."

Greta felt emotion well up inside her, everything she'd been denying since she'd agreed to get married. This is why she and Daphne were sisters. The ability to see the truth for one another and to speak it with kindness. She set down her glass and threw her arms around Daphne.

"Careful," Daphne said, setting down her own sangria glass. "Don't spill on Kurt."

Greta could hear the emotion in Daphne's voice that reflected her own. After a moment, they pulled apart.

"You have till Wednesday," Greta reminded her. "Then it's City Hall."

"For you, I could have had it done by tomorrow."

Three

Around two o'clock Sunday afternoon, Daphne walked Greta back to Rivet's offices, where Greta would review books and menus for the week. Olivia, Rivet's manager, sat at another desk in the room, a phone tucked behind her ear.

Greta promised to be available by cell phone when Daphne had questions about the wedding plans.

"You will answer when I call you," Daphne said.

"I always answer when you call."

"No, you don't. You get hyper focused on some nonsense and forget to answer the phone."

"I run two businesses," Greta said. "They're not nonsense."

Daphne snorted. "And I run a business too. But I answer when you call me."

"This is a ridiculous conversation."

Daphne put her hands on Greta's shoulders, reaching up a bit because, even though Daphne was five-foot-eight, Greta still towered over her. "Greta, when I call you this week, you will answer your phone. If you do not answer your phone, I will call someone else near you who will hunt you down." Daphne nodded toward Olivia. "I might share private information with that person in order to explain the urgency of the phone call."

"You wouldn't do that."

Daphne raised her eyebrows.

"You would do that to other people, but not to me."

Daphne waited a little longer.

"You would do that to me?" Greta shrieked. Then she lowered her voice. "You'd tell Olivia about my wedding to get me to answer the phone?"

Of course, Daphne would be inviting Olivia to Greta's wedding, but Greta hadn't made that connection yet.

"These are dire times."

"I'll answer the phone."

"Turn up your ringer."

"Fine."

"Do you need me to show you how?"

"Just get out," Greta said, pointing to the door.

Daphne strolled out of Greta's office, through Rivet's interior dining room and out the main entrance. While she waited for the valet to bring her car around, she dialed her phone. She smiled at the valet who brought her car—Sonia— and gave her a generous tip. Prior to Greta, all the valet workers had been men too.

Daphne hopped behind the wheel just as the man she'd been calling answered the phone.

"We have a problem," she said to him.

"Nice to hear from you, Daphne," the man said.

"I'm serious, Sandy!"

He laughed. "What happened?"

"Greta agreed to marry Timmy."

Sandy paused, and his voice grew serious. "And you are happy for her, right?"

Sandy's words held a speck of threat. He was protective of Greta. Although he'd grown to trust Daphne over the years, she knew he wouldn't let go of his protectiveness for anything.

"Of course I'm happy for her!" she hollered into her phone. "But she's not allowed to get married at City Hall this afternoon."

"Wait. She wants to get married today?" He sounded shocked and a little bit hurt.

"See?"

"You're on your way here?"

Daphne smiled. "Of course I am. I'm at Rivet. I'll be there in thirty minutes, tops."

Daphne tossed her phone onto the passenger seat and downshifted as she headed toward Sandy's home in Laurel Canyon. Ever since she'd gotten her first car in college, she'd loved to drive fast. She'd taken driver's education in high school without her overly-controlling father's knowledge—and explicitly against his wishes. So she'd held a license since she was old enough to do so in her home state of North Carolina. But her father had forbidden anyone in his household from driving the family Nissan except him. She hadn't driven much until she got to college. When she'd arrived at college, her boyfriends had let her drive their cars, and she'd loved it.

When she'd moved to LA, she'd owned a new-ish Honda Civic, a car she'd adored both because it was zippy and because she had been able to afford it. Now, she drove a flashy blue Audi S4 for the same reasons. She'd been able to buy the car outright, and the independence she'd felt that day had been bliss.

She was beholden to no one, not even a bank.

After crossing most of Hollywood, she started the climb up the curvy roads to Sandy's home. She hardly glanced to her left or right at the decadent glass castles tumbling down the mountainsides. She was aiming for one glass castle in particular.

When she reached Sandy's driveway, the gates were open, waiting for her arrival. She turned in and pulled up to the front door. The circular drive branched down to the right where his six-car garage nestled against the pines. The two nearest bays were open, one revealing Sandy's current Aston Martin (he always drove the latest model—and always in a dark pewter), and another revealing a classic muscle car in black. Daphne jumped from her car and headed down the hill so she could make it out. It looked like a 1967 Camaro. A pair of legs emerged from under the front. She guessed those belonged to Marlon, Sandy's handyman, mechanic, assistant and general guy Friday. Marlon lived in an apartment above Sandy's garage. He must have worked for Sandy for more than a decade, but the few times she'd met him, Marlon didn't seem much older than thirty.

She headed back up the driveway to the front porch, knocking loudly on the redwood door and then letting herself into the house. Two dogs, large, sleek and brown, came bounding up to her.

She spoke authoritatively. "Jodie. Foster. Sit." She touched her shoulder in a hand signal to reinforce her words.

The dogs' bottoms dropped to the floor, but their eyes remained imploring. Daphne set down her bag and kneeled in front of each one, rubbing their ears until their eyes rolled back in their heads.

Sandy stood in the doorway between his kitchen and his living room, watching Daphne with his dogs, always a little bit amazed by both her beauty and by how much she'd changed since he'd first gotten to know her. It was like a sheet of rigid metal had been peeled away, revealing even more beauty along with a precious fragility. He wondered if she'd mind the observation.

Back when he'd first met Greta and Daphne, Daphne had seemed the older sister, the leader, the one Greta looked up to. These days, in many ways, the roles had reversed. But Sandy had lived a long time—he could no longer say he was in his early fifties—and he knew how friendships changed over time. He also knew a real friendship when he saw one. So even though he gave Daphne a hard time sometimes, he knew she was for real when she stood by Greta's side. No one was more loyal to Greta than Daphne, and that was saying something. Greta inspired loyalty in everyone who got to know her.

"Those dogs are supposed to guard the place, you know," he said, entering the room.

"Not from me." Daphne stood, acting not the least bit surprised by his presence. He wondered if she'd known she'd been observed. "I'm a friendly."

"How could they possibly know that?"

"Multiple visits? My sweet demeanor?"

"But I'm the one who's supposed to tell them you're cool."

"After all these years, you've never told them I'm cool?" She sounded surprised rather than hurt.

"You don't need me to intervene with those dogs. Or with anything else. You never have."

"I might someday." She sounded sincere.

Sandy was taken aback. Daphne had never asked him for anything. Unlike Greta, Daphne worked in the film industry. Sandy, who'd won two Best Actors and been nominated for four more, could have given her a boost here and there if she'd needed him to. If she'd ever simply asked him. Hell, people asked him for stuff all day long. He had a feeling that doing a favor for Daphne would mean something.

"It would be my pleasure," he said.

At his words, she unleashed her megawatt smile, the one that left most men reaching for something to hold on to.

She turned back to the dogs. "Come here, kiddos," she said. They scrambled to her but never once jumped. At least the training he paid for counted for something. "We need to have a meeting."

"Let's sit in the kitchen," Sandy said. "Can you hang on while I make a call?"

❦

Daphne waited in Sandy's kitchen, although in Sandy's house, the kitchen, foyer and informal sitting area felt like one big space. It was the perfect floor plan for a party. No—for a wedding, she corrected herself. Through the archway leading out of the other side of the kitchen, she knew, was the more formal sitting room where Sandy was on the phone, and then the hallway that led to Sandy's private suite of rooms, which she had never seen. Off the main sitting room where she'd first entered was another hallway that led to another array of bedrooms.

Greta had told her once that the house was somewhere around ten thousand square feet, not counting the garage.

Daphne could believe it, even if all she saw right now was the proverbial tip of the iceberg. Sandy had earned his original wealth as a movie star in the seventies and eighties, but his business acumen had turned ordinary Hollywood money into real money. The kind of money that neither Greta nor Daphne could fathom, though on some late nights between beer and the Internet, they tried to wrap their brains around it.

Sandy reentered the kitchen, slipping his phone into his pocket. He gestured at a bottle of champagne already open on his kitchen counter, along with three flutes. There was also a carafe of what looked to be very freshly squeezed orange juice.

"Want some?" he asked.

"Sure," she said. "But between you and Greta, I'm going to be too drunk to plan a wedding."

"Rivet sangrias?" he asked.

"I limited myself to two."

While he poured the glasses, she noticed a new painting on the wall by the floor-to-ceiling glass doors leading out onto his deck. It looked like the work of the artist whose pieces hung in other parts of the house. *Barr*, the signature read. The canvas was large, maybe six feet square. She loved the scale of it, the scope, what could be captured in so much space. This one was predominantly blue, with a woman's face off-center. It reminded her of one of Picasso's Dora Maars, the way the woman stared at you plainly, almost ruthlessly. Daphne reached out to touch, her fingers nearly brushing the canvas, before she realized what she was doing.

"Sandy," she said. "This painting. I love it. It's the same artist, right? As the one in the foyer?" She kept staring at the woman, whom she called Dora in her head. "Who's this Barr artist? Anyone I could afford?"

"Probably," said a voice to the right, startling her.

She looked over her shoulder and saw Marlon.

"Didn't mean to scare you," he said.

"You didn't," she snapped, annoyed that he had, indeed, been able to sneak up on her. "Where's Sandy?"

"Here you go." Marlon handed her a glass of mimosa. "Sandy stepped out to take another call while you were looking at that." He nodded at the painting.

She marveled that she could have been so engrossed in the painting that she lost track of her surroundings. She took the flute from Marlon's hand. She could see that, although he'd washed his hands, he still had dirt and grease around the edges of his fingernails. *He needs to take a wire brush to his hands*, she thought.

Then she took a deep breath and reminded herself to stop being small-minded. She hadn't spent much time with Marlon. He tended to keep to himself. But he was Sandy's good friend. If you asked Sandy, Sandy might say Marlon was his best friend. Sandy had told her once that he tried to get Marlon to come with him when he came to Rivet, but Marlon always refused. Marlon had apparently said he couldn't stand the scene, or any scene really.

"So why does he live in LA?" Daphne had asked.

"He's from here," Sandy had said. "And he refuses to leave."

Daphne took a sip of her drink, turning back to the painting.

"You like it?" Marlon asked.

"I do." Daphne was eager to talk about it again. "Do you know where Sandy got it?"

"From his garage."

"He has a stockpile out there?"

"I have a studio in my apartment."

Daphne processed his words for a moment. "These paintings are yours?"

"The four that look like this one are, yeah."

"I know which four. They're lovely." She realized she sounded slightly breathless. "I didn't know you were an artist."

"I'm not. I'm a handyman and an assistant."

"So you don't try to show your work?"

"Nope."

"What does Barr stand for?"

"My last name is Barringer. I didn't want people to know the paintings were mine. So I use a pseudonym."

Daphne examined him. Marlon still stared at the painting, his arms crossed over his respectably broad chest. She'd been right about his age—the tight skin around his gray eyes proved he was no more than thirty. He must have started working for Sandy when he was twenty or maybe even younger. She wanted to know the whole story. Maybe Greta knew more.

Daphne also noticed that, under the overgrown haircut, with pieces of sun-lightened brown hair falling toward his face, under the scruffy growth of beard on his chin, under the fingernail grime and streak of grease on his sun-darkened forehead, Marlon was likely very handsome.

But he wasn't her type. She didn't date handyman-assistants, even ones whose lovely paintings hung in the homes of Hollywood royalty.

Marlon wasn't her match, she thought sadly. She'd chew him up, and then she'd blame herself for it.

I won't make the same mistakes I made with Dan, she thought. *The mistakes I made with any of them.*

She'd rather be alone.

"Great, we're all here." Sandy reappeared in the kitchen. "I hope you don't mind I invited Marlon to this meeting, Daphne. I always bring him in when there's an emergency."

"Of course not," she said. But she actually wished Marlon wasn't there at all. She didn't understand him, and that lack of understanding made her uncomfortable. She didn't want to be distracted when she should be concentrating on Greta.

The three of them sat around Sandy's enormous trestle-legged table that ran nearly the length of the room.

"What's the emergency?" Marlon asked.

"Greta's agreed to marry Timmy," Sandy told him. "She wanted to do it today, but Daphne convinced her to wait till Wednesday."

Marlon whistled. He seemed to know the significance of Sandy's statement. Daphne was intrigued.

"I've made a few notes," Daphne said, pulling out one of her business cards and setting it face-down on the table. She'd written five words on the back. "First, location. I thought you might want to have it here," Daphne said, gesturing around the house. "But if you don't, we can do it at Rivet."

Sandy smiled with genuine joy. "Yes," Sandy said. "Let's have it here."

"Could we have the ceremony out on the deck, you

think?" she asked. "Will everyone fit?"

Sandy's deck was enormous. It ran the entire length of his house, with doors into every room it touched. And it shot out from the house at least thirty feet. They could hold the entire party out there if they wanted to. Greta had told her that Sandy had done a lot of the construction himself, with Marlon's help, a long time ago.

"She'd love that," Sandy said.

"Done," Daphne said.

Marlon, Daphne noticed, was taking notes on a yellow pad in precise handwriting.

"Second," Daphne said, "people. I convinced Greta to let us handle the invitation list without having to run it by her. I figured time was of the essence. I could make a list today, and you could do the same. And then what? Invite by email? Is that too tacky?"

"Depending on how many invites there are," Sandy said, "we could hire a private stationery and courier service to hand deliver them all in the morning."

Daphne raised her eyebrows. Private courier. Hand delivered. Wow.

"Well, a private courier wouldn't be tacky," she said. "I'll have my suggestions to you via email tonight, along with text for the invitations. Review it, add yours, then get the list to your stationery and courier person?"

"Easy enough," Sandy said.

Daphne just shook her head.

"Third, officiant," she said. "Who should officiate?"

"I'm actually a legal officiant in California," Sandy said.

"Of course you are, you hippie," Daphne said. "But I thought you might want to walk her down the aisle."

"Do you really think Greta will want someone walking her down the aisle? Or that she'd want an aisle at all?"

"But how will she get there?" Daphne tapped her lip in thought. "Which brings up another question. What's the 'there'? Some magical wedding spot on the deck? How will we demarcate the altar-thing where the wedding takes place?"

"Do you really think Greta will want an altar?" Sandy asked, the humor leaving his voice. "Don't confuse what you want with what Greta wants."

Sandy's words hit her hard. That had always been her problem. So many times over the years, even when they were in college, Daphne had caused Greta pain by thinking she knew what was best for her. Daphne liked to think she didn't make this mistake any more.

When will I get it right? she thought.

She was angry with herself. She didn't let her emotions show, though. That was one of her gifts. Keeping her own negative feelings hidden so everyone else could remain happy and comfortable.

"You're right," she said, smiling. "No aisle. No escort. No altar. Just a magical wedding spot on the deck that you will somehow manifest before Wednesday." She smiled even more brightly. "I trust you, Sandy."

He reached across the table and squeezed her hand.

Daphne turned back to the list on her business card. "Next: food and booze. I figured we'd let Olivia arrange the catering through Rivet."

"I want to cover the cost," Sandy cut in.

"That's fine, but I'll let you figure out how to tell Greta." Daphne laughed. "Do you want to have a say in the menu?"

"Actually, Marlon knows a lot more about that sort of thing than I do. Would you mind working with him on that?"

"You free tomorrow?" Daphne asked Marlon. "I don't want to put this off another minute."

"What's the rush?" Marlon said. "I thought the party wasn't till Wednesday." He leaned back in his seat.

Daphne felt blood rush up to block her hearing. She rarely lost her temper, but she was about to lose it now.

"It is a wedding," she said slowly. "Not a party. The wedding of the most important person in my entire world. And if Rivet has to order special food to have it here by Wednesday, then I want to be sure they have plenty of time to do so. So I'm meeting with Olivia, the manager, as soon as she'll have me, out of respect for Greta. That's the goddamned rush."

At her harsh words, Marlon's expression turned quizzical, as though she'd posed a tough question he didn't know the answer to.

But, horribly, Sandy's face went blank, his happiness over the occasion apparently chased away by her nastiness.

She hated herself for her outburst. She just couldn't do anything right today. The same need to escape overcame her as it had back at Rivet. But this time, she gave in to it. She stood, her hands shaking as she picked up her bag and flung it over her shoulder. She was afraid to look at Sandy again, afraid of the disappointment she was sure she would see in his eyes.

Instead, she looked at the tabletop, speaking to Marlon. "If you want to talk tomorrow, I'll be at Rivet at three to meet with Olivia to set up catering for Wednesday." She turned to go. "Bye, Sandy," she said, nearly choking on the words. "I'm sorry."

She forced herself not to run to the front door. To walk steadily. To stop and pet the dogs where they lay by the couch, under another of Marlon's paintings. To ease out as though nothing were wrong, even though everything was wrong.

ೲ

"She's not having a good day, is she," Marlon said after Daphne closed the front door behind her. He picked up the card she'd left on the table. The remaining item on her list was Decor. He added it to his own list. Then he pocketed the card with her name and email.

"No, she most definitely is not," Sandy said.

"You always did say she was a little high-strung."

"I did."

"You also said she was, let's see, 'gorgeous, whip-smart and potentially lethal'—in a metaphorical sense."

"That sounds about right," Sandy said.

"But that girl looks like she's about to break into a hundred pieces," Marlon said.

Sandy just nodded.

"Any idea why?"

"Not really. But I'd like to know. She's one of Greta's most important people."

And Marlon knew Greta was one of Sandy's most

important people.

Of course Marlon was going to be at Rivet tomorrow at three o'clock because that was his job. But now he would be there, and he would be eager and fascinated.

Four

Later Sunday night, sitting at her usual table at Uptown Coffee, Daphne emailed her wedding invitation list to Sandy. Then she closed her laptop and waited for Dan to arrive. She remembered Greta's words from earlier in the day.

If Dan hasn't captured your attention by now, he never will, she'd said. *And if you're punishing yourself because of his failing to do so, that's just illogical.*

Was she punishing herself for Dan's failings? Perhaps. But there was more to it than that. She deliberately stayed with him because she could never fall in love with him. And if she could never be in love with him, she could never hurt him.

But she had to end it with Dan, if only for the sake of her soul. Cheating on him in order to stay with him made no sense. The betrayals only made her hate herself more than she already did.

Daphne hadn't spent much time alone. It seemed as soon as she broke up with one man, another was there, eager to take his place. And the next one always seemed good enough to spend time with. He was kind to her, charming, caring.

So she acquiesced.

But she'd never been in love with a single one of them. And now, knowing what a destructive force she could be, she was truly grateful she hadn't.

Through the tall, plate-glass windows, she watched Dan arrive. She watched him reach for the door. She watched as he entered the shop and said something to the barista that made her laugh and perhaps even blush. That was typical Dan. But Daphne didn't mind that he was a flirt.

After all, she slept with other guys.

What is wrong with me? she thought.

He picked up his order from the stainless steel counter and made his way past the glossy black tables where couples sat, past the glass display cases polished to a high shine full of decadent pastries. He made his way back to her.

"Babe!" Dan said, leaning down to kiss her. She tilted up her chin to meet his lips.

He sat across from her. She memorized his face, in case this was the last time they met. Dan's dark brown hair was nearly black, and he wore it slicked back like he was ready to pitch a campaign on Madison Avenue. He was forty-three but looked ten years younger. In fact, he'd lied about his age when he'd first met her three years before, knocking ten years off.

When she discovered his real age, he'd made her swear never to tell anyone how old he was. She'd only figured out his real age because she'd run a background check on him. Daphne had begun taking precautions after Greta was attacked.

She'd told him about her discovery, of course, because Daphne was honest about most things.

At the time Daphne discovered Dan's lie, they'd been going out about a month, and she'd known him about a year. Daphne still worked at Sony, so she and Dan could only hang out late in the evenings. He was already freelancing full time, and she was jealous of his freedom. They met at various places along San Vicente, places she could walk to after being cooped up in an office all day.

"Tell me more about yourself," she asked him that particular night. "When did you graduate from college?"

He gave her the correct school—UCLA—but he lied about the year. She already knew when he'd graduated from college and from where. In fact, she had his alumni record from UCLA pulled up on her laptop as they were speaking.

"Dan," she said. "There's something you need to know about me."

"I knew it!" he said with his usual bluster. "You're a lesbian."

She just shook her head. "One of the reasons Sony gave me a raise is because I'm the best researcher they have. I can find anything." She leaned forward and looked him in the eye. "Anything."

Dan's smile turned into a grimace.

She rotated her laptop so he could see the screen. There was the alumni record of UCLA, with Dan's name plainly listed next to his class year.

"Were you especially precocious? Did you go to college when you were, like, ten years old?"

"No."

"But you said you're only thirty-one."

Dan started shaking his head. "Shit," he said.

"I'm not trying to humiliate you," she said, shutting her laptop screen. "But there was no reason to lie."

"I knew you were in your twenties. I didn't think you wanted to date an old man."

"You're not an old man," she said. "But you did lie to me. If we can't be truthful with each other, we should probably end this now."

Dan reached out a hand but stopped just shy of touching her. "Don't leave," he said, a little breathless.

She looked up at him. "We can start again."

"Let's do the second one," he said with unvarnished hope.

Two months later, Dan invited Daphne to lunch with his agent. One week after that, Dan's agent sold Daphne's two scripts, the two she'd been writing on her own late at night. She'd made a pile of money and quit her job at Sony.

She had Dan to thank for so much. That's why she had to stop hurting him, even if he never found out about the hurting.

He set his demitasse on the table next to her closed laptop.

"What's wrong?" he asked.

"Greta's getting married on Wednesday," she said.

"Whoa Nelly. That's fast."

"Or, considering she and Timmy have been living together for five years, very slow."

"Is that what's bothering you?"

"I'm happy for her. I'm planning the wedding." She set down her cup. The ceramic clanked too loudly, as though making a warm-up noise for what she was about to say. "I think we're done, Dan. You and me."

He sat back in his chair. "No way."

"You're one of my best friends. But I don't think we're meant to last as lovers." She sighed, twirling a few strands of hair that hung over her shoulder. "I don't think we bring out the best in each other."

"Of course we do," he said. "We keep this up, one of us will win an Oscar!"

"Please take me seriously right now."

"I always take you seriously, babe."

Daphne realized that perhaps there was a clue to their problem buried in those words. She remembered what Greta would say: No human always does anything because no human is that consistent.

"It's over," she said.

"You're just freaking out because your friend is getting married."

"I'm not. I've been considering this for a while."

"I thought things have been great lately," Dan said, sounding hurt.

"They haven't been for me."

"Come on, Daph. Give us another chance."

"That's what I'm trying to tell you. I did give us another chance. The last few months have been chance after chance. And it's just not working."

"I don't believe you. This has to do with Greta." He seemed so certain.

Daphne had hoped to avoid doing this, but she couldn't get through to him. She grabbed Dan's hand and held it on the top of the table, stilling it. "I slept with someone else last night."

Dan paused. If she were transcribing his speech pattern in

a script, his pause would be the length of a triple beat.

"I don't care," he said, firmly.

"Don't be silly. You're a territorial caveman."

"OK, I care," he said. "But I forgive you."

"I didn't ask for your forgiveness."

"Then why did you tell me?"

"To illustrate how much we are over."

"You slept with someone else to push me away?"

"I slept with someone else because you were already gone."

"Ouch," he said, rubbing the back of his neck. "No need to be cruel, Daphne."

"I wasn't planning on telling you at all. But you weren't listening to me."

"You shouldn't have told me. Now I'll always think of you as a cheater."

His words stung. Daphne crossed her arms over her chest, assessing him. "Did you ever sleep with another woman while we were together?"

"What a ridiculous question!"

Daphne laughed with relief. He'd paused before he'd spoken, and then he'd given her a non-answer. He was lying again. Her suspicions were confirmed, her guilt assuaged.

"Dan, it's over. If we're both cheating on each other, what are we doing together?"

"But I really like you," he said with a pout.

"I really like you too." The words were true.

"I don't want to stop working together," he said.

Daphne and Dan worked together many days during the week. They wrote together, traded pages to perfect their drafts, even had agents at the same agency. Sometimes they attended each other's pitch meetings just to help out. When you were a freelancer, having another person to watch your back could be a huge benefit.

Daphne felt relieved that Dan didn't want to end their friendship. She didn't want to end it either. She wasn't ready for that much upheaval in her life.

Everything already felt disrupted.

"I'm planning on being at this table first thing in the

morning, just like always," she said.

"Then I'll see you here, just like always," he said. "Just not as early as you."

"Just like always." She smiled, but he didn't smile back.

He threw back the last of his coffee and stood. "You know, it was only the one time," he said. Then he turned from her at last.

Daphne gave Dan fifteen minutes to get on his way before packing up her own things and leaving Uptown. She had a ten-minute walk home. Even though it was dark out, the neighborhood was busy with foot traffic. She felt safe living here.

Of course, she and Greta had felt safe where they'd lived before, off Melrose, but they'd been wrong.

A Friday in December five years ago was the worst day of Daphne's life. Well, the worst day of her adult life. She arrived home late at night to find a pool of blood in the open doorway of the apartment she shared with Greta. Their landlord, Marcellus, told her that Greta had been attacked and had been taken to the hospital.

Then she arrived at the hospital, and Greta kicked Daphne out of her life. Greta could see what Daphne had done. Greta could see, in the special way she could always see things when it came to Daphne, that while Greta had been fighting to survive, Daphne had tried to destroy things between Greta and Timmy. Daphne would never forget the dead look in Greta's eyes. She had never looked at Daphne that way before. It was horrifying.

Daphne left the hospital alone and came home to the apartment on Melrose. By then, it was the early hours of the morning. She unlocked the door and stepped over the puddle of blood. The blood had darkened to a brownish color and seeped into the worn wood floor.

Automatically, Daphne reached under the kitchen sink for a cleaning bucket and a sponge. Daphne had grown up in a motel. She knew how to clean a floor. She knew how to clean anything off a floor. She filled the bucket with warm water and considered her options. Ordinarily, she wouldn't use harsh chemicals on wood floors, but these weren't ordinary circumstances. She poured a quarter cup of bleach into the bucket and set to work.

She scrubbed and scrubbed, dumping and refilling her bucket after the water turned pink, and scrubbed some more. She scrubbed until the sun came up on Saturday morning. And then she kept scrubbing. Her fingertips, she noticed numbly, were bleeding. Some distant part of her mind noticed that the bleach stung the torn skin. She saw the outline of reddish-brown on the wood floor, and she scrubbed harder.

Hours later, exhausted, she pulled herself onto the orange vinyl sofa that they'd dubbed "The Lifeboat" and fell asleep. A few hours after that, she woke to Timmy calling to say Greta wanted her things packed and ready to move out of the apartment.

"I'll take care of it," Daphne said.

Then she scrubbed some more.

Three months later, after living alone with that dark spot on the floor, Daphne found a small studio she could afford on the West Side of LA.

The day she moved out, Marcellus stood with her on the patio behind the apartment. "Thanks again for the lease extension," she said.

She had a lot more to thank him for, though. Marcellus had found Greta that awful night and likely saved her life.

Then, after Greta had moved out, Marcellus had offered Daphne a month-to-month lease. Daphne had let him feel guilty for renting them an unsafe apartment, even though she knew the attack had nothing to do with the safety of the neighborhood. Letting Marcellus feel guilty for her own personal gain was just another black mark against her. At that point, she figured, what was one more? She was irredeemable.

"It was no problem, Daphne," Marcellus said. "I will miss our talking."

"I'll miss it too," she said and gave him a hug.

"Daph, babe!" called a voice from inside the apartment. It was her former ex-boyfriend, once-more current boyfriend,

Federico. He was inside with some of his friends helping her move.

"Coming!" She dashed up the steps into the apartment. She refused to look down, refused to see the mark on the wood that she knew was there.

Federico stood with his two buddies by the lifeboat.

"Are you seriously moving this hideous couch?"

"Yes."

"*Pero, es muy feo*," he said.

"We see beauty differently," she said. "Please be careful with it."

"*Te amo, mi loca*," he said.

"I love you too," she said, wondering if she was indeed crazy to keep the orange couch that reminded her so much of Greta, and therefore, of what she'd lost.

While the boys wrestled with the couch, she entered her bedroom. Everything was packed except her bed. The mattress was stripped bare. For a moment, she considered leaving it behind. It had been a gift from someone she wanted to forget. But Daphne's thrifty nature wouldn't let her ditch a perfectly nice bed.

Daphne had been so wrong about so many things. And now Greta was gone, living who knows where, doing who knows what. Daphne just hoped she and Timmy had been able to work things out.

"Freddy," she called out. "Will there be room for my bed on the truck?"

"*Sí, claro*," he said from the other room. "I didn't rent a silly little truck for my princess."

She rolled her eyes. She hated being called a princess, but it was a nickname that had haunted her since college.

Daphne had started her new job at Sony shortly after Greta had moved out. The job was hard, harder than her first LA job had been. At Sony, she worked long hours and had no flexibility. But she was fine with long hours, with hard work. Plus, she had goals. She wanted to accomplish them, and for the first time, she felt like she had a way to do so. She could see the pathways to power.

So she spent her days sitting in meetings, taking notes,

getting coffee, doing whatever everyone with more power than she had told her to do, and spent her evenings sitting on the lifeboat in her cramped studio apartment reading scripts and books that someone else told her to read.

But she spent her nights working on projects of her own. She took what she'd learned at her job and applied it to her own stories. She worked on two scripts in secret. They were her own. She just didn't know what she would do with them yet.

Several months into her Sony job, on a Sunday afternoon in June, she got a phone call from a number she didn't recognize. She almost didn't answer it. Sunday afternoons were precious writing time for her.

But she did answer the call, and it made all the difference.

"Daph?"

"Greta?" Daphne's voice raised an octave. Surprise, hope, fear, all mingled.

"Yeah." Greta paused. "How are you?"

"I'm OK." Daphne was nearly breathless. "You?"

"Good."

A long pause.

"Where are you living now?" Greta asked.

"I moved to the West Side. Near Brentwood."

"Timmy and I have a place in Marina Del Rey."

"That's close to work for you," Daphne said.

"Yeah, about work," Greta said. "Do you have time for dinner tonight?"

Daphne felt her entire body go still, with both hope and a kind of desperation. "I do. Of course I do, Greta."

"OK then. Six o'clock. At Rivet."

Daphne spent the next two hours getting ready. She'd completely lost her ability to focus on writing. She went through her clothes. She tried to understand why Greta had called her now, out of the blue. She tried to understand why Greta had chosen Rivet for this reunion, a place that held terrible memories for them both.

At the appointed time, Daphne arrived at Rivet. She stood in front of the restaurant for the first time in months. The place looked the same as it had the last time she'd been there.

The same doormen—bouncers in fine clothing—stood at the doors. She valeted her car, and even the valet driver remembered her name.

"*Gracias*, Cristiano," she said.

"*De nada*, Miss Daphne."

She trod the walkway toward the double front doors as though in a dream. For a moment she wondered if this were some sort of set-up, revenge on Greta's part for what Daphne had done to her. Was Daphne about to be turned away, humiliated right here in front of LA's elite?

She certainly deserved it.

But no—the tall doors opened for her, and the doormen smiled and kissed her cheek as though no time had passed, as though her former friends waited inside at their usual booth.

But those friends, if they had ever been her friends, would be gone now. Rivet had new ownership. Daphne had heard that Sandy, a friend of Greta's, had bought the place.

That must be why Greta had asked her here, Daphne figured. Sandy owned Rivet now. So Greta could come here any time she wanted. Greta belonged here and could come and bring her friends. And now Daphne was walking in like she, too, belonged.

The feeling was surreal.

Daphne approached the host. "I'm here to meet—"

"Greta Donovan. Yes, of course," the young man said, and gestured for Daphne to follow, sneaking glances at her every few steps.

He led her down the short corridor and out to the covered patio. They passed table after table until they reached the farthest corner table where Greta sat alone. The host pulled out Daphne's chair for her and handed her a menu.

"Thanks, Stephen," Greta said to him as Daphne sat.

"Your description was accurate," the host replied, gawking at Daphne.

Greta sighed. "Bye, Stephen."

Stephen trotted off, past the tables and into the corridor.

Greta turned to Daphne with a pained expression. "When I asked him to keep an eye out for you, I told you were aberrantly gorgeous and Japanese. He clearly got stuck on the gorgeous part."

Daphne laughed. She laughed because Greta looked like Greta. Because her words were Greta's words. Because everything—well, not everything, not their sitting at Rivet, but they'd get to that—was so completely normal.

"I'm sorry, Greta," Daphne said.

"I know you are." Greta's manner was matter-of-fact, as always. "I knew that back in December."

A server arrived. He asked for their drink orders.

"Get anything you want," Greta said. "It's kind of on me."

Daphne raised her eyebrows in question.

"I'll explain in a minute," Greta said. "Should we get margaritas?"

"Well, yeah."

"Henry?" The server nodded, seeming pleased that Greta knew his name. "We'd like a pitcher of margaritas on the rocks please. Two glasses. No salt."

"Yes, ma'am. Um. Miss. Ah." Henry's face turned red as he stumbled over his words.

Greta cracked up laughing, but it wasn't mean laughter. She seemed as uncomfortable as he was. "Most people call me Miss Donovan, since I seem a little young to be called ma'am."

Indeed. By Daphne's estimation, Henry was likely older than Greta by a year or two, and Greta had just turned twenty-three in June.

"What are we doing here?" Daphne asked. "And if you say 'having dinner' I'll do something embarrassing."

"Sandy, Timmy and I all own Rivet now."

"What?" Daphne shrieked.

"Hush, Daphne. You said you weren't going to do anything embarrassing."

Daphne clapped her hand over her mouth and nodded.

"It's a little complicated, but Sandy and Timmy bought Marco out, and then they split the place between them, and then Timmy, against all reason, insisted on splitting his portion with me. It's not like we're married or anything. And when Sandy heard about that, he insisted we split three ways equally, which was even less reasonable, because why would he just give up more of his portion to me? So here we are. I'm one-third owner of Rivet for no apparent reason."

"You own Rivet?" Daphne nearly shrieked again.

"I own one-third of Rivet. Weren't you listening?"

"I'm so happy! We can come here all the time!"

And then it came crashing back. She and Greta weren't friends. This was the first conversation they'd had in six months. Daphne wouldn't be coming to Rivet all the time.

Greta would be.

But Greta grabbed Daphne's hand. "Daphne. That's right. That's exactly right."

Daphne met Greta's eyes as tears filled her own.

"If I have to hang out here all the time to keep up appearances then you have to come with me. It's only fair," Greta said.

Daphne nodded.

"I didn't ask for this responsibility," Greta continued. "Those two idiots just gave it to me."

Daphne nodded again.

"Stupid men," Greta said. "Acting completely against their financial self-interest."

Daphne started to giggle.

"What?" Greta demanded.

"Love makes us all do stupid things," Daphne said. "Someday you'll understand that."

৽৽৵

After that first dinner together, she and Greta decided to meet at Rivet every Sunday morning, no matter what. Soon, the Sunday brunches were sacred. Daphne didn't think Greta getting married would change their Sunday plans. Indeed, if Daphne suggested such a thing to Greta, Greta would only get annoyed.

Daphne was almost home from Uptown, the sidewalks dimly lit by the streetlights, the night air cool. She breathed deeply, enjoying the fresh smell of a sage plant nearby. She was grateful for the second chance Greta had given her. She hadn't deserved it. But she had taken it because Greta was the only thing resembling family she had. Without Greta, she had no one.

Five

On Monday morning, Daphne woke early like she always did, before the sound of her alarm. When she'd worked for others, she'd enjoyed the times she could sleep in, treasuring the luxury. Now that she worked for herself, each hour belonged to her. Each hour was a luxury.

She slept on the mattress that had been an uncomfortable gift many years ago. But the gift was nearly unrecognizable now. She'd acquired a low, wooden midcentury bed frame to hold her mattress and box spring. The headboard was a smooth, solid plane of wood, the grain telling a story with its curves and lines. The entire thing weighed a ton. Timmy and Greta had helped her move it after she'd found it at an estate sale, and even with all three of them, getting it inside her home had been a struggle. It was a good thing she didn't want to move again.

Her comforter was made of a pale blue cotton, a soothing color. Grasping it with both hands, she threw it from her body. Her alarm sounded at six o'clock, but she was already on her feet. She let the radio play as she got ready.

After a quick shower, she shook out her long hair to let it air dry and dressed in jeans and a thin black cashmere sweater. Then she slipped on her black booties, grabbed her neurotic bag and headed out on foot toward Uptown Coffee.

Her walk took her southwest down Montana to San Vicente. Every morning, she passed her neighbors who also liked the early morning hours. Mrs. Krumholz, who lived in Daphne's building, shuffled toward her on the sidewalk with a tiny Yorkshire Terrier, Guppy. Daphne gave Mrs. Krumholz a quick hug good morning.

"How are you feeling today?" Daphne asked.

Last Friday, Daphne had taken Mrs. Krumholz to a doctor's appointment, the first one since her former doctor had moved back to the East Coast after getting married. Daphne had insisted on the check-up when she'd learned that her neighbor hadn't seen a doctor in over a year.

"My hands feel so much better." Mrs. Krumholz held up hands that rheumatoid arthritis had twisted into knotted branches. "The new anti-inflammatory drug is a miracle."

"You don't have to suffer by yourself, Mrs. Krumholz. I'm not going anywhere."

"I knew you were a good girl when Guppy didn't bark at you the first time you met."

"Guppy is a wise creature," Daphne said. Guppy sniffed Daphne's feet, perhaps sensing Sandy's dogs. At the thought of her explosion at Sandy's yesterday, Daphne winced.

"Guppy is an idiot," Mrs. Krumholz said. "But she can smell a baddy."

Daphne wrapped her arms around Mrs. Krumholz's frail frame once again. "Remember that someone here worries about you," Daphne whispered into her ear.

"I don't know why you do," she said. "But I'll take it. Now I have to keep walking before Guppy craps on Mr. Dorsky's lawn, and he calls the cops."

Mr. Dorsky owned the next building over, and he spent an exorbitant amount on landscaping even by Los Angeles standards. The old woman and her dog made their slow way back home.

Daphne didn't have a blood family any more. She'd abandoned them when they had abandoned her. But she had worked hard to make a new one. Her neighbors. Greta and Timmy. Even Sandy. She took care of them.

Once again thinking of how she'd left things with Sandy,

she felt terrible. It was like remembering a bad dream. She hoped Marlon would show at Rivet that afternoon.

�❧

Daphne entered Uptown Coffee at six-thirty, right when they unlocked the doors. No one was surprised to see her. Not the barista, Rebekah, nor the owner, Tony. His last name was Upton—the coffee shop's name was a bit of a pun. Few knew that tidbit though.

"Good morning, Miss Daphne," Tony said to her. He worked the register most mornings, before heading to the back to prepare more baked goods. "Americano, as usual?"

"Yes please."

"Got it," Rebekah said from down the line at the espresso machine.

"I believe you are nearing the end on these two scripts, are you not?" Tony asked her.

"That's right. It's April. Just about time to start round two."

Tony kept up with Daphne's work. She wrote six scripts a year, two every four months. To many in her line of work, that seemed an ungodly pace. To her, it was plenty slow. Indeed, the pace was so slow it allowed her time to revise each script with her agent multiple times. She had time to ensure every single script she wrote sold for something, even if only fifteen thousand dollars. That was the least her agent would accept for work with Daphne's name on it.

Most of her scripts went for far more.

Two years ago, one of her scripts almost went all the way—the film itself was nominated for multiple Academy Awards. Not for best original screenplay though. But Daphne knew how the nominations worked. She was aware she had stepped on more than a few industry toes.

But enough people knew she'd written that script. Tony Upton knew. Hanging on the wall behind the register were autographed headshots of celebrities whom Tony admired. Daphne's was up there, just over his left shoulder.

That's why Tony never cared if she camped out at a table

in his café all day. He loved her work. He thought she classed up the place. She was part of the Uptown Coffee family. If anyone else tried to open a laptop, he'd fuss at them. But not at Daphne or at anyone who came in with her. He even kept an extension cord for her behind the counter.

"Here you go," Rebekah said, setting Daphne's mug on the counter. Daphne handed Tony a credit card to start a tab, then carried her drink to her table. She pulled her laptop from her bag and set to work.

Around nine o'clock, at his usual time, Dan showed up. Seeing his face, Daphne felt an immense sense of relief. Even after their harsh words last night, she hadn't lost her friend or her writing partner. In many ways, he was another member of her makeshift family, if only because she'd known him so long.

He dropped down into the seat across from her, breathless. "I almost got killed walking over here!" he said. "A blond breeder backed her land yacht right up onto the sidewalk."

"Really? Onto the sidewalk?" Daphne quirked an eyebrow.

"Nearly. You know how big the bumpers are on those things. It's amazing she didn't take my leg off."

"It's amazing."

Daphne was accustomed to Dan's exaggeration and crass language. Often, he was funny. But sometimes, he was just offensive.

Dan was good with words. He knew their power. He knew how to choose words with care. If he wanted to say something virulently sexist, or racist, or otherwise, then he was doing it on purpose. Sure he'd claim it was a joke. But jokes have power too.

Tony Upton himself brought Dan's cappuccino to the table, shaking Dan's hand in greeting. "How was your weekend?" Tony asked.

"I've had better," Dan said.

Daphne looked up from her laptop screen, suspicious.

"What happened?" Tony crossed his arms over his chest, waiting for the story.

"I got some unexpected bad news. Turns out someone I thought was reliable was doing bad things behind my back."

Tony shook his head. "I know the feeling. I had to fire someone recently for giving out free drinks to all of his friends. One or two, sure, but twenty a day?"

"You can't count on anyone it seems." Dan shook his head sympathetically.

Daphne rolled her eyes.

Tony headed back to the bar, and she glared at Dan.

"What?" He shrugged.

"I thought we were cool."

"Come on, Daph. I was just joking around."

"Dial back the asshole, OK?"

"I'm sorry, babe," Dan said. "I'm still messed up about last night. I lashed out."

She nodded, accepting his reasoning. She could take a little lashing out if it made him feel better about the bomb she'd dropped on him.

Years ago, Dan had done all he could to help her escape the studios. Sure, he'd wanted to get her into bed, but they'd also been friends. And for years now they'd been both friends and lovers. She knew what was in his heart. He was a forty-three-year-old man with both flaws and good intentions.

Dan got out his notebook and a pen. Dan wrote everything by hand and then paid a typist to transcribe his work. Daphne wasn't sure if he even knew how to type. He'd never sent her an email, and he didn't own a cell phone, although in a pinch he borrowed hers. He didn't like electronics and claimed they gave him headaches.

She'd confronted him about the cell phone thing once, when they'd been trying to meet up for a movie in Westwood. She'd arrived first, but the showing had been sold out. She hadn't known what to do—buy seats for the next showing? Skip the movie and wait for another night? She'd bought the late-showing tickets, hoping she'd done the right thing, and then waited for him to arrive.

He strolled up ten minutes late.

"It's a good thing it was sold out," she said, annoyed at his tardiness.

"It's sold out?"

"I bought tickets for the next showing. We have an hour to kill."

"Great plan!" he boomed, as though the later showing had been his plan all along.

"I didn't know what to do. It would have been nice to be able to call you."

"Nonsense! It all worked out perfectly."

"For you, Dan. Not for me. I didn't know if I wasted thirty dollars on tickets."

"You didn't waste a dime!"

"But I didn't know that," she said, her voice finally tightening with anger.

"Calm down, babe."

"Get a cell phone."

"You know I can't use a cell phone."

"You can use it to send text messages. Then you won't have to put the phone near your big head."

Dan considered her idea for a moment. "I don't think that will work. Just having it on my person makes me feel off."

She gave up then, handing him his ticket. She looped her arm through his, and they strolled down the street, and she never mentioned a cell phone to him again.

She accepted his foibles because that's what you did for people you cared about. Love was easy. Charity was hard.

಄಄಄

Dan observed Daphne. She was staring at her laptop screen, but her eyes and her fingers were still. She wasn't reading her typed words, and she wasn't adding to them. She was contemplating something, and whatever it was, it wasn't making her happy.

He refused to believe he was never going to be able to fuck this woman again. Daphne was amazing in bed. She was amazing to look at. She was by far the most gorgeous woman he'd ever dated, and he'd lived in LA for over twenty years so that was saying something.

When he thought of her sleeping with another man, he wanted to break the table in half. She'd called him a caveman, and she'd been right. Daphne was right about a lot of things. She'd always been able to see right through him. He hated and loved that about her. Mostly he loved it. He could truly be himself around her because there was no point in faking it.

What a relief that was.

He tapped his pen on his notebook, a test. Usually, his tapping drove her nuts. Right now, she didn't seem to notice, though. He wanted her to notice, to snap at him, to tell him to stop the infernal racket. Infernal. She always used such crazy words.

Late at night he liked to read *The New Yorker*. While they'd been together she'd usually lie right there next to him. (And usually naked. God, that body.) Every time he came across a word he didn't know, or a word he did know that he figured no ordinary person would know, he'd run it by her.

"Daphne," he said to her one night. She was sitting next to him in her bed, the blue comforter tucked up over her bare breasts, reading a novel she'd been hired to adapt into a screenplay.

She'd gotten money upfront for that job. Good money.

"Hmm?"

"What's a lepidopterist?"

"A butterfly collector." She never even looked up from her book.

"There's no way you know that!" He was incredulous. "You must have read this article."

She set down her book and looked at him. "What are you talking about?"

"This article on Nabokov. You read it. That's how you know that word."

"Everyone knows Nabokov collected butterflies."

"Everyone does not know that. Nor do they know that the scientific term for butterfly collector is lepidopterist."

She turned back to her book, ending the conversation.

"You didn't read the article?"

"If you want to know why I know a lot of words, you can just ask me to tell you the story."

He hadn't asked her to tell him the story. Instead, he'd tossed his magazine to the floor along with her novel and fucked her silly.

God they always had great sex. Outstanding sex. Surely she still agreed with him on that.

Only one way to find out.

"Are you going to miss it?" he asked her. Her eyes met his over the top of her laptop screen.

"Which part?"

"The fucking."

She rolled her eyes. "I won't miss the way you talk about it."

"There are the words, and then there is the deed. Answer the question."

"You and I were very compatible in bed."

He noticed she still hadn't answered his question, although her admission mollified him somewhat.

He had a decision to make: Was he going to try to win her back?

She'd started typing again, her hands flying over the keyboard so quickly it didn't even sound like she was making sense. But he knew she was. Daphne worked fast. She was a thoroughbred. Until yesterday, she'd been his thoroughbred.

Could he let her go?

He thought of another man's hands on her slender hips, on her slender thighs. Of her delicate arms wrapping around another man's chest while she rode him. He started seeing black spots over his vision.

Yes. He could let her go.

At least, he was pretty sure he could.

After his crass question about their erstwhile sex life, Dan finally let her work in silence. Daphne was grateful. She hit a rhythm with her work and barely noticed the time pass except when Rebekah brought her new Americanos, one every hour.

God, she loved this place. If she and Dan had to divide up Brentwood in the breakup, Uptown belonged to her.

Besides, Tony didn't have Dan's picture hanging behind the register.

Shortly after Rebekah dropped off Daphne's eleven-thirty coffee, she noticed someone nearing her table. Then, she heard a cleared throat. Daphne glanced up. Carrie stood next to her.

"Hey, um, Daphne," Carrie said, unsure what to call her. Daphne admired the girl for choosing to go with her first name instead of her last.

"Scram, Dan," Daphne said. "I have a lunch date with Carrie here."

Dan closed his notebook and dropped it and his pen into his leather satchel. He stood.

"Dan Morello," he said, offering his hand to Carrie.

"Carrie Ademola," Carrie said, shaking his.

Daphne watched while Dan appraised Carrie's obvious loveliness. Any man would. And Daphne knew plenty of couples with a greater than twenty-year age difference, especially in Los Angeles. But there was a predatory glint to Dan's toothy smile that she didn't like. She didn't bring Carrie here to throw her in the path of this particular wolf.

"Dan," Daphne said again. "Get out of here."

"I'm going. Jesus." He left his dirty coffee cup on the table. "Don't forget our pitch meeting tonight."

"Have I ever forgotten a meeting?"

"Never, babe. Never." He bent down to kiss her cheek, and then stopped himself inches from her skin. She could feel his warm breath on her, and then it was gone, and he was heading toward the door.

Daphne let out a breath she didn't realize she'd been holding.

"Have a seat, Carrie."

Carrie sat across from her, setting her small canvas satchel on her lap.

"That was Dan Morello?" Carrie asked.

"In the less-than-toned flesh." Daphne almost felt guilty about the dig, but then she saw the stars in Carrie's eyes and realized she didn't feel guilty at all.

"He wrote my screenwriting textbook," Carrie said, undeterred.

"A ghostwriter wrote your screenwriting textbook," Daphne said. "Her name is Rachel, and she's Dan's ex-girlfriend. He has a way of getting people to do stuff for him."

Not me, though, Daphne thought. *Maybe that's why we didn't work out.*

"Enough about Dan," Daphne said. "I want to learn about you. If you've never seen Dan at Rivet, then you can't have worked there long."

"Almost two months," Carrie said.

"And you write in your free time."

"Yes."

"Are you any good?" Daphne smiled a bit to take the edge off the question, but she wanted to see Carrie's reaction.

"Yes." Carrie gazed boldly back at Daphne.

"Let me clear this out of your way." Rebekah appeared at the table, sweeping away Dan's dirty mug.

"Would you like something?" Daphne asked Carrie.

"Coffee. Just regular coffee."

"Put it on my tab," Daphne told Rebekah, who nodded as she headed back to the bar.

"You don't have to pay for me," Carrie said stiffly.

"I know," Daphne said. "But I don't mind. So you should let me."

Rebekah returned with a large mug of black coffee for Carrie. Just like Daphne did, Carrie wrapped both hands around her warm mug and lifted it to her lips. They sat, facing each other and mirrored in gesture. Daphne was acutely aware of Carrie's internal feeling of urgency, of her need to succeed, because she'd once felt that way too. She'd sacrificed her friends—she'd sacrificed herself—to get what she'd thought she wanted. It was only by luck that she'd survived unscathed.

And, one could argue, she wasn't unscathed at all.

"How did you get your job at Rivet?" Daphne asked. She knew jobs at the exclusive restaurant were hard to come by, and new employees usually required a recommendation.

"My cousin is friends with one of the owners."

This detail caught Daphne's attention. Surely, by now, Carrie knew Daphne was friends with Greta. And she would also have figured out that Greta and Timmy—who was another owner—were together. There was only one owner left.

"You must mean Sandy," Daphne said.

"That's right."

"Is your cousin a colleague of his in the industry?"

Carrie giggled, and she looked very young. "Hardly. He's more like a handyman."

"Your cousin is Marlon." Daphne felt a small shock speaking his name.

Carrie nodded. "You know him?"

"Yes, of course."

"I guess you guys all know each other. Kind of an in-crowd over there."

"I don't know him well," Daphne said. "He never comes to Rivet."

"No one knows him well. He prefers it that way."

"Do you know him well?" Daphne asked.

"He's more like my brother than my cousin."

"How's that?"

"His parents died when we were still pretty young, and he lived with us until he turned eighteen. Our moms are, uh, were sisters." Carrie pointed at her brown forearm. "Our daddies looked a little different from one another."

In five minutes, Carrie had told Daphne more than Daphne had learned about Marlon in the last five years. He was an orphan. He was on his own at eighteen. He had family here in LA: Carrie, whom Daphne had taken a liking to, and Carrie's mom and dad, who lived in the Valley.

What Daphne inferred: Marlon was forever anchored to a city he didn't like at all.

Daphne checked her watch. It was noon. She really hoped Marlon would show at three. She had an apology to make.

"You hungry?" Daphne asked. "They have excellent food. Tony bakes anything a human can into a pastry."

"People still eat bread?" Carrie widened her eyes in surprise.

"It's a miracle he's still in business." Daphne glanced around at the packed restaurant.

"Sure, let's eat," Carrie said. "And then you can tell me why you invited me here."

So Daphne told her. And when lunch was over, they'd scheduled a meeting for two weeks hence, with Daphne, Carrie and Daphne's agent. Daphne would be at the meeting to make sure nothing went screwy. She felt protective of Carrie, the way she felt protective of her own younger self. She thought about when she herself had first arrived in Los Angeles, first started trying to make her own way, and she'd had no one to look out for her.

She wouldn't let anything happen to Carrie. It was a small gift she could give her.

Six

Daphne arrived at Rivet to meet Olivia just before three o'clock on Monday afternoon. The valet stand was empty, but she'd expected that. At this time of day, Rivet was closed to the public. She drove her car past the understated exterior of the building—Rivet had been a city-owned storage building in a former life—and parked her car in the valet lot. She strolled down the sidewalk to the restaurant. She climbed the steps and knocked on one of the two tall wooden doors. The pair looked like they'd been salvaged from an old French chateau.

After a minute, she could hear a bolt turning, and then a young man leaned his head out. Daphne gave him her winning smile.

"Hey," he said, opening the door farther. "Can I help you?"

"My name is Daphne. I'm here to see Olivia."

"I'm Ricky." He stood in the doorway, using his shoulder to prop open the door. Daphne was accustomed to this sort of behavior: men forgetting what they were supposed to be doing during a conversation with her.

"How long have you worked at Rivet, Ricky?" Daphne asked, humoring him.

"I just started last week."

That explained a few things, like his unprofessional

behavior at the door and his undesirable Monday afternoon lunch-to-dinner shift.

"How do you like it so far?"

"It's incredible," he said. "You'll never believe who I waited on last week."

"Hush." Daphne interrupted him. "You know you're not supposed to wait-and-tell. It's in the rules."

"Oh, right." Ricky ducked his head. "I keep forgetting."

"Pretend you're a doctor, and the guests are your patients. You can't break their confidentiality. Not for anything."

A car engine churned behind her, and she looked over her shoulder to see a dark pewter Aston Martin pull into Rivet's driveway.

Ricky let out a low whistle. "Sweet ride."

Daphne strolled down the steps to the car. Sandy rolled down his window. "Just dropping off Marlon before I head out to an appointment," he said.

Marlon opened the passenger door. He stood and met her eyes over the roof of the car, giving her a small smile.

"I'll keep you posted on our progress," Daphne said. "And on your catering bill." She gave an exaggerated wink.

Sandy touched the back of her hand where it rested on the car's windowsill. "You doing OK?"

She felt herself grow defensive for a moment. Sandy's question unnerved her. She was always OK. No matter what happened to her, she came through it all right. That was who she was.

"Sure," she said.

"It seems like Greta getting married has maybe brought up some stuff for you."

Daphne thought about the scene she'd made at Sandy's yesterday and felt ashamed. "I'm sorry for how I acted at your house," she said. "I was inexcusably rude—to you and to Marlon." She glanced at Marlon, who had turned his back to the car and leaned against it, as though he'd intuited her desire for privacy. "I'll apologize to him as well."

"I've been around a long time, and I've seen some things," Sandy said. "Like when a person feels she has something to make up for even when she doesn't."

"I just want Greta to be happy."

"She wants the same for you."

Marlon walked by her then and climbed the steps to the front door of Rivet. She watched him speak with Ricky. Crossing her arms over her chest, she turned back to Sandy. "Perhaps you're right," she said. "Greta and Timmy getting married has brought up some ugly memories. But I don't know how to make them stop."

"If I knew how to make the ugly memories stop, I wouldn't be living alone in that big house." He smiled at her and shook his head. "Do me a favor?" he asked.

"Of course."

"Give Marlon a ride home for me?"

Sandy lived half way up Laurel Canyon. Rivet was basically in Pacific Palisades. To give Marlon a ride home would take her past her own home in Brentwood—which was fifteen minutes east of Rivet—and another thirty minutes east and north into Hollywood and the hills above. In total, he was asking her to drive an hour out of her way.

"Sure I can," she quickly said. Such a small favor to clear her conscience over yesterday's detonation in Sandy's kitchen? She was delighted to have the chance.

Sandy sped off, and she watched him go, thinking of ugly memories, of a pool of blood that wouldn't come clean.

When she turned back to Rivet's entrance, Marlon and Ricky were still chatting. Joining them, she heard Ricky mooning over Sandy's car and over Sandy. Ricky still hadn't let anyone cross Rivet's threshold, though.

"Ricky," Daphne said, interrupting his gushing. "We're coming in now."

"What? Right. Sure." Ricky led the way into the building.

As she followed Ricky inside, Marlon chuckled over her shoulder. Her back stiffened. She had trouble reading Marlon, and she could read nearly anyone. She walked quickly, putting space between her and him.

Inside the restaurant, servers prepared for the dinner shift, changing linens and setting tables, engaging in all the prep work that goes on behind the scenes in fine restaurants before the patrons arrive.

She nodded to the bar manager, Quentin, who had worked at Rivet for almost a decade. She put Quentin in his mid-thirties, and she'd always found him handsome, with his black hair and bright hazel eyes. Quentin had watched the restaurant change hands five years ago, and considering the fierce loyalty he'd shown to the new owners, he seemed happy with Rivet's evolution. The new owners were far more trusting of their employees than the old ownership had been. For a bar manager, that trust meant more responsibility and also more freedom.

"Daphne!" Olivia came striding out of the manager's office and gave her a hug.

When Daphne had first moved to Los Angeles, she'd met Olivia. They'd worked together under very different circumstances. Back then, Olivia had seemed quiet and shy. But Olivia was also very observant. When Rivet had needed a new manager, Greta insisted they give Olivia the job. Turned out Olivia was only quiet and shy when she needed to act that way to survive.

"Can you believe it?" Daphne said.

"I cannot! But I'm so excited. Keeping it a secret from Greta is going to be impossible, even for three days."

"We can do it."

"Can we?" Olivia nodded toward Ricky, who was rolling silverware into linen napkins for the patio and bar place settings.

Just then, Daphne remembered who'd come with her. She stepped to the side, revealing Marlon.

Before she could introduce Marlon to Olivia, he held out his hand. "It's good to see you again," he said.

"You too," Olivia said, blushing, the pinkness spreading up to her natural blond hairline.

Daphne turned to Marlon. "I thought you never came to eat here."

"I don't."

"Sometimes we cater meals at Sandy's," Olivia said quickly. Too quickly. The catered meals were a truth, but they weren't the whole truth. Olivia, it seemed, had a small crush.

Daphne let the matter drop and returned to the business

at hand. "Speaking of catering, what are we going to do for this wedding?"

They sat at the bar, and Quentin made them spritzers with lime juice and some other mysterious ingredients from unlabeled bottles. Olivia had already come up with some ideas, and she laid out her plans on the bar. Daphne and Marlon sat on either side of her, examining the sketches and menus.

Marlon, despite having avoided Rivet as a patron, knew an awful lot about what kind of food the restaurant could produce. Sandy had been right to send him. After an hour, they were done. Marlon's knowledge of the floor plan of Sandy's house allowed Olivia to design the arrangement of buffet tables and bar stations. His knowledge of food, and Rivet's food in particular, allowed him and Olivia to put together a meal Daphne would be proud to serve Greta and Timmy.

She watched Marlon, his head tilted toward Olivia's, and she felt grateful, even warm. She thought about what Carrie had told her, about how he'd spent his teen years without parents, living in Carrie's home, and she wanted to know more.

"Ready?" She turned to him once Olivia had headed back to her office to set their plans in motion.

"What do you mean?"

"Sandy didn't tell you? He asked me to drive you home."

"Did he now?" Marlon looked like he would be having a conversation with Sandy when he got home.

"I'm happy to. Really."

"A bit out of your way, isn't it?"

Daphne checked her watch. It was a little after four. By the time she dropped off Marlon, it would be close to five. At six, she had a pitch-meeting-dinner-thing with Dan and a young producer she didn't know. Dan thought the meeting would be a great opportunity for them both to meet an up-and-comer. Dan was usually right about these things.

The dinner was in West Hollywood, not far at all from Sandy's place. She could just go early and kill time at the bar.

"Actually, tonight it isn't out of my way at all," she said. "I have a thing in Hollywood."

"A thing?"

"Yes."

Marlon chuckled again, the same sound he'd made coming into Rivet, the same unnerving sound that made her feel as though he knew far more about her than he let on, more than she ever wanted anyone to know except for the few people, like Greta, whom she trusted with her entire life.

She didn't trust Marlon with her entire life. She didn't even know him. Suddenly, the same anger she'd felt toward him yesterday came roaring back. She tried her best to stifle it.

They walked along the road to the valet lot to retrieve her car. The afternoon sun warmed her through her black sweater. The warmth felt good after the dark interior of Rivet. It energized her. She eyed Marlon, who smiled slightly as they strolled.

He looked smug. She wanted to know why.

"I had lunch with Carrie Ademola today," she said, watching him closely for a reaction. Marlon looked startled by her words. Daphne felt gratified that she managed to knock him off-kilter.

"Why?" he asked.

"I met her here." Daphne nodded at Rivet. "She and I have a lot in common."

"Doubt it."

Daphne smiled. It seemed he didn't know her so well after all. "Carrie told me about your parents. I'm sorry to hear they died when you were so young."

Daphne watched his reaction. At her words, Marlon pressed his mouth closed, the skin around his eyes tightening.

When they got to her car, he stopped, not opening his door. He rested his hand on the roof, looking her dead in the eye. "You sound genuinely sympathetic."

"I am," Daphne said, taken aback by his skeptical tone.

"But we both know there's more going on here."

Daphne, recognizing a worthy opponent, nodded.

"You wouldn't be using the death of my parents to make a power play here would you? To try to get some sort of upper hand?"

Daphne felt tears sting her eyes, and not just from the

dust of the road or from the late afternoon sun in her face. Of course she'd been making a play. She had indeed wanted to get the upper hand, to let him know that as much as he might think he knew about her, she knew things about him too. That he wasn't so mysterious. That he shouldn't seem so self-satisfied.

She wanted him to feel like she did: unsteady. So she'd been manipulative. Mean.

She didn't recognize the person she was around this man. She barely recognized the person she was at all the past two days. Whoever this strange Daphne was, she didn't like her.

"I'm sorry," she said.

Marlon relaxed, running his hands through his hair. "I think you and I need to start fresh."

"Yes," Daphne said, grateful that he'd stopped her from using her knowledge against him, and grateful that he'd forgiven her for trying.

Sandy was right. Something was wrong with her. She was out of control in the ways that she was usually the most in control. It was important to Daphne that she not cause pain to the people close to her. But that's all she'd done the past twenty-four hours.

She didn't know how to make it stop.

"Hop in," she said.

She pulled out of the lot, and they headed north to Santa Monica Boulevard.

Daphne took the roads in her normal fashion—as fast as she could until other cars slowed her down, shifting as easily as breathing.

After about ten minutes, Marlon spoke.

"Can you slow down a bit?"

Taken aback by his request, Daphne slowed to just a few miles above the speed limit. "Sure. Sorry. My car does prefer to take these turns at speed."

"I'm not a huge fan of driving fast."

Daphne remembered the day before, seeing Marlon working on the Camaro. "Aren't you rebuilding a muscle car?"

He laughed. "Sure am. And I plan on cruising nice and slow in it. Perfect for all that traffic on Sunset."

"I thought men bought muscle cars specifically so they could drive fast."

"My mom died in a car accident. Speeding seems an unnecessary risk."

Daphne thought of her own incessantly speedy driving.

"What are you driving while you rebuild the Camaro?" she asked.

"Nothing."

"You don't have a car?" Daphne worked to keep the incredulity out of her voice. Typically, Daphne was a master at hiding her emotions, especially when they might make someone else feel bad. She didn't want Marlon to know she was judging him for living in Los Angeles without a car when he could clearly afford one. But anyone would find his car-less status completely strange.

"I had one. It stopped working. Now I'm building a new one."

"And in the meantime?"

"I don't need to go many places. I can walk to the market from Sandy's place, and they have most of what I need. Plus, I don't have a lot of friends." He gestured around them as they sped by the life on Santa Monica. "Don't you find that, despite all the millions of people that surround us, you just end up with your few friends, and your few favorite places?"

Daphne thought about her small world in Brentwood, of Greta and Timmy, of Rivet, of even Dan and of Sandy. There just weren't that many people who were terribly important to her. Or that many places she ventured to.

Marlon was right.

"What about Carrie?" she asked.

She noticed Marlon stiffen again. If he had a weakness, it was his adopted sister.

"What about her?"

"Don't you want to see her more?"

"We meet up for coffee every week."

He sounded almost defensive to Daphne, as though he had something to make up for, but Daphne didn't know what.

"Well, that's good. Greta and I get together every week too." Daphne tried for a reassuring tone. "Carrie still lives in

Westwood, right? Near UCLA?"

"In her crappy college apartment with twenty other kids," he said. "I can't stand going there. Did you ever live like that?"

"No, actually. Greta and I lived together our junior year, and then we graduated a year early."

"Running from or running to?" Marlon asked.

Daphne laughed, a little shocked at both his perceptiveness and his directness. She turned north onto a side road that would take them to Sunset. He kept her perpetually unbalanced. There was only one way to handle the problem. Head on.

"You are one of the few people I've ever met who can constantly surprise me," Daphne said. "Part of me wishes you would stop it."

"Who is the other person?"

Daphne sighed. "That right there. That was a completely unpredictable reaction to what I said."

"Not really. I just think you misjudged me."

Daphne shook her head, wondering if he was right. "The other person is Greta."

"You're telling me that the other person who keeps you on your toes is your best friend?"

"Yes."

"Then why on Earth would I stop?"

Daphne turned left off Sunset to head north up Laurel Canyon. She loved how her car handled the steep climb. She wished she could take the curves faster, but she didn't want to upset Marlon.

"I really am sorry to hear about your mom dying," she said. "You know Greta's mom died a few years ago."

"I did not," Marlon said. "Is that your secret to share?"

"It's not a secret," Daphne said. "When she died, it wasn't sudden, but it was still horrible. There's nothing OK about losing your mom."

Daphne thought about her own mom, whom she hadn't spoken with in years. She wondered if it was possible to lose someone before they died.

"Thank you," he said. "She was everything to me back then. Losing her was the worst thing that's ever happened to me."

Daphne downshifted to head up a particularly steep curve. She passed the house where she'd acquired her sideboard from the side of the road. She couldn't help but glance every time she passed, hoping to find more treasures.

After a few minutes, Daphne turned right onto a small road off Laurel Canyon, headed downhill a bit and then turned into Sandy's driveway. Instead of stopping in the circular drive at the main house, she cruised down the hill to the garage. All the bays were closed. She parked in front of the second bay, where she knew the non-running Camaro was located.

Marlon opened his door. "When is your thing tonight?" he asked, before stepping out of the car.

"At six. It's not far from here."

"What time is it now?"

"I'm guessing you don't wear a watch?"

Marlon shook his head.

"No cell phone either?" She thought of Dan then, and the frustrations that followed from his refusal to embrace any modern technology.

"Are you kidding? Of course I have a cell phone. I just didn't want to fish it out of my pocket when you have a clock right there on your dashboard."

Daphne tried hard to suppress her smile. "It's ten to five."

"Perfect. You have time to come up and have a beer on my deck."

"Isn't it Sandy's deck?"

"I'm not talking about Sandy's deck. I'm talking about my deck." He closed the passenger door, then headed off, as though expecting her to accept his invitation.

Daphne turned off the car and grabbed her bag, following him around the side of the garage. A gravel path lined with jade plants led to an exterior staircase that climbed the back of the building. He unlocked a metal gate, then led her up the steps. At the top was a smaller version of the deck that graced Sandy's house.

But Marlon's deck wasn't small—the garage had six bays, after all. Suddenly, Daphne wondered just how big Marlon's digs were. Did his apartment take up the entire top of the garage? The deck extended the full length of the building, and like the deck on the main house, there were doors leading into the living quarters every few yards.

"You built this?"

"Sure did."

"Wow."

"Have a seat." He gestured to a pair of lounge chairs with a table between them.

The furniture, she noted, matched the furniture on Sandy's deck. Sandy spared no expense to keep his assistant-handyman in style. Daphne sat facing the canyon below, where she could see the tops of houses and then, farther off, the city, whose lights were beginning to shine as the sun approached the horizon.

Marlon disappeared into the apartment and reemerged a little while later with two open beers. He handed her a bottle, and she examined the label. It was a Rocky Mountain microbrew that looked tasty.

"Don't you think a girl like me would prefer wine?" she asked.

"Not a chance." He sat on the lounger to her right and gazed into the distance.

"Why's that?"

He turned his eyes on her then. "You drive like you'd prefer a dirt track to Indy. I've seen you choose a burger over filet mignon. I think you do like fine things, but you like to be a little uncivilized too."

"When did you see me get a burger? I thought you never went to Rivet."

"Timmy's birthday dinner here at Sandy's last fall. I handled the take-out order. You and Greta got burgers."

"Why didn't you join us? Surely Sandy invited you?"

"Didn't feel right." He sipped his beer.

"Because you didn't know us all that well?" Daphne paused, thinking. "But that can't be true. You knew Sandy and Greta. Even Timmy."

"Busting in on a tight circle like that, on someone else's family, that's not something I do if I can help it."

Daphne thought then of a young Marlon, left on the

doorstep of another family when his own had died on him.

He must be so alone now, Daphne thought. *And he does it to himself.*

Daphne reached out and touched his left arm, resting her palm there for a moment, as though she could tell him with her touch what she couldn't say with words. That he wasn't alone. That Carrie loved him like a true brother—Daphne had seen it herself. That even though Daphne had been rough on him the past twenty-four hours, she could see him more clearly now. And she liked what she saw.

In fact, as the sun set further, she liked what she saw more and more. The light glinting off his hair. His cool gray eyes, such a strange and lovely color. He'd even scrubbed his hands, she noticed with a smile.

He leaned into her hand a bit as though in response to her touch. Then she pulled her hand away.

She drank more of her beer, the coldness of the drink settling her thoughts. She remembered her dinner plans. She remembered her commitment to Dan. She looked at her watch.

"I have to go," she said. "I have my thing."

"You could go," he said. "Or you could stay up here and watch the sunset. I have a feeling it's going to be a good one."

"What?" she said. "No."

"I can usually tell. It's a gift."

"I'm not talking about the sunset."

"You should be. What's the point of working for yourself if you can't watch a perfect sunset when one comes along?"

"The reason I'm able to work for myself is because I don't skip important meetings." Her voice snapped more than she intended.

She didn't particularly want to go to dinner with Dan that night. In part it was because memories of the things he'd said to her last night (*I'll remember you as a cheater*) and that morning (*You can't count on anyone it seems*) lingered. But it was also because she didn't want to leave Marlon.

She really didn't.

Marlon set his beer on the table and stood. He took hers from her hand and set it next to his, then pulled her to her feet. He rested both of his hands on her shoulders, his thumbs brushing her neck.

She let him touch her.

"Sandy's worried about you," he said. "He thinks you're having a hard time. Maybe because of Greta's wedding, maybe because of some other stuff too."

"Sandy asked me if I'm doing OK, back at Rivet."

"What'd you tell him?"

"I told him I'm having a hard time."

"Cancel your thing," Marlon said. "And then you can tell me what's wrong."

"Why would I tell you?" She felt the heat of his hands through the soft fibers of her sweater. "We're basically strangers."

"Don't you know that strangers are the easiest people to talk to?"

Daphne thought of yesterday morning, waking up next to John. She didn't even know his last name. She thought of the other anonymous men she'd shed her problems upon, physically if not verbally.

She nodded. "I need to make a call."

He leaned forward, brushing his chin across her temple. Then he released her shoulders. He sat back down in his chair and lifted his beer to take another sip.

Hands shaking, Daphne fished around in her bag until she found her phone. She dialed Dan, hoping he hadn't left home yet.

"Babe!" Dan said. "I was literally walking out the door, but I just knew it was you. Wanna ride together?"

"I hate to do this to you, but I have to cancel. You'll be fine without me, right?"

"What do you mean you're canceling? This is the opportunity of a lifetime!"

Daphne rolled her eyes. With Dan, it was always the opportunity of a lifetime.

"Sorry, Dan. I can't make it. But I'll be at Uptown tomorrow as usual, and you can tell me all about it."

"Are you with someone?" His voice switched from bombastic to worried and jealous.

Daphne felt bad. She didn't want to hurt him. "What do you mean by that?"

"Are you with whomever you were with last weekend?"

"No, Dan. I'm not."

"You're lying. You're with a man."

"I'm at Sandy's house planning Greta's wedding, and things are running late." She kept her voice light. "Stop being an ass."

Dan was silent for a minute, apparently mulling the veracity of her words. "What you did was really fucked up."

"I'm sorry I hurt you," she said.

The line went dead.

She lowered the phone from her ear and realized she was shaking even more now. She glanced at Marlon.

He wasn't watching the sunset. He was watching her. Closely. "This Dan fellow. Is that the guy you were seeing? The guy at Timmy's birthday dinner?"

"Yeah. We broke up yesterday."

"You did the breaking up."

Daphne nodded.

"And he isn't taking it too well?"

Daphne nodded again.

"How long were you two together?"

"A year and a half? I have to think about it. We sort of eased into our relationship," she said. "We started out as work friends."

"And now it sounds like you guys aren't much at all."

Daphne sat down next to Marlon again and chugged the rest of her beer. She set the bottle on the table, then leaned back in her lounge chair and shut her eyes.

"You can't watch a sunset with your eyes closed," he said.

"No. But I can feel it."

Seven

Marlon Barringer didn't like taking risks. He drove slowly. He wore light-colored clothes when he took walks so drivers could see him. He had plenty of money in his savings accounts. He wore safety goggles when woodworking, and he never put his left hand in front of a chisel. He knew his risk-averse behavior stemmed from the deaths of his parents when he was young, but he was OK with that. Being driven by the past was only a problem when it was a problem.

Like right now. He looked at Daphne Saito, lounging next to him on the long, brown-cushioned chair, eyes closed, black ponytail hanging loose over her shoulder, unaware of his examination. Of his fascination. He'd managed to keep at least that much under wraps.

He'd meant it when he'd said she couldn't read him right because she'd misjudged him. He knew that she thought he lacked motivation. She thought that was why he didn't try to make a career showing his paintings. Truth was, he was extremely motivated. And he did have a career with his paintings. He just didn't need to have a show. Each one was sold before he'd picked up a brush.

Marlon made a very good living.

She also didn't understand his relationship with Sandy. That was clear enough. She would figure it out soon, though, once she spent more time with him.

His relationship with Sandy was basic psychology. When Marlon had been eighteen, he'd met Sandy, and the childless man had taken him in. But Marlon wasn't just Sandy's assistant. Marlon and Sandy were family, and neither man had much family.

"You want another beer?" Marlon asked.

She tilted her head in his direction. She opened her perfect brown eyes to gaze at him.

He wondered what ends he would go to in order to keep her on his deck.

"Yes," she said. "Bring the rest of the six-pack."

"The beer will get warm out here."

"The sun is setting." She pierced him with her eyes. "Bring the six-pack and a blanket."

She turned her head to the sky again and shut her eyes. Marlon remembered Sandy's description of Daphne: *gorgeous, whip-smart and potentially lethal.* Not exactly the girl for the risk averse.

He entered the door that led into his kitchen. The garage apartment resembled Sandy's house. When Sandy had remodeled his house (with Marlon's help), they'd done both spaces at the same time. The apartment had the same stone countertops, the same custom cabinetry. Marlon had insisted that putting such fine materials in a guest house was a wasted expense, but Sandy had seemed delighted by the idea.

Marlon had only been a junior in college.

It wasn't until Greta had come along that Sandy had seemed to take an interest in another person. Greta had captured Sandy's attention much like Marlon had—he was protective of her and treated her like a favored niece or even a daughter. Greta had quickly won over Marlon too. She was also part of his family.

But Marlon had never had much occasion to get to know Daphne.

He'd seen her from a distance many times. Passed her coming and going. Noticed her, of course—how could a man not? She was a knock-out. That much was undebatable. But she always seemed busy, and she always seemed taken. So he'd kept his distance.

He opened his fridge. Inside were all the fresh ingredients he had purchased at the neighborhood market. Sandy hadn't said as much, but the reason he was having Marlon handle the wedding catering was because Marlon knew his way around a kitchen.

In the refrigerator door was his collection of beers. He liked to try new ones every time he went to the store. After hesitating a moment—the phrase "potentially lethal" crossed his mind again—he grabbed the remainder of the six-pack. He snagged the quilt from the couch and made his way back out onto the deck.

He set the beers on the table. On her lounger, Daphne had kicked off her shoes and tucked her sock-clad feet up under her bottom. She opened her eyes when she heard him approach. He stood there with the blanket in his hands, unsure of what to do with it.

Draping it over her himself seemed far too intimate.

"Scoot your chair next to mine," she said. "Then we can share."

Clearly the two of them had different ideas of what constituted intimate.

But it didn't seem as though Daphne were trying to seduce him. Quite the contrary. She seemed to be curling into herself, looking inward for comfort. But he was flattered she felt relaxed enough to do so around him. He knew what kind of trust it took to let down one's guard around someone new.

He moved the table out of the way and pulled his chair adjacent to hers. The armrests touched. After sitting down, he flung the quilt over both of them, and it settled over their chairs, brushing the deck on either side.

Daphne ran her hands over the material. "This is beautiful."

"My mother made it."

Daphne paused, seeming to take in his words. "Did your mom make many quilts?"

"One a month, it seemed. She gave most of them away. I have a few of them left."

"What was her name?"

"Isabella."

"Italian?"

"Very. She named me after Marlon Brando."

Daphne giggled. Then her face turned serious. "I'm sorry I laughed."

"No, it is hilarious. My mom had stars in her eyes. Thought I could be a movie star or something, growing up in Los Angeles. But you look at Marlon Brando—I mean, just the tragedies with his kids—one a killer, one committed suicide. Life must have been awful for him."

"It wasn't easy for you either," she said. But there wasn't any pity in her voice, and he found himself liking her even more because of it.

"Maybe the name was a curse," he said.

"What happened to your dad?"

Marlon paused, unsure of how much to share with this beautiful stranger.

It had been so long since he'd shared anything. Sure, he'd met girls—and women—here and there, and many had even seen the inside of his bedroom. But he'd hung onto none of them. He'd certainly never shared anything about his childhood. He thought of Carrie and smiled, feeling a little disgruntled. His cousin-by-blood but sister-in-spirit had taken the choice out of his hands by telling Daphne more than he would have volunteered. He wondered if Carrie had done it on purpose, matchmaking without his consent.

"My father died young. But before he died, he wasn't around much. He was trying to start his own company."

"Doing what?"

"Fine carpentry. Cabinet making. The fancy woodwork you see in houses like these." Marlon waved his hand at the hills below. "He'd leave early, at like five-thirty in the morning, and wouldn't get home until after we were asleep. Once I got old enough to swing a hammer, I realized the only way I'd ever get to see him was to work with him. So that's what I did."

"How old were you?"

"Eight."

"What did Isabella think about that?"

"She was just glad to know he didn't have a mistress."

"But he did, didn't he? In a way? Just not the human kind."

"Yeah, you could look at it like that. He got a few good jobs, but it didn't take. He blew through our family savings in a couple of years. And then he just died. Heart attack. I was twelve."

"Do you have any brothers or sisters?"

"Yeah. Carrie."

Daphne nodded, seeming to understand a bit of what he was saying about his adoptive family.

"My mom died two years later," Marlon continued, "and then I showed up on Aunt Donna's doorstep with two duffle bags."

Daphne ran her hand over the quilt again, tracing the pattern with her delicate fingertip.

"Thank you," she said, finally.

"Well, strangers are the easiest people to talk to," he said.

"Am I still a stranger?" she asked.

Her eyes poured into his, and he felt lost. Then he remembered her phone conversation, the dinner she wasn't having right then, and drew back. He certainly didn't want to be her rebound.

"I've known you for a long time, but it's true we've never become friends," he said. "I'm glad we finally have."

"Me too," she said, looking back at the sun as it neared the horizon. "What time is sunset?"

"Around this time of year? A little before seven-thirty."

She looked at her watch. "What would you normally do for the next thirty minutes?"

"Eat."

"I skipped dinner for this," she said, raising her eyebrows.

"Then I'll be back shortly." He stood, and this time he tucked the blanket around her, intimacy be damned.

Daphne watched the sun dip closer toward the horizon, barely marking the passage of time.

After a while, Marlon returned to the deck with a gigantic platter covered in a Caprese salad. He set it on her lap. She took in the beauty of it before gazing up at him in wonder. "You truly are an artist," she said. "Where's my fork?"

His smile made her stomach flip, and she wondered if the feeling was influenced by the beer. He held out a fork, handle first.

"Is this all mine?" She gestured to her lap.

"I thought we might share," he said. "It's an awful lot."

"Are you just going to eat off of me?"

As soon as she said the words, she wanted to fall off the deck in embarrassment. Marlon just gave her a closed-mouth grin, one that told her he knew what she was thinking, that he was thinking it too, and that they could be grown-ups about it and move on.

She sighed, unsure if she was grateful for his maturity or not.

She ate the salad, the tomatoes so red as to seem cartoonish, the white mozzarella, creamy, the basil, richly pungent—did he grow it himself somewhere?—the olive oil, liberally applied.

After what seemed like only a few minutes, the salad was gone. Marlon produced napkins from the table next to his chair and handed her one while he took the platter from her lap.

"Did you know I'm from North Carolina?" she asked.

"I did."

Daphne was surprised, but then realized she shouldn't have been. Marlon knew about Greta. Therefore, he knew a few things about her.

"Then you know I'm a tomato connoisseur. It's what we do there. Well, tomatoes and pork. And those were amazing tomatoes."

"I buy most ingredients at the market down the hill."

"The one you can walk to."

He nodded.

Daphne passed the shopping area on her way up to Sandy's every time she came, but she paid it little mind. She supposed the handful of stores mattered a lot to the people who lived here, and even more to someone like Marlon who didn't have a car.

"What else can you make?"

"Just about anything originating in Italy. Most things from France. A lot of things from Spain."

"You're a chef," she said, delighted.

"I like to cook."

Daphne felt it again, the tingle of allure that she knew would transform into full-blown attraction if she let it.

She wanted to let it.

But she didn't trust herself. She knew she was reeling from Dan. She was also reeling from Greta's marriage to Timmy. Plus, Sandy was important to her, and Marlon was important to Sandy. Obviously, Marlon was like a son to him. She couldn't screw things up. She couldn't, no matter how much it would make her feel better now.

She looked at her watch. Seven-fifteen.

"We're getting close," she said.

He reached over and took her hand where she had been unconsciously tracing the starburst pattern of the quilt.

God, she was done for.

As the sun dipped beneath the horizon, they huddled under the blanket for warmth, tucking their hands beneath but not letting go.

He started this too, she said to herself. *It wasn't just me.*

She turned to face him, resting her head on the lounger, and he did the same. His gray eyes held so much warmth and caring. She realized these emotions were his status quo. She wanted him to feel those feelings for her.

But she shouldn't get too close. Marlon was too special to all of them. What would Sandy think—or Greta—if Marlon got hurt because of her?

She couldn't be the one to start this. But she could wait here on this chair. She could wait here all night. She'd always been patient, even as a little girl.

He reached his free hand over and tucked a lock of hair behind her ear. He let his hand rest on the curve of her neck. Still, she said nothing. Did nothing.

Marlon let go of her hand. He stood. He gathered the

dishes, the empty beer bottles and the napkins to carry inside the house. He left her alone on the deck, and she felt bereft. How could he not know what she was feeling, the emotions bursting for him?

He came out again and stood next to her chair. He lifted her to him, quilt and all, wrapping his arms around her, placing her sock-clad feet on the deck. Then he kissed her as though he hadn't kissed anyone in years.

He pulled back from her, studying her face. She recognized his expression of deep consideration. This was not a man who made snap decisions. Maybe he could break her curse. Maybe his supreme vigilance could overcome it.

"Come with me," he said, his voice rough. He guided her into his home. She followed, holding his hand like a lifeline.

Inside, the apartment was brightly lit, with floor-to-ceiling doors and windows reminiscent of those in Sandy's house. "You can leave the quilt there," he said, pointing to a brown leather couch by a fireplace.

She folded the quilt carefully before draping it over the back of the couch. She wanted to take her time, to give him the opportunity to change his mind and tell her to go.

He leaned against the kitchen island, watching her. She leaned against the couch's back, wary under his assessing gaze.

"Come here," he said, holding out his hand.

She placed her feet carefully on the polished floors, not because she was tipsy, which she had been earlier but was no longer. No, she stepped carefully because she wanted each step to mean something.

She took his hand, and he led her to his bedroom.

The room was sparsely furnished. A bed with a metal headboard sat beneath a painting that looked to have come from his own hand. The bed itself was covered with another handmade quilt. A set of sliding doors opened onto the deck. There wasn't an item of clothing out of place, she noticed, wondering what he would think of her own messy bedroom.

"Can we open that?" She pointed to the door.

He flicked the lock and slid the door open. Cool air washed into the room. She wrapped her arms around herself and sat on the edge of the bed.

Then he was behind her, and he was pulling her back to his chest, and he was wrapping his arms around her. Their heads were on the pillows, facing the night world beyond.

"Why are you having a hard time right now?" His voice brushed her ear.

The warmth of his body radiated along the entire length of her own. She pressed closer to him, shivering.

"I broke up with my boyfriend, and he's being an ass— but you already know that." At the thought of Dan, of John, of how much she seemed to hurt men even without meaning to, she pulled away from Marlon slightly. Cool air kissed her back through the loose knit of her sweater.

She didn't deserve his warmth.

"I get the feeling you can usually handle breaking up with a man."

She laughed. "Usually. But I'm off my game this week. I think Greta getting married has affected me more than I thought it was going to."

"You usually know how things are going to affect you?"

"Yes, actually."

"I guess that means you're rarely surprised."

"The few times in my life I've been surprised have turned out terrible."

Marlon pulled her close again. He kissed her on the temple. Such a vulnerable spot.

"Take a nap, Daphne. Let someone else worry about the surprises for a little while."

She shut her eyes. Cooled by the night air, warmed by Marlon's arms, her feet tucked under his shins, she fell asleep.

Eight

Daphne opened her eyes. She was alone in a strange bed, covered by a quilt. She was fully clothed, down to her socks.

The memories came back. She sat up quickly, glancing at her watch. It was two o'clock in the morning.

"Marlon?" she called out.

"One sec," he called back from another part of the apartment.

He came into the bedroom wearing a paint-streaked T-shirt and jeans. Both were riddled with holes and fit him snugly from too many washings. She caught herself staring at his upper arms a little longer than was appropriate.

What was appropriate, though, given that she'd just woken up in his bed?

"Why are you awake?" she asked.

"Inspiration got a hold of me."

"You've been painting."

He nodded.

She stood, then peered out onto the deck to where she'd left her shoes and bag. They were gone.

"I brought them into the house once you fell asleep," Marlon said. "They're in the living room."

He led her through the open door to the kitchen, to where her things waited for her on the leather couch.

She pulled on her shoes, then slung her bag over her shoulder.

"That's a heavy bag," he said. "You always have that much stuff with you?"

"Always," she said. "Just in case."

She followed him out onto the deck. But instead of heading left toward the stairs, she went to the railing and leaned out, looking into the night. She glanced to her right, past the dimly lit bedroom doors, and saw, at the very end of the deck, another set of doors. Light poured from them. His studio, she figured.

She turned to where he stood, leaning against one of the chairs with his hip, hands tucked in his pockets. She thought about their bodies curled together on the bed, of the warmth of him pressed against her. Of the single, blistering kiss.

"Why?" she asked. "Or rather, why not? I would have said yes."

He rubbed his chin with his hand, considering. "It just didn't seem like what you needed."

"Are you sure that's the whole reason? Altruism?"

He smiled ruefully. "Nope."

"Did Greta tell you precisely where I grew up?"

"She did not."

"She wouldn't have," Daphne said. "She knows I don't like to tell people. But you can know."

"Hit me," he said.

She smiled. "I grew up in the manager's cottage of the beach motel my parents owned."

"Owned? Are they still there?"

Daphne debated how much to tell him. Then she decided she had nothing to lose. "I would imagine so. But I don't know for sure. I haven't spoken to anyone in my family in years."

"I heard something similar about Greta's father."

"Yeah, she doesn't speak to him at all. But all Greta has is her dad. I have three sisters and two parents." Daphne took a deep breath—it still hurt her to speak the words. "And ever since my birthday, two years ago, I've been dead to them."

"They abandoned you?"

"I don't want to make myself out as a victim," Daphne said. "You could say that we abandoned each other."

She wondered what Marlon would think about leaving behind such a large, living family, when his family had all been taken from him. She wondered if he would judge her.

"So, you grew up in a motel?" he said, seeming to accept her words. But Daphne knew better. There would be another conversation if Marlon had his way.

She explained her childhood. "I worked the check-in counter from the time I was tall enough to see over it. I met a lot of people. I took their money, and I gave them keys," she said. "After years of doing this, I learned to figure out what they were there for." She pushed away from the railing and stood straight. "What they wanted."

"You're saying you're good at reading people."

"I told you I'm rarely surprised."

"You also told me I kept you on your toes."

"I've spent more time with you now."

"Good thing or bad thing?"

She paused in consideration. "Good thing."

"So what have you learned about me?"

"Altruism is part of why you left me alone to sleep tonight. You're a good person, and I don't know many of those." She nodded toward Sandy's house. "I can see why Sandy adopted you."

"And the other part?"

"You don't like to gamble. Not with anything. And I seem like a huge gamble to you."

He was in front of her in two strides, his hands wrapped around her shoulders. "God help me, yes. You do." His mouth was on hers, then, burning away the evening chill.

When he pulled away, she laid her palm against his cheek. "Congratulate yourself. Your instincts are working. I am indeed a terrible bet."

She turned to flee, but he caught her hand.

"Wait," he said. "Answer one question, and I'll let you go."

She nodded.

"Why did your family abandon you?"

"You don't want to know."

"I really think I do."

Daphne looked down at her hand, still caught in his, then at his face. "My father hurt me when I was a girl. He... sold me to a guest for a large sum of money. Our family would have gone bankrupt if he hadn't. I never spoke about it afterwards, not for years."

Shame encased her. She couldn't meet his eyes, so she looked out over the canyon instead. "Two years ago, I flew my mom and sisters out for my birthday—it's in March. I told them what happened, but it was like they didn't believe me. Except the weird part was, they did believe me. They were just angry at me for speaking of it. They chose him over me."

Marlon was silent for a long while after she finished speaking.

Finally, she looked at him, desperate to know what he was thinking. She'd never told anyone this secret except for Greta. What had possessed her to tell Marlon, a stranger? She started to panic. "Will you please say something?" she demanded.

"I'm trying to figure out how you can blame yourself for your mom and sisters cutting you off when you needed them most."

"It's not their fault, not completely. My dad is very controlling and persuasive. Plus, I was the most rebellious daughter."

"Still sounds like you're blaming yourself."

She could sense his sympathy, and it scared her worse than his silence. "Marlon, you have to let go of my hand." She could hear the desperation in her voice.

He did.

She strode away fast, practically running down his stairs. She turned the knob to unlock his metal gate, then held it so it wouldn't clang shut behind her.

Once in her car, she took the turns down the canyon as fast as she wanted, windows down, wondering what it would be like to release her grip from the wheel and fly.

∽∾

Twenty minutes later, Daphne used her clicker to open her garage door, then pulled her car into the parking space under her condo. She climbed the steps from the garage to the metal gate that connected her garage to her front doorstep. Closing the gate behind her, she jumped back, startled.

Someone was asleep in her front porch alcove.

She looked more closely and determined the person was a woman. She looked closer still and realized she knew the person. The woman was dozing on a coat, her head resting on a backpack.

"Miranda?" Daphne said, amazed.

Miranda sat up quickly, looking dazed. When Miranda saw Daphne, she rushed to her feet.

"Hey. Crap. I didn't mean for this to be so weird." Miranda used her fingers to make sure her dark blond hair wasn't totally mussed, and rubbed her cheek where the backpack had imprinted on it. "It just got so late, and everywhere was closed."

"I know what time it is," Daphne said. "How did you find my house?"

Miranda George lived in North Carolina just like so many of the other people Daphne had left behind after college. Miranda wasn't supposed to turn up in Los Angeles uninvited. She wasn't supposed to surprise Daphne, especially this week.

"I just looked you up. Under Daphne, I mean. Did you change your name legally?"

"I did it five years ago," Daphne said. "What are you doing here?"

"I heard this is where a person comes when her mother dies."

Daphne exhaled slowly. She took in Miranda's stony face. Miranda looked bored sharing the news of her mother's death, in fact. Daphne's instincts fired. Something was very wrong.

"What happened?" Daphne asked.

"Alcohol poisoning," Miranda said. "Again. But this time she died."

The way Miranda described her mother, it sounded like drinking was something her mother had done a lot. Daphne had never known this tidbit about Miranda.

"When did you get to LA?"

"This afternoon. My mom's funeral was this morning, and I drove straight to the airport after."

"Do you have a place to stay?"

"Not really."

"Is that all you have?" Daphne asked. Miranda's backpack might hold enough clothes for a week, but that was all.

"Yeah. But you know I've never been one to wear a variable wardrobe."

It was true. In college, Miranda had tended to wear jeans and black T-shirts. Or jeans and black tank tops. Or jeans and black sweaters. She could probably survive a while on the clothes in that bag.

"Come on," Daphne said. "You can stay in my guest room till you figure things out."

Daphne unlocked the door, and Miranda followed her in. She led Miranda to the guest bedroom, which Daphne always kept prepared even though she rarely had guests. She also had a desk in the room where she could set up her laptop, but she didn't mind giving up that workspace. She rarely used it.

Daphne pointed at the desk. "You can put your stuff here," she said. "Everything you need you can find in the bathroom cabinets." She pointed to the guest bathroom off the bedroom. "In the morning, you'll tell me everything."

Miranda sat on the edge of the bed. "There's not much to tell. After college, you took off, and I didn't. I worked in my parents' law firm to make money, dodging the law school question while writing freelance stuff to build a portfolio. I actually have a lead on a job out here if I want to stay."

"Do you want to stay?"

"I have no idea. I just know I don't want to go back."

Daphne had a feeling that going back referred to a lot more than a geographical location.

"We'll talk more after you've slept."

"Thanks for taking me in. I have nowhere else to go."

Daphne heard a nearly unbearable loneliness in Miranda's voice. But she also knew Miranda would reject any and all pity. "I figured," Daphne said. "You look like complete shit."

"You should smell me. Gross." Miranda headed into the

bathroom. Daphne heard her turn on the shower.

Daphne shut the guest bedroom door behind her. Then she grabbed her cell phone and texted Greta: "Miranda George is here. Unexpected arrival. Call me when you get up."

Greta would call in the morning as soon as she received the message.

Daphne entered her own room, closing the door behind her.

She listened to the shower running. Miranda was here. Memories from college flooded back, especially the memory of a particular moment, when Miranda had asked for Daphne's help, and Daphne had failed her.

Daphne couldn't have known the stakes, then. Couldn't have known what failing Miranda would have cost. But the cost to everyone had been high.

She and Miranda had been close friends once. She wondered if they still were, or if Daphne's home was just a place for Miranda to escape to.

Daphne pulled off her clothes, tossing them to the floor. She glanced at her sweater, crumpled on top of her jeans, then picked it up again, holding it to her face. She inhaled. Yes. She could still smell him—mineral spirits, olive oil and Marlon.

Wistful, she climbed into bed. She and Marlon might have worked out in another time, another place.

Nine

Marlon woke Tuesday morning to his phone ringing. Sandy.

"Morning, sir." He sat up, holding his phone to his ear with his shoulder. He glanced at the side of the bed where Daphne had lain the night before. He put his hand on the pillow.

"Meet me in the screening room?"

"Give me twenty minutes."

Marlon tossed his phone on the bed. He showered, dressed and made his way over to the lower entry of Sandy's house. He climbed the stairs to the main floor, then up another level to the top floor. The screening room was a large, windowless space that looked like a miniature movie theater. It held four rows of five narrow, reclining leather chairs, each row elevated. At the back of the room was an A/V booth with a projector, and at the front was a projection screen.

Sandy sat in the middle of the second row holding the remote control in one hand and a coffee cup in the other. He was watching what looked to be a police procedural.

Marlon sat down next to him.

"This is a pilot for a new series I've been asked to invest in," Sandy said. "Tell me what you think. There's a coffee for you."

Marlon glanced down at the cup-holder in his arm rest, and indeed there was a tall coffee cup from the café at the bottom of the hill. He took a sip and watched the show. He knew Sandy got investment requests like this almost daily but that he only considered a few of them. And he rarely brought Marlon in, not because he thought Marlon had little to offer, but because Sandy didn't want to waste Marlon's time.

No, Sandy had brought him here this morning to talk about something other than the pilot, and Marlon had a feeling he knew what that something was.

The show ended, and Sandy used the remote control to turn off the projector and turn up the lights.

"What'd you think?" Sandy asked.

"Good casting for the leads. I wouldn't have thought a former sci-fi leading man could make the transition to detective, but I was wrong."

"He's got good charisma," Sandy said.

"It goes a long way," said Marlon. "He's gained some weight though. Almost looks chubby, especially next to her."

"Good old Hollywood double standards," said Sandy.

Marlon said nothing, thinking of his little sister and the shit he knew she would have to put up with living here and trying to make a living in the film industry. God, he worried about Carrie constantly.

"I saw a car parked by the garage when I got home last night," Sandy said.

"Yep."

"It wasn't there when I got up this morning."

"Nope."

Sandy took a long sip of his coffee. "You think you can handle her?"

"Not in the slightest."

Sandy laughed. "At least you have a sense of your own limitations."

"I always have."

"A person could say she's done some terrible things."

"Not lately." Marlon was startled by his need to defend Daphne.

"Not lately, no."

"You're the one who stranded me with her yesterday. Don't tell me that wasn't deliberate."

"I hoped you might find out what was eating at her. Not take her in for the night."

"Pulling strings on me, sir?" Marlon was officially annoyed.

Sandy sighed. "Don't be mad at me. I'm just feeling protective."

"That's unnecessary."

"I suppose if Greta and Timmy can forgive her, then anyone can," Sandy said. "Just be careful."

Marlon hooted with laughter.

"Yes, yes I know," Sandy said. "You always are."

"I've got a wedding to pull off by tomorrow." Marlon stood. "See you around?"

Sandy nodded, still looking thoughtful.

That made two people who'd warned him away from Daphne: his paternal stand-in and Daphne herself. Marlon wondered if he shouldn't start listening.

But, lord help him, he didn't want to.

 споء

Daphne woke to her phone ringing. She looked at the screen: Greta.

She jumped out of bed and opened the door to peek into the hall. Miranda's door was still shut, the light still off.

"Greta, hey," she said.

"What's she doing there?"

"Her mom died. Alcohol poisoning, she said. The funeral was yesterday, and she just took off afterwards."

"She always was impulsive."

"What should I do?"

"What did she ask you to do?"

"Good point. Nothing."

"That's the other thing about Miranda," Greta said. "She doesn't ask for much."

"Except that one time when she did," Daphne said with regret.

"Except that one time," Greta agreed.

It seemed like all of Daphne's past mistakes were going to torment her this week, when all she wanted to do was focus on Greta's happiness. Her mistake with Miranda happened a long time ago, back when they were in college. Miranda had asked her for help, and Daphne hadn't given it. Daphne hadn't realized then how rare it was for Miranda to ask for help.

Maybe Miranda's appearance last night was fate giving Daphne a second chance.

"See you this afternoon?" Daphne asked.

"Yep," Greta said. "And Daphne?"

"Yeah?"

"I don't think she was close to her mom, but still. This death ruptures her understanding of how everything maps onto everything else. When a parent dies, it's hard to make sense of things." Greta was speaking from experience now. "Give her a hug for me."

"I will."

After they hung up, Daphne showered and dressed, throwing on jeans and a navy blue cotton blouse, then sat at her kitchen table with coffee and her laptop. Even though things had ended uncomfortably with Dan on the phone last night, she was determined to be at Uptown before nine o'clock in case he showed up looking for her. She'd said she'd be there, so she would be there.

After half an hour—at seven o'clock—she heard noises in Miranda's room. Miranda opened the door. She'd obviously gone to sleep with wet hair, because now it hung in bent tangles. Her eyes looked less tired, but no less haunted.

"You're up," Miranda said.

"I always get up early."

"It's late back east. I can't believe I slept this long."

"You had a long day yesterday."

"I'll be out in a minute."

Miranda emerged a few minutes later wearing black, body-skimming jeans and a tight black T-shirt, her hair pulled back in a severe ponytail. Her full lips were painted dark red. She plopped into a chair next to Daphne. Daphne raised her eyebrows.

"What?" Miranda said. "I'm in mourning."

"Nice lipstick."

"I'm starving. Do they serve food in Los Angeles? From what I've seen of the women, I can't tell for certain." She smiled darkly, eyeing Daphne's skinny frame. "No offense."

Daphne laughed. Miranda's sense of humor not only took no prisoners, but often fed those prisoners to hungry carnivores.

"Let me show you around the neighborhood," Daphne said. "I have some meetings today."

"I can look after myself." Miranda sounded defensive. Daphne knew that underneath that defensiveness were some deep wounds.

She touched Miranda's arm. "I know you can."

She encouraged Miranda to bring her own laptop with her, and she gave Miranda a key to the condo. Then they strolled down to San Vicente together. They stopped at Didier's, a French bistro that happened to serve breakfast. It was, as usual, packed.

"You OK sitting at the bar?" she asked Miranda.

"Please. I've been sitting at bars since I was in diapers."

Daphne saved her response to Miranda's statement until they were settled at the bar with two menus.

"Tell me what happened," Daphne said. "I seem to be missing an important part of your biography."

"My mom's been a drunk my whole life. It's a miracle it didn't kill her sooner." Miranda leaned against the back of her barstool, hooking one elbow over the top of it—a casual pose to hide deep pain, Daphne suspected. "There's nothing more to tell."

"You never talked about this in college."

"Not with you, no. Not with most people. Honestly, it was too embarrassing."

Daphne knew what it was like to be embarrassed by her family. The only friend who had ever visited her family home was Greta, and that was only once.

"Don't you think your dad will want you around?" she asked Miranda.

"He's got my little brother."

"Why leave home now? Why not last week? Last year?"

"No reason." She shrugged. Again, though, her eyes were haunted.

"I think you're leaving out some crucial stuff, dear."

"And I'm doing it on purpose," Miranda snapped. "Please just let me eat one meal. Tell me something happy."

Daphne forgave Miranda's angry tone. And happy she could provide. "Greta and Timmy—that's her boyfriend of the last five years—are getting married tomorrow."

"No shit?"

"No shit."

"I bet you are neck deep in wedding planning," Miranda said.

"I am."

"I have the worst timing," Miranda said, resting her face in her hand. "Or rather, my mother has the worst timing. Why couldn't she have waited till next week to off herself?"

"Don't say that," Daphne said, unnerved.

"Why not? None of this is new to me."

It was true, Daphne knew. Unexpected death wasn't new to Miranda. She might seem like a mouthy brat, but shadows followed her everywhere.

"Tell me about the job you have a lead on."

"Actually, I already have the job. I would start next Monday."

"Wow. Doing what?"

"Writing for an entertainment website."

"How did you get the job?"

"We went to Cameron University, Daphne. It has, like, the alumni network of the gods."

"I don't know what that means."

"I emailed someone at the company who is a Cameron alum, he asked for my résumé and portfolio, and I got the job."

"That's it?"

"There was a phone interview, but yeah, that's it."

"Holy crap, that's awesome."

Miranda smiled, and it was the first real smile Daphne had seen since she'd found the girl on her doorstep. "Thanks. It was nice to accomplish something that wasn't tainted by my parents. They didn't even know I was applying for jobs."

"You applied for more than one?"

"Yeah—all over the country. I didn't plan on coming to Los Angeles necessarily. I just planned on getting out of Winston-Salem. I only came here because my mom died."

"You can stay with me if you want, while you try out your job. Give LA a test run."

"I can pay rent," Miranda said, her defensive tone returning.

"Of course you can," Daphne said, soothing her. "We'll have a landlord-tenant meeting after the wedding."

They ate their breakfast—croissant sandwiches, plus plenty of coffee and fresh-squeezed juice—and then Daphne stood.

"I have to go to my first meeting now. It's at Uptown Coffee, just down the street. I work there a lot. You'll be able to find me there later, maybe, but I'm also running around preparing Greta's wedding." She handed her card to Miranda, and scribbled her phone number on the back. "Call me at some point so I have your number."

"OK."

"And you're invited to the wedding. So you should probably buy something to wear."

"What's the dress code?"

"For you? Just wear black."

Miranda watched Daphne leave the restaurant, then turned back to the coffee in front of her. She considered pulling out her laptop and finishing up a contract job she had due for a web client. But she didn't feel like doing it. Writing web copy was more fun than she'd thought it would be—and it beat the hell out of following in her parents' lawyerly footsteps—but it was still a job. And right now, she didn't feel like doing her job.

"Can I get a mimosa?" she asked the bartender.

Miranda had never drunk in college, when the kids around

her had been blasted all to hell. Part of her had been scared that she'd turn out like her mother. Part of her, well, had just been scared. She'd seen what happened to people when intoxication hit.

Now, she was a drinker, just a very deliberate one. Even on a Tuesday morning.

"Um, excuse me?" A man spoke to her right.

She looked up. A guy stood there, about her age, tall—taller than she was, and she was five-ten—and on the good-looking side of things.

"What's up," she said.

"That girl you were with, who just left. Was her name Akane?"

Miranda tilted her head to examine the guy more closely. He seemed a little out of sorts. Something was up. Daphne hadn't gone by Akane in five years. She'd said so last night.

"No," Miranda said. "Who are you?"

"Oh. I'm John." He looked even more disoriented. "I was just having breakfast with my friend there," he pointed over his shoulder with his thumb, and Miranda spied another guy about John's age sitting at a table. "And I thought I recognized her from a—" he paused, searching for the right word it seemed, "from a night out recently."

"How recently?"

"Saturday."

That was indeed recently. Miranda narrowed her eyes. She was pretty sure John had met Daphne on Saturday night, and Daphne had not wanted John to meet her again. What Miranda couldn't figure out was why. Daphne was usually very straightforward. Lying, sneaking around—that was not Daphne's style.

"I'm Miranda," she said. "Sorry that wasn't your friend."

"She, uh, wasn't a friend. Just someone I met. Briefly."

Miranda worked hard to keep a smile from her face. She wondered exactly how brief John had been if Daphne was trying so hard to avoid him now.

Then Miranda did something she knew she shouldn't have done. She felt like it wasn't her mouth speaking or her body acting. She knew Daphne was a good person—she had just taken her in after all these years—and she shouldn't want to hurt her. But thinking of her mother's body rotting in the ground, thinking of the past few years after college putting up with her mother's shit while Daphne lived as a glamorous writer here in Los Angeles, thinking of the one time she'd really needed Daphne's help and Daphne had run out on her much like she'd run out on this John fellow, Miranda's willpower broke.

"Do you want to have a seat, John? I seem to be on my own today, and I'm new in town." She smiled her red-lipped smile. It would either work, or it wouldn't.

"Oh, well, sure," John said, revelation dawning on his face. "Let me just go say good-bye to my buddy."

Really, Miranda thought. *Men.*

She lifted her mimosa to her lips. Delicious.

ക്ക

Around nine o'clock Tuesday morning, Dan Morello entered Uptown Coffee. He placed his order with Tony, the owner, and stared at Daphne's signed headshot while he waited for the barista to bring him his cappuccino. In the photo, she was smiling her open smile, her radiance shining for the world to see, and he wondered if she would ever smile at him like that again. He wished he hadn't been such an ass to her last night on the phone.

He turned to scan the room. She'd said she'd be here this morning to debrief about the dinner she'd skipped last night. And there she was, typing away at her usual table in the back corner, her laptop plugged into the only outlet in the place. He considered turning around and leaving, never speaking to her again. He wasn't sure if he could keep his cool around her any more.

But his practical side won out. She was a gifted writer, and more than that, she was charismatic. Everyone loved this girl. If he burned her, it didn't matter that he had fifteen more years in the business than she did. She'd come out on top. Plus, a long time ago they'd been friends. Maybe they could figure out how to do that again. It would be hard as hell, but he could give it a go.

He wove through the closely set tables until he reached her, then dropped his bag to the floor. When she met his eyes, she didn't seem surprised to see him. Ah. So she'd watched him come in. Had he fled, she'd have noticed. Of course she'd have noticed. She noticed everything.

"Good morning," she said, as though he hadn't slammed the phone down in her ear the night before.

"Yeah, you too," he said. "You missed the most amazing dinner last night."

"Did I?"

"Once in a lifetime. The food, the kid, everything."

"You did say that."

He'd said that? Said what? What was she talking about? She'd been saying the strangest things lately.

"Anyways," he continued, "the kid said he has a budget to option just about anything he's interested in right now. And he's heard of you. Can you believe it!"

"Yes."

"That's it? That's all you have to say?"

"Why wouldn't he have heard of me? He agreed to have dinner with me."

She was acting like he'd just said something to piss her off. Why on Earth would she be pissed off at him? She was the one who dumped him.

"Regardless," she continued, "I appreciate you having the meeting without me. Should we share his info with our agents as a go-to person?"

"Yeah," he grumbled.

"What's the matter?"

"Where were you last night?"

"I told you. I was at Sandy's."

"Are you fucking Sandy?"

"Oh Christ. Stop it."

"He's not that much older than me."

Actually, according to Dan's sources, Sandy was exactly fourteen years older than he was, and thus, significantly older. But Sandy was a seriously good-looking dude. And right now, Dan couldn't see straight where Daphne was concerned.

"Do you want to have this conversation?" She sounded tired.

"Not really." And he didn't. He was tired, too, and he did feel old. Maybe she was right to dump him.

"Good." She eyed him hard. "Because I was about to invite you to Greta and Timmy's wedding. Which will be at Sandy's house tomorrow." She leaned forward, eyeing him again. "Do you understand?"

"Of course, babe. Calm down. I get it." She seemed so pissed off with him. She'd always been so patient. Maybe he'd pushed her too far.

"I'm inviting you because you've been friends with Greta and Timmy a long time. But there will be bouncers from Rivet at the wedding. I won't be afraid to use them on you."

"Jeez, babe. What do you think I'm gonna do?"

"I have no idea, Dan."

∽✖✣

During her conversation with Dan, Daphne had kept her phone in her lap, set to silent mode. The last thing she needed was Dan asking her why her phone kept buzzing. She'd been receiving texts and phone calls from all sorts of people: florists, Olivia, Sandy, Greta, even Timmy. Wedding frenzy was in overdrive.

And then there was Marlon. Marlon had called twice since she'd arrived at Uptown. She'd ignored both calls.

Now that she and Dan had both turned to their work, she looked down to see another text message arrive. This one from Marlon. "Are you ignoring me on purpose?"

She was. She knew she shouldn't be ignoring him because she was supposed to be planning a wedding with him. She'd thought the meaning of her words to him last night was plain: *Keep away. I'm trouble.*

But her words hadn't gotten through. Two phone calls and one text message later, she wondered if she should answer him, just to make sure there wasn't some wedding crisis she needed to deal with. But if that were the case, then Olivia's text messages—even Sandy's—would have said so. No. She had a feeling Marlon's messages were not related to wedding business.

She deleted both of Marlon's voicemails and the text message.

She had trouble concentrating for the next thirty minutes and considered calling Miranda to see if she wanted to go shopping for a dress to wear to the wedding. She was just closing the lid to her laptop when she gasped. Marlon. Standing right next to her table, arms crossed over his chest.

"What are you doing here?" she asked.

Dan looked up. His eyes narrowed. He, too, crossed his arms, leaning back into his chair.

Daphne stifled a groan.

"I thought you might have lost your cell phone," Marlon said. "So I came to find you."

"Nonsense!" Dan said. "Daphne's cell phone is attached to her body. It's like her freaky sixth toe."

"You have a sixth toe?" Marlon asked her.

"Would it be a problem if I did?"

Dan cracked up laughing. Then he stood, sticking his hand in Marlon's direction. "Dan Morello," he said.

"Marlon," Marlon shook Dan's hand.

Dan gawped at him.

"How did you get here?" Daphne asked.

"Sandy lets me drive his car."

"You know Sandy?" Dan asked.

"Yeah," said Marlon.

"You drove his Aston Martin?" Dan asked.

Marlon glanced at Dan, an impatient look in his eyes. "Yes. The Aston Martin."

"Who are you?" Dan asked.

"Sandy's handyman."

Dan glared at her then. Daphne knew at that moment Dan had figured out the truth about where she'd been last night. She wanted to run from the restaurant, to let these two animals have their fight. But she wouldn't. Uptown was her territory.

Instead, Dan picked up his bag and hung it over his shoulder. He took his time packing up his pen, sliding the lid on it with a loud snick, folding closed his notebook, then tucking both into his bag. He strode out, not saying good-bye, not saying anything. He was, she believed, whistling.

Daphne got a bad feeling.

Marlon sat in Dan's seat.

"Ugh, Marlon. Why are you here?" Even though she was annoyed by his unexpected arrival and annoyed that it set off Dan, she couldn't help feeling pleased that he was here, sitting across from her, down from his hilltop sanctuary.

She buried that emotion.

"Sorry about that," he said. "I thought you guys broke up."

"We did break up, you idiot. You heard us yourself when I called him. But now he knows I was with you last night." She put her face in her hands. Her friendship with Dan now seemed irreparable, and she just didn't have many friends.

She looked at Marlon, angry now. "How would you feel if your girlfriend of many years was with another man the day after breaking up with you?"

"Not good."

"Not good! I don't want to hurt him. I just don't want to be with him."

"I've been trying to get in touch with you, but you won't even text me back."

"It's only eleven o'clock."

"Fine. Tell me you weren't ignoring me, and I'll go."

Daphne squeezed her fingers together into two fists. She couldn't lie to him. She just shook her head, refusing to speak.

"Why?" he asked.

"Didn't you see Dan? I hurt people, Marlon. It's what I do. But you're special. I don't want to hurt you too."

"You think I'm special?" He sounded delighted.

This time she did groan. "I thought you didn't like taking unnecessary risks."

"You and me might be risky. But I think you have a good heart. I don't think you hurt people on purpose."

"Of course not—I don't do it on purpose." She pressed her hands against the sides of her face in frustration. "But we both know accidents happen. Like, when this guy you've been hanging out with somehow improbably tracks you down at your favorite coffee shop and humiliates your ex." She paused, realizing something. "Wait. How did you find me?"

"Carrie."

"Carrie? That stinker."

"Fair's fair. She told you about my parents."

"Do you think she's matchmaking?"

"Absolutely."

Daphne laughed, and her face relaxed into a smile.

"Do you want another coffee?" He waved at a server.

"It's OK. I've had plenty this morning." She nodded at him. "What did you want to tell me so badly?"

"I talked with Sandy this morning. He saw your car at my place late last night."

"Oh no!" She covered her face with her hands again, embarrassed.

"Oh yes. He told me to be careful around you."

"He's right, you know."

"Yes, you've told me. About eighteen times now."

"So you came here to warn me that Sandy knows about us?"

"That was one reason."

"What was the other?"

"It's in the car," he said. "Come on."

He stood and headed out of the café, expecting her to follow. Then she threw her things into her bag and hustled after him.

Ten

Marlon drove Sandy's car slowly not because he was worried about damaging the car. Sandy wouldn't care if Marlon got in a fender-bender. Sandy had told him as much the first time he'd loaned Marlon the keys, saying, "When it's in the shop, the dealer always loans me the newest model. It's like having a fling." Sandy hadn't wanted Marlon to worry. Marlon had been nineteen years old.

No. Marlon drove slowly because he always drove slowly. Los Angeles was a city packed end-to-end with cars, and those cars carried people in unbearable hurries. How miserable. He refused to live that way. So he drove at his own pace and planned carefully so he would never be late.

Never needed to be in a hurry.

Never needed to rush things.

Plus, right now he had Daphne sitting in the car next to him. She was an added reason to take his time.

They headed east on San Vicente. "Turn left up here," she said, pointing to Montana. He did. After a few more blocks, she directed him to turn left again and head around back of a two story building. He waited a moment while she opened her garage to let him pull into the empty spot next to her Audi.

He climbed out of the car, standing in the cool shade of the garage with her.

"Do you... um... I don't suppose you want to come inside?" she asked.

"I think I need to," he said.

"You do?"

He nodded, loving her adorable look of confusion.

"Just hold open the door for me, OK?"

"OK," she said, and she trotted up the stairs.

He heard a metal door clank open at the top of the stairs. He opened the rear hatch of the car and withdrew the large wrapped item, taking care not to bump it on anything.

He met her at the top of the stairs where she held the gate. She eyed the package in his hands, and he could see her guessing—likely accurately—as to its contents.

She unlocked her front door and led him into the foyer, then firmly locked the door behind them. She took off her shoes by the front door, adding to the fancy sneakers, glittery flats and boots of a variety of heights piled there. He set down the package and then did the same. Then, picking it up again, he followed her inside.

Her home was a tribute to the midcentury era. He knew purchasing that high-end furniture would have cost a fortune. But he also knew she probably hadn't spent a fortune on it. It didn't seem like something she would do.

"Where did you find all this stuff?" he asked.

"Thrift stores. The side of the road."

"That's what I thought. That couch though. Wow."

It was a blazing shade of orange. Traffic-cone orange. Safety-vest orange.

"That's the lifeboat. Timmy and Greta bought that a long time ago. It set the tone for the rest of my house."

She must have been referring to the couch's midcentury styling, not the color. "Then why don't Timmy and Greta have it now?"

A look of pain crossed her face. "It just became mine one day."

"Sure, OK," he said. "Got a place where I can put this down?"

"Through here."

She led him into her kitchen and through to her dining

table.

"It's clean," she said, seeming to sense that cleanliness was important. "For once."

He set the package down flat, and it covered an awful lot of her six-person table.

"I'm guessing you've figured out what's in here," he said, gesturing at the brown wrapping paper.

"I think so." She sounded as nervous as a bird.

"All right then," he said. "I guess I'll leave now." Perhaps if he gave her some space, she'd come around.

"No, don't go."

Her words surprised him.

"I mean," she said, "if you have some place to be, I don't want to keep you. But, if you don't need to leave, you can stay."

"I don't have some place to be."

She reached forward with both hands to grab the edges of the paper. Then she pulled slowly, revealing the painting underneath. It was the painting he'd stayed up all night finishing while she'd been asleep in his bed last night. He wasn't supposed to give it to her. He was supposed to give it to the man who'd already paid for it. But it didn't seem right. This painting was Daphne's.

This painting was Daphne.

"Here, let me." He reached for the painting.

Because the oils were still wet, he'd encased the canvas in a three-inch-deep frame for transport. He lifted the frame from the canvas, leaving it bare on its wrapping paper.

She reached to touch the canvas, but stopped just before her fingers could brush the raised paint strokes, sensing that they were still damp. She traced the air a hairsbreadth from the painting, a portrait of her on the lounge chair, the sunset exploding behind her.

"When?"

"You know when."

"But, so fast?"

"I'd already started it. I just didn't know how to finish. Who belonged on it."

"So this part is still wet?" She gestured at the center where her portrait appeared.

"Yes. I'd done most of the work this past month, and I knew it would be a portrait. I knew how most of it would look. But not how it would end."

"You talk like you're writing a story."

"It's kind of like that I guess."

"Will you hang it for me?"

"You got tools?"

She dashed to the hall and opened a closet door. She pulled out a sturdy red toolbox, holding it out to him. "Greta put this together for me. It should be well stocked."

He opened the box and found a hammer, a tape measure and the rest of what he'd need, and he put items in various pockets of his jeans.

Then he reached wide and picked up the canvas by its edges, letting the brown paper fall to the floor. He carried the painting to her room, following her lead. She kicked aside a pile of clothes to make a pathway for him. Her room was delightfully messy. Then she stepped up onto her bed, pointing above her headboard.

"Here." She gestured at the bare space there.

He leaned the painting against the wall. He climbed up on her bed, eyeing the space. He took his time measuring, ensuring the picture was even over her headboard and not too high. When he finally let the canvas frame's wire catch on the hanging hardware, he heard her sigh behind him.

He stepped back, taking in his work.

Earlier today, when he was deciding what to do about Daphne, he'd considered keeping the painting. He'd thought if he were going to let her go, he'd at least have the painting to remember her by. But when he decided to not let her go after all, he knew she should have it. She should have it, and no one else should. The portrait was too intimate.

It belonged right here above her bed. He would have suggested she hang it there if she hadn't figured it out for herself.

He turned and looked at her. She stood, leaning back against the wall, her mouth covered by her hands. "It's so lovely," she said. "Is that really how you see me?"

"Don't you know you're not supposed to ask questions of the artist?"

"I'm sorry."

He stepped off the bed, which was another fine piece of craftsmanship. He pulled her to him, wrapping his arms around her slender shoulders. "Yes," he whispered in her ear. "Yes, of course that's how I see you." Then he kissed the corner of her mouth. When she kissed him back, he really wished he didn't have something else he needed to work on that afternoon.

A click sounded from the front of the house, the front door unlocking. Opening. Daphne stepped away from him.

"Daphne? You here?"

"I'm here!"

"There is an ever-loving sweet DB9 parked in your other parking space. Oh." Miranda saw Marlon and stopped in the bedroom doorway. "I guess that's your sweet DB9."

A girl stood there, a whirlwind of black and red and a dark blond ponytail that hung almost to her gorgeous rear end. She was tall—though not as tall as Greta—and striking, with her enormous eyes and full, red lips. Marlon was certain he'd never seen her before.

"In a way," Marlon said.

"You steal it?"

"No."

"Borrow it?"

"Yes."

"Then it's not yours. Bummer."

"Marlon, meet Miranda," Daphne said with a sigh.

He glanced at Daphne, who looked pained. He knew Daphne didn't have a roommate. Miranda was company then. The unexpected kind?

"How do you two know each other?" he asked.

"We went to college together," Miranda said.

"Ah," he said. "Another Cameron girl."

Miranda frowned, seemingly displeased with the moniker. "You don't have to put it like that."

"Why not?"

"None of us liked it there very much," Miranda said.

"I thought everyone loved Cameron," Marlon said. "What do they call it on ESPN? Blue Heaven?"

Miranda made a gagging noise.

Daphne spoke. "Not us. We're like a secret club."

Miranda laughed. "Is it secret?" Then she held up a shopping bag to show Daphne. "I got a dress for the wedding. You should give it your fashion diva approval before tomorrow."

"I'll see you later, Marlon," Daphne said. "I have to take Greta out to buy her wedding dress, then I'll come by Sandy's so we can finish arranging the space. I might be late—like around seven?"

"He doesn't have to go," Miranda said. "He might have excellent fashion sense."

"I do not," Marlon said. He nodded at Miranda. "Nice to meet you."

He headed out, through Daphne's living room and into the foyer, slipping on his shoes at the door, listening to the girls talk in low voices in Daphne's bedroom. He couldn't make out what they were saying.

He felt a stab of self-consciousness. Perhaps giving her the painting was too grand a gesture. Daphne had a face he was certain men had painted before. Had photographed. Had captured for eternity. What was one more depiction of her perfection? One more penitent worshipping at her altar?

He opened her front door silently and slipped out, making his way to Sandy's car. He started the drive back home, heading north.

He'd seen them, the men who'd come with her to Sandy's house, men like Dan Morello. He'd known who Dan was long before shaking his hand at the café this morning. That's what Marlon did. He paid attention to things, to the people who came and went from Sandy's house. To the people who were important to the people who were important to Sandy. He might only watch from a distance most of the time, but he watched closely.

He drove north until he hit Sunset Boulevard. He knew Wilshire was probably the faster route from Daphne's house, but he preferred the rolling hills of Sunset. He liked to pass by the northern edge of UCLA, where, like Carrie, he'd also gone to college. This was the route he'd taken to school, driving down from Sandy's house where he'd lived during most of his school years instead of in college housing. He thought of Carrie's current nasty living arrangements and smiled. He was glad she was living within her means, working hard at Rivet while working on her dream. Too many beautiful girls in Los Angeles thought they could find easier ways to success, thought they could cut corners. But they couldn't. Not without losing parts of their souls.

Just look at Daphne. Five years later and she was still a wreck. He wondered if she knew just how much he knew about what had transpired between her and Greta all those years ago. But Daphne had grown stronger for it, if a little fearful. In fact, the reason he was willing to take a gamble (as she'd put it) on her was that she was more afraid of him than he was of her.

He had an idea. He pulled into the parking lot of a restaurant, closed at this time of day, then pulled out his phone. He hoped she would answer this time.

"Marlon? Is everything OK?" Daphne answered after two rings.

"I had an inspiration."

"Another one?"

"Let's get together, you, me and Carrie."

"OK," she said. "That would be nice."

"Great. I'll call her and see when she's free."

ɷ

Daphne hung up. She had the sense to recognize that Marlon inviting her to get together with him and Carrie was a big deal. Like meeting his parents, except he didn't have parents.

Miranda was in the guest room, changing into her dress. It wasn't that Miranda was modest—she would have stripped naked right in front of Daphne without a second thought—but she wanted to surprise Daphne.

Out she came, flinging open the door dramatically. She'd

let down her hair from its ponytail so it hung around her in long, dark blond waves. The dress was, of course, black, with spaghetti straps, a fitted bodice, and a tea-length skirt. The color made the fair skin of her arms and chest glow. The slim-fitting cut exaggerated her curves.

"Well? Is this Hollywood-wedding-appropriate?"

"It's perfect," Daphne said. "On you."

"Compliment?"

"Yes." And it was. Miranda was dressed to kill. In fact, Daphne thought she recognized the designer. "It's, ah, really nice," Daphne said. "Did you get it at one of the boutiques on Montana?"

"Yes! How did you know?"

"Fashion diva, remember? I know this is nosy, but you didn't come here with much. Are you sure you can afford it?"

"Here's the deal, Daphne." Miranda suddenly looked fierce, staring down at Daphne with blazing brown eyes. She reminded Daphne of the Sumatran tiger she'd once seen at the San Diego Zoo. "I have my dead mom's credit card. It's the same color as this dress. I used it to buy a plane ticket to get here. I used it to buy this dress. I'm going to keep buying stuff with it until my father cancels it or I hit its preposterous credit limit. And I'm not going to feel the slightest bit guilty about it."

Daphne smiled faintly. "I won't tell anyone."

The fierceness left Miranda, and she slumped. "Cool."

"I'm going to meet Greta at the Beverly Center," Daphne said. "That's our shopping mall. She's going to buy her wedding dress. Do you want to come with us?"

"Nah," Miranda said. "I think I'll take a nap. Don't worry about me."

But Daphne couldn't help worrying about Miranda. She might be fierce, but she was also a creature in pain.

Daphne pulled into the parking deck at the Beverly Center. She was meeting Greta at Bloomingdale's. Greta refused to shop at boutiques like the one where Miranda had purchased her dress.

Greta had once said, gesturing at her own body, "The salesgirls look at me like I'm a freak who won't fit into their clothes. And they are not wrong."

But for her wedding dress, even Greta had agreed to go to a nice department store. To Daphne's joy, she'd even agreed to shop the designer dress department. Daphne could barely contain herself.

Daphne found Greta waiting on a bench in the mall just outside of Bloomingdale's, sipping a cup of coffee.

"Fortifying yourself?" Daphne asked.

"Why would I need to do that? You assured me this procedure would take minimal time and energy."

"I'm so excited!"

"Of course you are. That's why we're doing this."

But Greta was smiling too, and she and Daphne looped their arms together.

"Where's Miranda?" Greta asked. "I figured she'd come along."

"I invited her. But she was tired after all of her exploring of Los Angeles. She's trying to decide if she wants to stay here."

Greta chuckled. "Miranda in Los Angeles? Her dark humor will create an event horizon."

"There was a time when you thought you wouldn't fit in here either."

"That's true. I guess she just needs to find her people."

"You and me—we kind of are her people."

Greta nodded.

"I'm glad you feel that way because I invited her to your wedding."

"Of course you did. You have a kind heart."

Daphne snorted. "At least that way we can keep an eye on her."

"How's she doing?" Greta turned serious.

"Not well." Daphne remembered the moment when Miranda's snarky facade had fallen and her bitterness had shone through.

They browsed the departments of different designers,

Daphne opting for dresses that were sleeveless and even strapless.

"But it's cold right now!" Greta said.

"It won't be at five o'clock tomorrow. And we'll get you a cardigan to wear over it." She pulled a cream cashmere piece off the rack. "This one."

Greta rolled her eyes. "This outfit is going to cost more than everything else I own put together."

"Not if you count your shoe collection."

"Oh. Do I get to buy new shoes for this?" Greta asked.

Greta loved shoes.

In the end, Greta bought an ivory strapless dress that stopped at her knees, the cashmere cardigan "so she wouldn't freeze her ass off," and a new pair of strappy heels in a pearl-colored leather.

Outside the store again, they hugged. Daphne felt particularly ardent: protective, loving and grateful all at once. She backed away from Greta but held on to her hands. "I'm so happy for you," she said, and then burst into tears.

"Daphne," Greta said, leading her to the mall bench. "What's the matter? If this is simply an oversupply of emotions because your best friend is getting married, I understand. But I'm sensing that's not the case."

"I don't want to burden you the day before your wedding," Daphne said, more in control.

"If it weren't for you, I wouldn't even be having a wedding. This whole rigmarole is your fault."

"Thanks for letting me have a rigmarole."

"Tell me what's wrong."

"I will," Daphne said. "After."

Eleven

Miranda George did indeed want to take a nap while Daphne took Greta out to buy a wedding dress. But that wasn't the only reason she declined to go to the Beverly Center. Miranda had plans for the evening.

She slept the afternoon away, finally feeling refreshed after her travels the day before. Then, she climbed out of bed and dragged herself into the shower.

Earlier that day, she and John had shared mimosas at Didier's. They'd discovered that they both worked in the same field—new media—although he was a programmer and she a content creator. Like her, John was new in town, but not as new as she was. He had his own place, steady work and a group of friends, one of whom she'd met at Didier's. When they'd finished their drinks, he'd asked her out to dinner that night. She'd agreed.

She was well aware of the chaos that dating Daphne's recent one-night-stand might introduce into her own already unbalanced life.

But honestly, she thought as she stepped out of the shower, *what was a little more chaos?* She dried off, looking at her face in the mirror. She looked like shit. She wished she could borrow Daphne's concealer to deal with the under-eye circles, but their skin tones were too different. Whatever. She'd wear red lipstick again. It served as an excellent tool of misdirection.

Miranda's thoughts returned to chaos as she headed into the bedroom to dress. She'd watched Daphne break away from sucking face with that Marlon guy earlier. Seeing how easily Daphne made all guys fall in love with her, seeing how charmed her life was—Miranda didn't feel guilty at all about introducing a little chaos.

Well, she thought as she slipped into her skinny black jeans, maybe she felt a little guilty. Daphne had taken her in without hesitation, and that had helped Miranda a lot. If Miranda had been forced to use her mom's credit card to pay for a hotel for a couple of weeks, she'd have taken a big risk— after all, she didn't know when it would get cut off. And she just wasn't ready to sign a lease. Not in Los Angeles, not anywhere.

Miranda didn't know where she was supposed to be. She was unmoored.

She checked the time on her cell phone. She had fifteen minutes to make it to Didier's, where she'd said she'd meet John. He was going to pick her up and take her to dinner someplace. She didn't want to give him Daphne's address. She might embrace chaos, but she wasn't stupid.

Dan Morello sat alone at Rivet's bar eating one of their famous steaks. He wasn't a filet mignon guy, though. He preferred the strip. He had a glass of whiskey next to him, and he made small talk with Quentin, the bar manager. Quentin had been at Rivet since the day the place opened, and he knew everyone. He knew everything. He was like Yoda with a martini shaker, except better looking (could have been an actor and had probably tried at one point) and less cryptic. Dan thought he'd enjoy hanging out with Quentin, but the few times he'd dropped such a hint, Quentin had pretended not to understand.

Perhaps Quentin thought he was too good to hang out with Dan. Dan shook his head. That wasn't possible. No way some bullshit bartender believed he was better than Dan

Morello.

He'd also recognized someone else that evening. Working an indoor section of tables was the girl he'd met with Daphne at Uptown Coffee the previous morning. Casey? Carrie? Carrie. Yes, that was it. Carrie something. She had an impossible last name. But she was foxy, that's for sure. Amazing tits.

He would say she was a bit young for him, except this was Hollywood, so there was no such thing.

Carrie came up to the bar to hand a drink order to Quentin.

Dan called to her. "Carrie, right?"

She looked at him, and her face brightened. "Dan?"

"That's right. I didn't realize you worked here."

"Working here is how I met Daphne."

Hearing Daphne's name, Dan frowned, his hurt and anger almost overtaking his ability to think rationally. Sandy's handyman? Daphne had betrayed him for that goon? He couldn't believe it.

"Well, I should get back to work," she said. Dan realized he'd taken too long to pick up his end of the conversation.

"Of course you need to work!" he said, trying to sound jolly. "I wouldn't want you to get in trouble."

Carrie's face relaxed into a smile.

He lowered his voice. "You going tomorrow night? To the wedding?"

"Yeah, I am."

He lowered his voice to a whisper, forcing her to lean closer in order to hear him. "Wanna go together?"

She looked uncertain, but interested. He wondered what the hang-up was.

He added, "Just as friends."

"Sure." She sounded more interested.

He handed her his card. "Call me later—I'll be home around ten. We'll make plans then."

She smiled. "Sounds cool." She turned to head back to her tables, giving him a nice view of her long, long legs.

Dan lifted his whiskey to his lips and took a sip. The burn felt good.

๛

Daphne took the curvy roads up the canyon to Sandy's house at a good pace, loving, as usual, the feel of her tires gripping the pavement. She pulled into Sandy's driveway and then headed down to the garage. The first bay was open, revealing Sandy's car. The last bay, the sixth one, was open as well. She parked in front of the closed door of the second bay, blocking in Marlon's non-running car. She climbed out, tucked her cell phone and keys into her pocket, and headed for the open sixth bay, which she'd never before seen the inside of.

The sixth bay was partitioned from the rest of the garage. This bay wasn't a garage at all, but a wood shop. Large power tools stood on wheeled stands. A giant dust collector snaked along the ceiling. A workbench with upper and lower cabinetry ran along the entire side wall. It appeared both well organized and well used.

In the middle of the workshop floor, Marlon was working on a wooden arbor. The sides of the arbor resembled French doors with unglazed panes. The top was covered with a small pergola.

He was rubbing the arbor with a white cloth dipped in oil. Daphne stood at the entry of the wood shop, watching him work the oil into the wood grain.

"I hope you can keep a secret," he said.

"What is this?"

"I made it for Greta. You mentioned needing a magical wedding spot on the deck. So I made one."

"You made this?" Daphne was astonished. "When?"

"I started it Sunday night after you left."

"But it's so extravagant." And it was. She didn't understand how so much detailed work could have happened since Sunday night.

"Sandy's got a spot in his garden for it. It won't go to waste."

"But you're not making it for Sandy. You're making it for Greta."

"Greta's always been good to me."

Daphne paused at his words. Marlon said Greta's name in

almost the same tone he used for Carrie's. A little less protective, perhaps, but brotherly nonetheless.

"You were here that day." Daphne realized an important truth. "When she first got released from the hospital."

"Yeah." He used his fingertips to work the finishing cloth into the corners of the windowpanes on the side of the arbor. The detailed work seemed to take a lot of his concentration.

"Greta and I have never talked about those first few days... after." For the first time, her and Greta's silence on the topic struck Daphne as horrible.

"I don't think anyone likes to talk about it," Marlon said. "Why dwell on bad times?"

"Will you tell me what you remember?"

He looked at her, squeezing the cloth in his hand. "Why do you want to know?"

"Because it was my fault."

"That she got hurt?"

Daphne nodded.

"I thought some nut job did it."

"But it happened because of me."

Marlon dipped the cloth in the can of finishing oil. "It seems Greta forgave you for whatever you think you did."

"She did."

"But you haven't forgiven yourself."

"I don't want to talk about me," Daphne pleaded. "Please just tell me what happened."

"Fine, OK." Marlon resumed his work. "But I'm not sure it's going to give you the answers you're looking for."

Daphne dragged a stool over from the workbench so she could sit closer to him.

"Sandy picked up Greta when she was released from the hospital and brought her straight here. You know that?"

Daphne nodded. "She wouldn't let me or Timmy see her after that first night in the hospital."

"When she got here, she looked beat all to hell. But you know what she looked like."

Daphne nodded again, feeling the sting of tears in her eyes. Five years and the pain felt the same. She would never forgive herself.

"She couldn't do anything for herself because her arm was all torn up. She was also freaked out. I think she was afraid that the person who got her would come after her again." He paused, working oil into a particularly tight spot. "So Sandy didn't want to leave her alone for very long. He had me pick up food from Rivet, all sorts of soft foods that she could eat even though her face was smashed. Soups, mashed potatoes, you know."

"I know," Daphne whispered.

"I helped get one of the rooms ready for her. I unpacked her bag with her stuff from the hospital." Marlon looked at her. "I guess you would have been the one who packed that bag."

"Yeah." Daphne choked out.

"So mostly we made sure she took her pain medicine, ate enough food and rested. We kept her clothes washed, filled her prescriptions and did everything else we could imagine that would help her not feel like her world was ending."

"Because she must have felt that way. God." Daphne put her face in her hands and cried.

"Hey." Marlon wiped his hands on a cloth and came over to her, kneeling. "I shouldn't have told you."

"No, no. I'm glad you did. I'm glad to know you guys were here for her when I wasn't."

"As I recall, Timmy wasn't here for a lot of that time either. Took him a week to come back around."

"But that was my fault too." She stood and strode into a patch of sunlight just outside the garage, arms crossed tightly across her chest. Light slanted through the tall pines that clung to the side of the mountain. She needed to be in a warm place. The sun on her dark blue shirt thawed her from the outside in. She stared at the tree line, the living wall that provided privacy for Sandy's home. Sandy had told her once that his original gardener had started to clear out some of the forested areas of his property without his permission. He'd fired the guy for it. Now, Sandy and Marlon just let the small forested areas grow wild.

"Do you want to help me with the arbor?" Marlon interrupted her thoughts, standing beside her. "The work's not too messy. And if you drip oil on yourself I can help you get it out of your clothes. I've got practice."

"Yes. OK." She took the finishing cloth Marlon handed her, dipping it in the oil the way he showed her. She knelt on the floor, taking on the lower portion of the arbor, using her fingertips to push the cloth into the corners and sweep across the wood, watching the surface darken slightly as it absorbed the oil.

"What kind of wood is this?"

"Redwood. Sustainably grown, of course."

"Of course. Sandy is such a hippie."

They worked together in silence for a while, dipping and rubbing, working the oil into the smallest nooks on the arbor, making the whole thing glisten.

When they were done, they stepped back from it together, taking in the finished piece.

"Did you learn how to do this from your dad?" she asked.

"Yep."

"I'm glad he taught you, even if the price was high. You have a gift."

"I can also make canvas frames faster than anyone in the UCLA art department, so there's that."

"You majored in art, then."

He nodded. "I wouldn't have done it if Sandy hadn't encouraged me to." He took her cloth and dropped both cloths in a bucket. Then he handed her a towel to wipe her hands on. It smelled like mineral spirits, but it got her hands clean.

She stepped closer to the arbor until she stood beneath it. She looked up, admiring the pergola, and turned in a circle, measuring the space with her body, feeling what a structure made of love, made for love, felt like. She closed her eyes.

She knew she herself would never stand under anything so lovely, made just for her.

Then her elbow brushed the side of the arbor. "Oh, crap," she said. She looked at her sleeve. A dark mark marred the fabric where it had absorbed oil from the wood surface. "Did I hurt the arbor?" she asked.

"Nah. It's fine. But you need to treat the oil mark right

away. Come on."

She followed him to the back of the wood shop and through a door. It led to a patio under the deck and a garden beyond. A spiral staircase at this end of the patio led straight up to the deck. She climbed behind him until they reached his deck. Her breath caught for a moment as she remembered the night before, as she remembered leaving him, telling him to stay away from her. Yet here she was, back in the same place again.

Even weaker than before. Even more unable to say no to him.

"This way," he said. "I have good stuff in my laundry room. But we need to get you another shirt."

Mutely, she followed. She felt so selfish. She knew where this walk would end, and she wanted it to end there.

Marlon slid open a glass door, and they entered his bedroom. She removed her shoes at the threshold as he closed the door behind them. The room was lit only by the remaining daylight entering through the glass. Daphne sat on the bed, watching Marlon move through his space, remembering what it felt like to sleep with him here, how she'd fallen into a sleep so deep and relaxed she hadn't even dreamed.

She couldn't remember the last time she'd slept so well.

Marlon pulled open a drawer to reveal rows of neatly folded shirts. He extracted one, long-sleeved and black, and set it on the bed next to her. He stood facing her. She glanced at his face, then at his feet.

"Daphne. Look at me."

"God, Marlon. I can't."

"You can't look at me?"

"I can't hurt someone as wonderful as you."

"You plan on hurting me sometime soon?"

"I would never hurt you on purpose. Never." She burst to her feet. "But it just happens. That's what happened to Greta. Just being near me almost got her killed."

"You two are still friends, though."

"She was lucky to escape with no permanent injuries. And I was lucky she is so forgiving."

"Or Greta just doesn't let you push her away." Marlon

lifted her hand, then turned her arm over, examining the oil mark. "Change your shirt. Let me fix it."

࿙

To Marlon, Daphne's eyes looked wretched. When he let go of her hand, he wanted to grasp her to him, not in an embrace, but to hold her together so she wouldn't break into pieces. But he didn't. He turned to go, to give her privacy. But before he could leave she moved.

Daphne unbuttoned her first button. By the time she'd unbuttoned the second, Marlon was spellbound, her delicate fingers tripping across the fabric. He didn't deserve this. He knew he didn't deserve this gift.

She slipped the shirt from her shoulders and held it out to him, standing before him in a plain black bra, the dips in her clavicles catching the evening shadows, her narrow waist making him want to fall to his knees.

He took the shirt, clenching it in both fists.

Now what?

She sighed, a velvety sound in his dimly lit room, and reached for his T-shirt.

He threw her shirt to the floor.

Pulling her to him, he kissed her lips, kissed her neck, kissed her shoulder. He thought of how much he'd studied human anatomy for studio art, and he wanted to find and name all of those places on Daphne's body and more, and then he wanted to worship them.

"Wait here," he said, leading her to the head of the bed, pulling back the covers. It was the same place she'd lain the night before. The pillow still held the impression of her head. "I'm going to go wash your shirt."

He left her standing there by the bed. He knew he was taking a risk. He might come back to find she'd changed her mind, spouting more nonsense about how he should keep his distance. He might come back to find her gone completely.

But this was the sort of thing he did: He took things slowly and carefully. He had faith that if he did so, the right thing would happen. She would either be there when he got back, or she wouldn't.

And if she were there, then being with her would be right.

He brought her shirt into his laundry room and treated the stain with a concoction he'd been using on oil stains since college, then rinsed it in cold water. He hung it on a wooden rack. It would be dry by morning.

He hoped she would be here in the morning.

He stopped in the kitchen to grab two beers, a hard cheese, a knife and a cutting board. Food first. She needed care as much as she needed love.

He paused and made a wish.

Then he walked into his bedroom. The door to the deck was open again. He looked out, hoping to see her there, staring at the valley below. Hoping that she hadn't left him. Then he saw his T-shirt, still sitting on the bed where he'd placed it. A few seconds later, he heard the faucet in the bathroom to his right. She stood over the sink, splashing water on her face. Then she turned to his bath towel and rubbed her face dry, pinking her cheeks.

Relief washed over him.

She saw him and smiled.

"I thought you might be hungry," he said. "It's nearly seven o'clock."

"I can tell." She nodded toward the open door. "The sun is getting ready to set."

He set the bottles on the bedside table and the cheese board on the bed. "Come eat."

Daphne grabbed a beer and joined him on the bed. She lounged opposite him, the cheese board between them. She still wore only her bra and jeans. She'd removed her socks at some point, so her narrow bare feet peeked out from the bottom of her jeans. Her toenails were painted a pale pink.

They ate in silence, studying one another. He cut her a slice of the hard cheese, an Australian cheddar, holding it out to her. She ate it, looking thoughtful. But she didn't see fit to share those thoughts with him.

Finally, when the block of cheese was almost gone, when the beers were nearly empty, he spoke. "I can't decide if it would be better or worse to tell you what I'm really thinking."

"I'm a fan of honesty," she said.

"But I think we both know there are lots of ways of stating the truth."

Daphne smiled.

"I could tell you, for example," he said, "that no woman except you has ever slept in this bed. And that would be the truth."

Daphne nodded. "I figured I wasn't the first woman to be in this bed. But sleeping is far more intimate than having sex." She chewed a bite of food, thoughtful. "And I would respond to your statement with a question."

Marlon raised his eyebrows.

"Why me?"

Marlon didn't know the names of all of the boyfriends Daphne had brought with her to Sandy's house for dinner parties over the years, but he knew who all of them were. First there'd been a young, handsome one, dashing even, clearly wealthy, who seemed to worship her. Greta hadn't liked him much, though, calling him Slick Rick behind his back. He hadn't lasted long. Then there'd been the guy who played for the baseball team. Marlon hadn't recognized the guy because really, who has time for baseball, but Sandy had told Marlon at one point. Apparently the guy wasn't a dumb jock though— and he led a lot of community investment projects in East LA where he'd grown up. After the baseball player had come Dan Morello, who, despite his macho attitude, was a successful screenwriter and producer and seemed to care a lot for Daphne.

Thus, from a certain point of view, Marlon could easily be asking Daphne the same question she'd asked him. Why Marlon, when it seemed she could have anyone?

But Daphne didn't care at all that someone was a famous screenwriter, or producer, or actor like Sandy, or professional athlete. And that was part of the reason he wanted her.

So he started there. "You don't care about status symbols or someone's income. You don't care that I'm a handyman."

"To be fair, I don't actually think you are a handyman."

"You didn't correct me when I said that I was to Dan Morello."

"Of course I didn't."

"Why not?"

She bit her lip, appearing confused.

"Because you actually don't care whether I'm a handyman."

She nodded. "I wouldn't care. That's true."

"But you do care whether I have a shot at happiness, or fulfillment, or whatever you want to call it. That's why you said what you said about showing my work."

"Yes, of course," she said, appearing confused again. "Why else would I have said it?"

He laughed sourly. "There are lots of self-serving people who have made a similar suggestion for self-serving reasons."

"Oh," she said. "You didn't think that about me I hope."

"No. Because the only thing you care about is your friends. And that right there is the answer to your question."

"You're wrong." She took the last sip of beer from her bottle, then handed it to him to place on the table. "I care about myself too. I refuse to be financially dependent on others. I own my home, my car, everything that's important to me. It's all mine and only mine. I'm horribly selfish."

"Wanting security isn't selfish. That's sanity." He reached over and placed both bottles and the cheeseboard on the bedside table. Then he yanked his own T-shirt over his head. He turned back to her, and in a quick motion, rolled her beneath him until their noses almost touched, until their bodies pressed so close that he nearly lost his mind. "I'm the same way."

She reached up and ran her hands through his hair. "So the only reason I was allowed to stay here last night was because I don't care about status symbols and I'm loyal to my friends?"

"Looking like a goddess doesn't hurt your case."

He ran one hand down the side of her rib cage, down to the curve of her waist, to her hip, to the top of her jeans, and groaned.

She smiled, a secretive smile, close-lipped, looking like the portraits of Persephone just before her abduction that he'd studied in school. Perhaps he shouldn't have invoked a deity.

He pushed his luck too far.

But no. She was reaching down, unbuttoning her jeans. She was lifting her hips and sliding them off. Jesus.

He came to his knees and pulled her jeans from her legs, working each pant leg down, pausing at each foot to admire her pink toes. Finally, she was lying before him in only her black bra and panties, pushed up on her elbows, her ponytail draped over one shoulder. She was smiling, a real smile, not a sad one like he'd seen earlier.

He stood and took off his own jeans. She stood too, on the opposite side of the bed. She grabbed the covers and sheet, and he did the same, and they pulled them from the bed. They came together on his cool white sheets, their mouths meeting first. He wrapped his arms around her lower back as they stood on their knees. Then he lowered himself onto his back and brought her with him, draping her across his chest.

"You're a good person, Marlon."

"I'm not perfect."

"I only said you were good," she said. "Goodness is rare."

Then she was slipping his boxers from his legs. Then she was kicking off her panties.

"Top drawer," he managed to croak, and she located a condom there and handed it to him.

Then she was on top of him. And then he was lost.

❧

Around eleven o'clock Tuesday night, Daphne realized she had to decide whether to stay or go home. She stood in the open doorway of Marlon's bedroom, looking out into the night. Marlon had made it clear she was welcome to stay. Plus, she was meeting Greta here at Sandy's early in the morning.

Greta's wedding day.

A simple text message to Greta to ask her to grab her dress for her would solve the logistical problems tomorrow, and Daphne would avoid the hour and a half of traffic she'd have to sit in during morning rush hour.

Plus, she really wanted to stay here.

Marlon was sitting up in bed texting with Carrie. He was arranging a mid-morning coffee date at the café down the hill from Sandy's. Apparently Carrie met Marlon there a lot, so coming around was nothing new for her. The new thing would be seeing Daphne with Marlon.

Daphne was nervous.

"It's all set," he said, looking up from his phone. "We just need to give her twenty minutes' notice, and she'll be there. She's working a double at Rivet tonight so she's off all day tomorrow."

"Great," Daphne said. "I really like Carrie."

"I'm still not convinced you meeting up with Carrie was coincidence," he said. "I think it was all part of your grand plan to land me."

"Have I landed you then?"

Marlon set his phone on the table. "Yes."

"Aren't we jumping to conclusions?"

"Nope."

"Are you afraid of scaring me off with your straightforward confessions?"

"Absolutely."

"I'm starting to feel like you aren't afraid of anything."

Marlon flew from the bed, stopping in front of her. "I'm afraid of everything, Daphne. Everything." He wrapped his arms around her, pressing their bare bodies together while the night air whispered over them.

They climbed back into bed. Daphne picked up her phone and dialed Miranda.

"Hey, Daphne. What's going on?" Miranda said.

"I got hung up at Sandy's house with wedding plans," she said. "I won't be making it home tonight. Are you going to be OK without me?"

"Oh sure. I don't cook, so a kitchen fire's unlikely. You have forty-five deadbolts, so a burglary is unlikely too. That just leaves vandalism by me, but I'm way cleaner than you are, so mostly you have to worry about me hiding your stuff in places where they belong like drawers and closets."

"Good night," Daphne said, suddenly happy that Miranda was visiting.

"Yeah, you too."

Daphne set her phone down and turned to Marlon. "That phone call just raised an important issue."

"What do we tell people."

"Can we wait till after the wedding?"

"Of course."

Then she curled into his arms and fell asleep.

Twelve

Just before eight o'clock on the morning of her wedding, Greta pulled her green pickup truck into the circular drive by Sandy's front door. The truck was an antique at this point. But for some reason she couldn't fathom, in Los Angeles, its age, combined with its excellent upkeep at her hands, made it cool. She saw Sandy's perfect car nosing out of the garage at the bottom of the driveway. Sandy's car was cool. Her car was only kept from jalopy status because of her willpower and automotive knowledge. Once again she wondered if all the residents of this overly large city were deranged.

Then she noticed another car parked farther down the driveway, a blue Audi S4 sedan with nineteen inch wheels and Pirelli tires. It was a car she would recognize anywhere. Daphne was here already, but she wasn't parked at Sandy's house. She was parked at Marlon's.

Greta climbed the steps to Sandy's front porch, then let herself inside. Five years ago he'd given her a key, and he'd never asked for it back.

Earlier that morning, she'd received a text message from Daphne with a request. Daphne needed her to stop by Daphne's home to pick up her clothes and makeup for the wedding. Daphne's condo was essentially on Greta's way, so it wasn't a big deal. Greta had hoped to say hello to Miranda as well, but Miranda had still been sleeping when Greta had arrived.

Greta entered Sandy's kitchen and made her way to his espresso machine, a professional model similar in size and function to the one they had at Rivet. She deftly ground the beans and compressed them into the portafilter, then locked it into place. She set a cup under the spout and pressed the brew button. While the machine churned, she heard the front door open and a voice call hello. Daphne.

"In here!" Greta called out over the noise of the machine. "I'm making us fancy coffee."

Daphne came in, setting her bag on the counter. She plopped on a bar stool.

Greta didn't pay much attention to clothes. But she knew without a doubt that Daphne was wearing the same shirt she'd worn yesterday at the Beverly Center.

"Where's Sandy?" Daphne asked.

"Getting breakfast take-out from down the street. We're supposed to wait for him here."

Greta added cream to the Americanos she'd brewed, then handed one to Daphne. Both took a moment to sip their coffees. Greta waited for Daphne to offer up information about Marlon, but she wasn't forthcoming.

"So you broke up with Dan," Greta said, sitting on the stool next to Daphne.

Daphne looked up at her over the top of her mug, then nodded.

"Did it go OK?"

"It was fine." Daphne sighed. "He was annoyed more than anything."

"Annoyed about being dumped? That's a predictable reaction, I suppose."

"I think he was more annoyed that I cheated on him."

Greta raised her eyebrows in surprise. "How did he infer that?"

"I told him."

"Why did you do that?" Greta asked, incredulous. "What outcome could you have possibly hoped for?"

"He was very resistant to me breaking up with him. It was

like he couldn't hear the words."

"Dan isn't unintelligent. What happened?"

"I told him, Dan we're breaking up. And he said, I don't understand your words. And I said, Dan we're breaking up. And he said, Your words make no sense to me because I'm an early hominid."

"He wouldn't listen, so you raised the stakes."

"Correct."

"You tried to force him out by admitting your infidelity."

"Yes."

"Did it work?"

"Sort of. At first he offered to 'forgive' me!" Daphne shook her head. "And now, he still seems to want to work together. And that's what I want too, in my fantasy version of these events. But his wanting the same thing seems too good to be true."

"Because he's an early hominid."

"He was tetchy at first, but then things seemed like they were before, back when we were friends." Daphne set down her mug. "And I don't have many friends. I'd prefer to keep him as one."

"I understand," said Greta. And Greta did understand. She didn't have many friends either.

"I invited him to the wedding. I hope you don't mind."

"I don't mind."

"How did you know I broke up with him?"

"Because Marlon would never spend time with a girl who had a boyfriend. That's not his way."

Daphne shrieked and smacked Greta on the arm that wasn't holding a coffee mug. "You knew about Marlon and didn't say anything!"

"Daph, it didn't take deductive genius. Between your car and your shirt, even someone who wasn't your best friend could have figured it out."

"I'd hoped to be in here before you arrived and to have come up with some nonsense for why I was parked all the way down there by Marlon's apartment."

"And the shirt?"

"Yeah, that I'd just hoped you wouldn't notice."

Greta rested her hand on Daphne's forearm, letting the warmth of her hand seep into Daphne's body. Daphne had taught her that words weren't the only way people spoke to one another. "Is Marlon why you were crying yesterday?"

Daphne paused to consider the question. "Yes and no."

"You still want to wait to talk about it until after the wedding? We have some time now."

"I want to wait."

Greta knew Daphne had some silly notion about not wanting to spoil Greta's special day. And Greta didn't want to make things worse by insisting the day wasn't that special and pressing Daphne to talk.

Greta had known Daphne long enough to know when to wait.

As Greta made a second round of coffee, Daphne played with Jodie and Foster, who were in the kitchen hoping for treats. When the front door to Sandy's house opened, the dogs trotted out to the foyer. A few minutes later, they followed Sandy back into the kitchen.

Sandy was holding a large brown shopping bag stamped with the insignia of the market down the hill. He must have walked there, Daphne figured. His car had been in the garage when she'd come up to the house.

She thought of the many times Marlon must have walked to the market as well. Indeed, the market and the restaurants around it seemed like the heart of this small nook of a larger neighborhood. The thought of Marlon walking down the hill to buy tomatoes made her smile.

"I see trouble has already arrived at my kitchen table," Sandy said, setting down the bag. He reached in and fished out three to-go boxes. "I just got three of the same thing."

Inside each box were croissants, eggs and even some sort of sausage.

"I know you two eat actual food," Sandy said. "So I went big."

The girls sat side-by-side and dug in.

"There's no way this is pork sausage," Daphne said eventually. Not because of the flavor—it tasted really good. But because of the principle.

"Agreed," Greta said.

"Chicken, I think," said Sandy.

"That's a gastronomical fallacy," said Greta.

She and Greta ate until all their food was gone, and then they ate the food Sandy had left in his box too.

"I always underestimate how much you two can eat," he said with a chuckle. "I should have doubled the order. Come on. Let's go outside."

Daphne and Greta grabbed their coffee mugs and followed him.

He led them out onto his deck overlooking the valley. Daphne glanced to her right, to a smaller version of this deck that jutted from the garage apartment.

"So, my girls, it's down to us," Sandy said. "We're getting invaded in a few minutes, but right now, having just the three of us here feels nice."

"What do you mean by 'invaded'?" Greta asked.

Daphne smiled. Greta still didn't understand the scope of the party they'd planned for her and Timmy.

"Greta," Sandy said. "You're finally doing this thing?"

"Yeah." Greta leaned back against the deck rail.

"Why now?" he asked.

"I'm at a sensible age to get married. I'm twenty-six. I'll be twenty-seven in June."

"So you made him wait five years until your age was sensible?" Sandy asked.

"Getting married at twenty-one would have shown demonstrably poor judgment," Greta said.

"But you loved him then," Daphne said. "You love him now. What's changed?"

"Nothing's changed." Greta sounded impatient. "That's why we're getting married."

Sandy laughed. "That's my girl."

Something settled inside of Daphne. She realized Greta had become a solid thing, more so than she'd ever been, and that was saying something. Greta had always been dependable.

Now, Greta was like one of the cosmic bodies Greta had studied in college, of immense, nearly immeasurable gravity. Daphne felt herself leaning toward Greta's shoulder, finding comfort in her solid presence. She rested her cheek there, her body relaxing.

"OK then," Sandy said. "I approve."

Greta snorted. "Thanks, superior-version-of-dad."

Daphne laughed too, imagining Greta's horrible father back home in North Carolina. When Greta had moved in with Daphne just before their third year of college, Greta's dad had thrown Greta out of his home—and moved his mistress in. Greta's mom, dying of cancer, had still been living upstairs.

Yet, despite his many bad actions, Jim Donovan was Greta's only living family. Daphne wondered whether she should have invited him to Greta's wedding after all. It would have been appropriate. Of course, giving him three days' notice would have been too risky—he might actually have come out from North Carolina just to be an asshole. But calling him today—the day of—there was no way he'd be able to get here in time. After all, even though it was eight o'clock in LA, it would be eleven on the East Coast.

"Greta," Daphne said. "Do you want me to call your dad? Give him a wedding announcement?"

"Ugh. How about an email instead?"

"If we send an email, then you'll spend all your time worrying that he might call when he receives it."

"That's true," Greta said.

"If we go ahead and call, then you won't have to worry."

"Fine," Greta said. "Let's call him."

"Right now?"

Greta nodded, sitting on one of Sandy's lounge chairs, identical to the ones on Marlon's deck. "Right now."

"I'll go back in and start handling wedding invaders," Sandy said. "Holler if things get out of hand. Fake dad will take care of real dad." He headed back into the kitchen, sliding the door shut behind him.

"Should I make the call?" Daphne asked, sitting next to Greta and pulling out her phone. "I could pretend you aren't sitting right next to me. Then, if he seems reasonable, I could pretend to go and find you."

"Sure," Greta said. "Fine." Now that the prospect of talking to her father had become closer to reality, Daphne could see Greta's shoulders growing stiff, her eyes blinking a little too fast. She looked like a hunted animal.

Daphne dialed the number she still had saved in her phone. After a few rings, a familiar male voice answered. Daphne would never forget what Jim Donovan sounded like. She made a point to remember details about her enemies.

"Hello?"

"Mr. Donovan? This is Daphne Saito. I'm not sure if you remember me."

"I remember you." He cut her off. "Did something happen to Greta?"

"Um, no." Daphne was startled by the concern in his voice. "Greta's fine."

Jim Donovan's voice turned cold then. "What is the purpose of this call?"

"Greta's getting married."

Silence met her words.

Greta was watching her carefully for any sign of Jim's reaction. So Daphne held out her hand, palm up, shaking her head. She mouthed, "Nothing."

"I see," Jim Donovan said, finally. "When?"

"At four o'clock," Daphne said. "Today."

"Where?"

"At a friend's house."

"She's getting married in a house?" He sounded like he was sneering.

"It's a big house," Daphne snapped. And then, against her better judgment, she told him to whom the house belonged.

Greta's eyebrows shot up, nearly meeting her hairline. "What are you doing?" she whispered.

Daphne mouthed, "I'm sorry."

"I see," he said again. "Thank you for informing me."

He hung up.

"That went fantastic." Daphne recounted the conversation for Greta. "We won't be hearing from him for a while. He sounded so pissed."

"I think your assessment is correct," Greta said. "He's unlikely to call me again."

"He couldn't get off the phone fast enough."

She rested her head back against her lounge chair, and Greta did the same.

"Families are the worst," Daphne said. "Better to make new ones."

"Agreed."

"And you're making a new one today. With Timmy."

Greta reached over and took her hand. "You and I have been making a new family since we met at the Cameron University pool."

She and Greta sat like that, holding hands in the cool morning, looking out over the valley below, waiting for the day to begin.

ھوجی

Marlon stood in the kitchen with Sandy, listening to some detail about when Olivia was going to arrive with her crew from Rivet. But he was having trouble paying attention. Through the tall glass windows of Sandy's kitchen, he could see two people lying on lounge chairs—Daphne, Greta—and he could see their clasped hands dangling between their chairs. He kept trying to look away from those interlaced fingers, but the fingers kept drawing him back.

"They're remarkable together, aren't they," Sandy said.

"Totally," Marlon said. "Wait. What?"

"If sisters could be born of different families and be lucky enough to find one another, you'd be looking at them right now."

"I know a thing or two about siblings born of different families."

"I know you do. That's why you can appreciate what you're seeing. Family reborn."

With that, Sandy left him standing in the kitchen, the visual feast now a solo one.

The girls released their hands. They stood. They laughed about something together, something so funny that they both reached to grab hold of the handrail for support, and he could hear their laughter through the double-paned glass. He wished he knew what they were laughing about. He wanted to be a part of it. Of their closeness.

They opened the door into the kitchen and entered. Greta spied him and smiled. Daphne entered behind Greta so she didn't see him at first—after all, Greta was really, really tall—and when she did see him, she looked startled.

"Morning, ladies," he said. "Sandy told me to be at your beck and call."

"Oh great," Daphne said. "Cook something. I'm starving."

"Didn't you two just eat?" he asked.

"Sandy never gets us enough food," Greta said.

"We always tell him. And it's not like he doesn't watch us eat all the time." Daphne sounded exasperated. "When will he learn?"

"What do you want?" He smiled at their verbal volleyball.

"Anything!" This word they spoke in unison.

"*Huevos con chorizo?*"

"Oh God yes," Daphne said.

"I'll make more coffee." Greta took Daphne's mug. Daphne's eyes got dreamy when she spied Greta at the espresso machine.

Marlon wondered how on Earth there could have been a time when these two women were not this close.

He pulled some chorizo sausage from Sandy's fridge. He knew the sausage was there because he had put it there the day before. He grabbed the eggs too.

He remembered the story he'd told Daphne yesterday, of the day when Greta had arrived from the hospital after being attacked. He remembered talking to Greta back then, and Greta telling him that she'd lost everyone in her life. She meant Timmy, and she'd meant Daphne.

It hadn't taken long for Timmy to come back around. It had taken a little longer for Daphne to reappear—six months or so if he were remembering correctly. What had happened during those six months?

As he sliced the chorizo and tossed it into a frypan to

brown, he thought of the interlocked hands.

He thought of himself at age fourteen, alone in a bedroom that was and wasn't his, with a family that was and wasn't his.

He thought of Daphne's mother and sisters, choosing her abusive father over her.

He scrambled eggs in with the chorizo, turned down the heat and served up two heaping plates. He slid the plates in front of the girls, then handed them forks. They ate like wildcats, greedy and uninhibited. Greta's auburn curls and Daphne's black waves were so different, but both girls wore their hair pulled back in loose ponytails.

He considered leaving the room because their togetherness seemed to require so much privacy. Then he remembered what Sandy had said to him earlier. Family reborn. Greta and Daphne weren't lovers who wanted to be alone. They were family, and if Marlon had learned anything in his life, family like Greta and Daphne was hard to come by.

God, Daphne.

He thought of their morning together, just a couple of hours earlier. She'd woken up next to him, slightly frantic, worried about Greta finding out she'd spent the night.

"I just don't want her to have another thing to worry about on her wedding day," she said to him, dashing off a text message to Greta.

"She doesn't seem worried at all to me. You do, though." He tugged her arm so she fell back to him on the bed. He wrapped his arms around her.

"How can you know for sure that this isn't a mistake?" She'd asked him some variation of that question three or four times throughout the night.

"I don't think we can know anything for sure. We can just make good guesses."

She slapped his forearms in frustration.

"I tend to guess well." He kissed her neck.

She turned to face him. "I'm scared, Marlon."

"I know you are. It's plain as anything."

She hugged him then, so tight he thought she might break her bones. Then she let go and dashed from his room to grab her shirt from the laundry room. She threw on her clothes, ran her fingers through her hair, and pronounced herself "drab but presentable." Then she left to walk up to Sandy's house.

Marlon remained in bed a while longer, holding a hair of hers he'd found on the pillow. It was twenty inches long, easy—and so strong. He pulled on it, even wrapped it around his fingers. As he tugged, it held.

Daphne ate her second breakfast with Greta and appreciated every minute she could spend with Greta on her wedding day. But she never forgot Marlon's presence on the other side of the kitchen island, standing by the sink while she and Greta sat at the bar wolfing down the eggs and chorizo.

She feared his presence would cause her to lose her cool. But instead, he had the opposite effect. He soothed her. She should have been feeling anxious about the upcoming ceremony and party. But she knew Marlon would help her handle anything that needed handling. She didn't have to do it alone.

She looked at him and caught his eyes. They were gray like a cloudy sunrise back home. God. She could fall in love with him. She'd never felt this way before.

Greta leaned back in her chair. "Sandy gave me a room to use as my bridal prep area or whatever. I hung our dresses in there and set up our makeup bags on the counter."

"You don't have a makeup bag," Daphne said.

"Shows what you know," Greta said.

"What does it look like?" Daphne asked. "Where did you get it?"

"Black and I got it at Bloomingdale's."

"Greta having a makeup bag is way more shocking than Greta having a wedding," Daphne informed Marlon.

"Not to Timmy," said Greta. "In any event, I feel like I should take a nap."

"It's still morning. It's not nap time," Daphne said.

"I was at a show late."

"Greta! You went to a show after we bought your dress? How could you!"

"It's my job?"

Greta had worked a show for Pac Lighting late into the night before her own wedding? Daphne was appalled.

"Stop judging me, Daphne, and let me take a nap. I'm fed. Soon I'll be rested. And then I'll be coiffed. The laws of Daphne's universe will no longer be in disarray."

"Fine. Go sleep. Which room is it?"

"Um, the one with the green comforter?"

"I know which room," Marlon said to Daphne. "I can show you later."

Sandy had an obscene number of bedrooms. It could have been nine. It could have been more.

Greta stood and hugged her. "Talk to you soon. I'll call when I wake up. I'm sure you have plenty to do." Then Greta left the room and headed to the bedrooms off the living area.

Daphne turned to face Marlon. "Hey." She gave him a private smile.

"I understand now," he said.

"What do you mean?"

"Why you wanted to know what happened to my family."

Daphne cocked her head, questioning.

"Greta is for you like Carrie is for me," he said.

"Yeah. She is. She's my sister."

"Speaking of which," Marlon said, fishing his phone out of his pocket and dialing. "Carrie?" he said. "You free now? Yeah. Perfect."

"Our coffee date?"

"She'll meet us there in twenty."

They headed out the front door, Daphne petting the dogs one last time for courage.

They strolled together down the hill, holding hands. They kept to the side of the road—there were no sidewalks here—for the fifteen minutes or so until they reached the café. The café was part of the small cluster of shops that served this nook of Laurel Canyon. Marlon led her in under the striped awning and to a round table. He ordered for them at the counter, returning with two mugs.

"You know, I used to only drink tea," Daphne said. "I never drank coffee."

"I just watched you and Greta almost break Sandy's espresso machine."

"I know. It's crazy. Things changed when I started writing all the time in coffee shops. The smells of coffees intrigued me. So I tried different ones. And then the flavors became more and more appealing. And now here I am. A complete addict."

"You started writing in coffee shops when you left the studio?"

"Sometimes I'm surprised you know so much about me," Daphne said. "And then I think about it, and I realize I shouldn't be. All these years, you've always been there in the background."

Marlon just nodded.

Carrie blew into the café then. Her hair was piled atop her head, her smile broad. She wore a white T-shirt and black leggings with booties.

"Morning, Cee-Cee." Marlon stood to give Carrie a hug.

"Hey Daphne," she said. "Let me grab a drink. I'll be right back."

"She looks happy." Marlon sat back down. "I think I know why."

"Because of us?" Daphne asked. "Really?"

"Yes, of course. She's tried to play matchmaker a few times over the years. This is the first time it's worked."

Carrie returned and plopped in the third seat at the table. "Daphne, it's so good to see you. I've been writing like a madwoman since we got together."

"You should be," Daphne said. "Only a week and a half till our meeting."

"What meeting?" Marlon asked.

"Daphne is introducing me to her agent!" Carrie's eyes brightened. "Didn't she tell you?"

"No, she didn't." Marlon looked at Daphne with surprise.

"Carrie deserves the chance," Daphne said, defensively. "Her ideas will hold up."

"Forget work!" Carrie said. "Let's talk about the wedding. How exciting. I've never been to Sandy's house."

"You'll get to cater a party there if you work at Rivet long enough," Marlon said.

"But tonight I'll get to be a guest! I even have a date."

"Really?" Daphne was concerned because none of the nearly seventy wedding guests had received a plus-one with their invitation.

"Don't worry, Daphne. I wasn't raised by wolves," Carrie said. "I'm going with another invited guest."

"Who would that be?" Marlon asked.

Daphne heard the brotherly concern in his voice. The protectiveness.

"Dan Morello."

Every muscle, every tendon, every moving part in Daphne's body stiffened. Her brain spun. She looked at the young girl in front of her, with her two bright front teeth the centerpiece of her brilliant smile, the big brown eyes, the rowdy curls. The unbelievable innocence in every gesture.

This was not a creature Dan Morello could ever be allowed to spoil.

Marlon spoke first. "How did that come about?" He kept his voice calm.

"I saw him when I was working at Rivet last night. He asked me then."

"Why'd you say yes?" Marlon asked.

Carrie bristled. "Why wouldn't I?"

"He's old? He's a jerk?" Marlon said.

Daphne wanted to laugh but instead kept her face perfectly still. Marlon's low opinion of Dan, though, was perhaps influenced by more than just his interest in Carrie.

"We're going as friends. And besides, he's brilliant."

"Only as friends?" Marlon scoffed. "I can promise you there is more to his side of the story. You just don't know it yet."

"Someday you're going to have to stop being so protective, Marlon, and accept that I'm all grown up."

"I agree with Marlon, Carrie," Daphne said. "Dan's a little rough around the edges."

"He seemed nice enough for you to hang out with." Carrie's tone was accusing.

Marlon interrupted before Daphne could reply. "Daphne

is older than you. She's been through a lot more than you have. It's a long road between twenty and thirty."

Carrie laughed, then she threw back the last of her coffee. "I'd hoped to have a nice little get-together here to admire my matchmaking skills, since you two have obviously hit it off. Instead I'm getting lectured about my fake date for the wedding." Setting down her mug, Carrie stood.

"Don't go, Carrie," Daphne said. "Please."

"It's OK. I'll see you guys tonight. This argument is so ordinary it's boring. If you're going to hang out with Marlon and me, you might as well get used to it." She sounded almost cheerful as she left the café.

"That went awesome," Daphne said.

"You need to call Dan and tell him to stay away from my sister."

The intensity in Marlon's voice startled Daphne.

"Oh, OK. Sure," Daphne said, her tone appeasing. "As soon as we get back, I'll call him."

"You make sure he leaves her alone." Marlon wouldn't meet her eyes.

"Marlon." She waited until he looked at her. "I'll handle it, OK? Don't worry."

"Good." He stood and exited the café, leaving her alone at the table.

She found him outside, standing impatiently with his hands on his hips. He wasn't talkative on the walk back to Sandy's house. She asked him a few questions about the wedding planning, and he answered with brief, precise answers.

When they reached Sandy's front porch, she stopped. "I'm going to move my car down the street to make room for guests to park," she said. "I'll call Dan now too."

"Good." Marlon entered the house, his stiff shoulders telling her how upset he truly was.

She dialed Dan's house as she headed down the hill toward her car, praying he would answer.

"Hello?" He answered after six or seven rings.

"Dan," she said. "It's Daphne."

"What can I do for you?" he said cheerfully.

She got in her car and started the engine, tucking her phone behind her ear.

"Right now," she said, "you can call Carrie Ademola and tell her you will not be her date to Greta's wedding."

"What are you talking about? That's a done deal!"

"Nonsense," she said, gritting her teeth to keep the anger from her voice. "Cancelling will only require a simple phone call. Everyone around here is pretty upset about it, actually." She pulled her car out of Sandy's driveway and turned right up the hill to park, about a hundred yards from Sandy's house.

"Who is everyone?" Dan asked.

She parked her car in first gear, set the brake and then turned off the engine. "Dan," she said. "If I ever meant anything to you, please do this one thing for me."

"You certainly did mean a lot to me, Daphne." He sounded hurt. "But you showed me just how little I meant to you."

He hung up. She tried calling back, but he didn't answer.

She walked down the hill to Sandy's, wondering how she would explain her failure to Marlon. Perhaps, Dan would reconsider. Surely he'd realize that entering Sandy's home with Marlon's little sister on his arm—after an explicit request not to—would be a really bad idea. Given how much power Sandy wielded around town, doing so could hurt his career. Surely Dan's own self-interest would lead him to that conclusion.

Surely Dan would figure it all out before tonight.

Thirteen

It was two-thirty, an hour and a half before the wedding, and Daphne was taking stock of the final details.

Three Rivet valets would direct parking. At the moment, they were setting up a temporary valet stand on Sandy's front porch. The valets would fit as many cars in Sandy's driveway as possible by parking them tightly. But at the same time, the valets would be able to move cars around as necessary so folks could leave. Not ideal, but it would work. Folks who needed to depart earlier in the evening might have to wait twenty minutes for their car to be extracted from the parking situation, but these guys—and girl—were pros. If you needed to be out, they could get you out.

Luis, the head doorman from Rivet, walked around the exterior of Sandy's home, examining the property. He was excellent at security, and only the best would do for tonight. He had two more guys with him to assist.

Olivia had outdone herself with the catering. Small buffet tables were grouped around Sandy's spacious living area as though they naturally belonged among the swanky furniture. Two bars—supervised by Quentin himself—would serve beverages. No one would have to wait to eat or drink.

And out on the deck, a supernatural event seemed to have occurred and transformed the place into, indeed, a magical wedding spot. White flower petals covered the deck boards. A white flowering vine coiled around the railing of the deck, turning it into a living thing.

Except Daphne knew it hadn't been a supernatural event. She knew it had been Marlon. She could see him now through the glass doors of the kitchen, the doors that would be left open throughout the evening to allow guests to come and go as needed.

He squatted on the deck, wrapping the same flowering vine around the arbor. The arbor, of course, was the centerpiece of the deck.

She slid the door open and stepped through, and a delicate fragrance emanated from the entire outdoor space.

"It doesn't just look amazing, does it?" Daphne took a deep breath through her nose.

Marlon didn't look up when he spoke. "White jasmine vines. Same with the petals on the ground. They're pretty fragrant. You reach Dan?"

"I did. I don't know what he's going to do."

"What happened on the phone?" Marlon wouldn't look at her.

"I asked him to call it off. And then I begged him."

Marlon glanced up at her then. "You begged him?"

"I don't want him near Carrie. He has his good qualities, but he's a jaded old man in a jaded old town. Carrie shouldn't be around that. Not yet, anyway."

"Someday, maybe." He spoke with something like understanding in his voice.

"Only after she has some experience of her own."

Marlon stood. "Thanks for calling him. I know that wasn't easy for you to do."

He wrapped an arm around her shoulder and pulled her to him, resting his nose against her temple and inhaling, as though she smelled as deliciously fragrant as the jasmine.

৬৩৫

Daphne and Greta dressed in the bedroom Sandy had set aside for the bride. Daphne opted not to tell her friend about the situation with Dan and Carrie. Greta didn't need to know about that on her wedding day. Besides, Dan and Carrie's date would probably come to nothing. Even Marlon didn't seem too worried, and Marlon worried about everything.

Daphne pulled on her navy blue dress. It was classy but understated—she hadn't wanted to outshine Greta.

"Zip me?" she asked, and Greta complied. The dress was fitted throughout, with cap sleeves, a scoop neck and a hemline just past her knees.

"Your turn," Daphne said to Greta.

Greta pulled off her bra and slipped the pale dress over her hips, tugging the straps over her shoulders. Daphne zipped her up. Then they pulled on their shoes and made sure their hair hadn't gotten mussed getting dressed. They'd done their makeup first to ensure they didn't get any on their clothes.

They were ready.

They each held a cardigan to ward off the evening chill. "Give me yours," Daphne said. "I'll find a place out there to stash them."

"Nothing better happen to that. It cost a fortune."

"But you love it." Daphne grinned.

"I'd love it more if it were a darker color and therefore less likely to get grease stains on it."

"If you get grease stains on it I will pay to have it professionally dyed."

"Deal."

They hugged then, and Daphne felt joy.

"I have to go greet guests," Daphne said. "And you have to stay hidden here. Do you want me to send Olivia back here to keep you company?"

"I brought my laptop," Greta said. "I was going to quote a show while I waited."

"Here I was, worried you might be nervous before getting married."

"Like I said, Daphne, nothing's going to change. So there's nothing to be nervous about."

Daphne smiled. "I'll knock on your door right at four o'clock when it's time for the ceremony. Make sure it's me before you open the door. I don't want anyone else to see you." Daphne shut the door behind her and took a deep breath.

It was time to find Timmy.

She and Timmy had grown close over the past few years, despite the rough beginning to their friendship. Back when Daphne had thought she'd been losing Greta to a man who wasn't worthy, Daphne had taken desperate measures.

She'd taken aim at Timmy.

And then it had turned out that Timmy was, in fact, worthy of her friend.

But it had taken a long time for Timmy to accept Daphne back into his life, to trust her again. She understood. She wouldn't have trusted her either after what she'd done.

Despite the passage of time, and the happy memories they'd created, all Daphne could think about today was that one awful night. And she had a feeling Timmy would be thinking about it too.

She saw him standing in Sandy's living room, looking out through the open door to the deck. He stared at the arbor, dressed in its gown of jasmine vines. Daphne's throat constricted. She joined him, standing beside him and gazing outside.

"Hey," he said.

"Hey. It's about time to start greeting your guests."

He glanced at his watch. "Wow, yeah. Time is flying." He nodded toward the deck, then looked around the room. "I can't believe you pulled this together so quickly."

"I had a lot of help."

"Maybe. But this has Daphne written all over it."

"Is that a good thing?" she asked, uncertain.

He turned to look at her and seemed to carefully consider his words. "What you did will never be OK."

Daphne looked at her feet. She knew that already. He didn't need to tell her.

"But we've forgiven you over and over. I've forgiven you. You don't have to hurt yourself with it any more."

"I didn't do all of this for your forgiveness."

"I know," Timmy said. "You did it because you love Greta. Even a dope like me can see that."

He put his arm around her and hugged her to his side. "Let's get lined up, sis."

At promptly three-thirty, guests started arriving at Sandy's house. Daphne had mentioned on the invitations that the doors would open at that time and not a minute sooner, and people had listened. Good. Things were already running smoothly.

Sandy, Timmy and Daphne stood in a line by the door. Greta's newly made family took the place of her real one. They each greeted the guests as they entered. Sandy was first in line, as this was his home. Timmy, as the groom, was second. Daphne, the bridesmaid, was third.

Timmy's parents arrived, along with Timmy's uncle Brian and his wife. Olivia arrived, looking smashing. She'd left for an hour to freshen up. More guests arrived, friends from Rivet, friends from Timmy and Greta's work, friends from six years of living in Los Angeles.

And then Miranda arrived. She had an uninvited date in tow—problem number one. And that date was John, the guy Daphne had spent the night with last weekend—problem number two. Daphne took an inadvertent step backward, John's presence kicking her off-balance.

Miranda and John shook hands with Sandy and then with Timmy. By the time they got to Daphne, Daphne's hands were twitching with anger at Miranda. Somehow, she knew Miranda hadn't brought John here by accident. Miranda knew exactly who John was to Daphne.

Miranda and John stopped in front of her. Miranda looked gorgeous in her designer dress and flashy lipstick, her mane of hair hanging around her shoulders in waves. She could have been standing on a red carpet in that outfit.

Miranda smiled like a viper, making the formal introduction. "John, I want you to meet my current temporary roommate and old friend from college, Daphne." John's eyes widened when they met Daphne's.

Ah. He hadn't known what he was getting into either.

Daphne shook John's hand, but she glanced at Miranda while she did so. Miranda, she saw, was watching John.

"Nice to meet you, John," Daphne said. "What do you do here in LA?"

John laughed at the inside joke. She had displayed a distinct lack of interest in his profession last Saturday.

Daphne refused to let her smile waver.

"I design websites," he said.

"How did you meet Miranda?" Daphne asked.

Miranda interrupted. "We met at Didier's, after you left me there yesterday morning. We got to talking and realized we work in the same field. We just hit it off. I figured you wouldn't mind if I brought a date since I don't know a single one of these jerk-offs."

"Don't be impolite," Daphne said, using a condescending tone designed to make Miranda bristle and run her off. She could tell by the other girl's expression that it had worked. Daphne glanced at her watch. "I have to go check in with the caterer. I'll see you in a little while."

Daphne dashed to the bathroom. She had to get over her surprise at John's presence and Miranda's unexpected betrayal. In the bathroom, Daphne stared at herself in the mirror. Her makeup was perfect. Her lipstick was an understated neutral tone. This was a wedding, not a cocktail party, despite Miranda's flashy appearance. Daphne couldn't let John's presence unsettle her. But no, John had seemed as surprised to see Daphne as she'd been to see him. This was about Miranda, not John.

What was Miranda trying to do to Daphne? And why was she doing it here?

After a few minutes, Daphne returned to Sandy and Timmy. Tonight wasn't about her bad decisions. It was about Greta. She had to keep calm.

Then Dan and Carrie walked through the door, together.

Sandy greeted them both, his polite smile never faltering. But he snuck a glance at Daphne, a severe frown marring his handsome face.

His unspoken words were clear: Solve this problem.

She whispered to him: "I'll handle it. Just as soon as the

ceremony is over."

He patted her arm in thanks.

Carrie greeted Daphne coolly. "Hi Daphne. That's a good color on you."

"Thanks, Carrie," Daphne said. She wanted to win the girl over. Otherwise, later, Carrie wouldn't listen to her advice. "You look even more fabulous when you aren't dressed as a waiter. I didn't know that was possible." Daphne pretended to leer.

Carrie giggled.

The fact was, Carrie did look gorgeous. She wore a short baby-doll style dress with spaghetti straps and an empire waist. The color was a cornflower blue that set off her medium-brown skin tone in epic fashion.

Dan, naturally, was staring down at Carrie's cleavage.

"Dan." Daphne spoke to draw his attention. "Good evening."

"Hey, Daph." He seemed genuinely happy to see her.

As Dan and Carrie made their way into the house, she glanced around for Marlon. She knew he would be upset. She wanted to call Rivet's doorman, Luis, over and have him throw Dan from the wedding. She considered doing so, but then an even bigger disaster walked through the door.

"Holy fuck," she whispered to Sandy and Timmy.

"Who is it?" Sandy whispered back.

"That's Greta's dad."

"Jesus Christ," Timmy said.

"What can you do?" Daphne asked Sandy.

"This one I can handle for a minute," Sandy said. "Daphne, go to Greta's room and warn her. Stay with her until it's time. Timmy, get your parents and your aunt and uncle. Give them the run-down. They're going to be Greta's shield tonight. At least one of them stays with this guy every minute he's here, and the rest stay with her."

"I can do that." Timmy headed to where his family stood in a cluster.

Daphne watched Sandy approach Jim Donovan. Jim stood in the doorway, surveying Sandy's spectacular home with a mild expression. But Daphne knew that behind the mild expression lurked a man who would betray his own daughter without a thought.

He had done it before.

When it came to machinations, though, Sandy outclassed Jim Donovan. Sandy outclassed everyone. Jim Donovan might be able to hide his expression of shock at shaking hands with an Oscar winner of Sandy's caliber, but he wouldn't be able to fool Sandy about his intentions. And if his intentions toward Greta were anything but peaceful, Sandy would have Luis carry the man bodily from his house. Hell, Sandy would probably have the man in jail within the hour. And Greta would never, ever know. Not till she was back from her honeymoon, anyway.

Daphne left Sandy and Jim talking by the door. Ten minutes till show time. She headed toward Greta's room, wondering if Jim Donovan were the one thing that would ruin what should have been a perfect night.

ঙ৵

After John and Miranda got drinks at the bar, John touched Miranda's arm. "Can I talk to you in private for a second?"

She followed him to an alcove off the living room.

"Did you know?" He sounded mostly sad, but a little angry too.

Miranda replayed the scene by the front door. She'd seen the flash of shock pass quickly across Daphne's flawless face. For a moment, Miranda had enjoyed Daphne's shock, her discomfiture. She had enjoyed this tiny revenge.

If Miranda had thought of Daphne a year ago, even a month ago, she'd have said she'd forgiven Daphne for what she'd done back in college. But seeing Daphne again Monday night, seeing her life here, seeing how perfect everything had turned out for Daphne when everything in Miranda's life was shit—it had brought those awful memories back. Turned out, Miranda wasn't over it.

So she'd used John to humiliate Daphne, and it had been fun. For a moment.

It wasn't fun now, though. Now, Miranda felt confused. She didn't want to fight with Daphne. And she didn't want John sad or angry with her.

"I suspected," she answered. "Daphne's name used to be Akane. She changed it a long time ago."

"You could have said something at Didier's."

"Why?" Miranda snapped. "So you could track her down and try to win her over?"

"That's not how it would have gone. You and I had a great time the past two days."

"That's exactly how it would have gone!" Miranda was fuming now. "You came up to me because of her. Not because of me. Daphne outshines everyone, you idiot."

Miranda hated how bitter she sounded.

"Miranda, listen to me."

"Just let it go, OK?" She took a deep breath. "I understand if you want to leave."

"Why would I want to leave?"

She didn't know if he wanted to stay because of her or because he was at an exclusive party at the home of a semi-reclusive superstar.

She decided she didn't care. She threw back her drink and headed to the bar to order another.

ॐ

Daphne knocked on Greta's door.

"Yep?" Greta called out from the other side.

"It's Daphne."

After a minute, the door cracked open, and Greta peered out at her. "You're early."

"You have somewhere else to be?"

"I wanted to finish this CAD today."

Briefly, Daphne almost forgot the awful news she had to share. Greta was too precious.

"Let me in. I have something important to tell you."

"Ominous, you mean."

Daphne shut the door and leaned against it. Greta stood in front of her.

"Yes. Ominous." Daphne wanted to yank her hair out of its bun so she could pull on it. "Your father is here."

Greta sat on the bed. "Wow."

Daphne sat next to her. "How the fuck did he get here so fast? We called him this morning!"

"Time zones in his favor and limitless funds."

"Jesus, Greta. I'm sorry."

"His appalling presence is hardly your fault."

"I'm the one who suggested a phone call."

"You had a logical reason for it, and I agreed to it."

Daphne stood and started pacing. "We've made a plan. Sandy is handling him now."

Greta, impossibly, started laughing. "Yes!" she exclaimed.

"Why are you laughing?"

"Because Sandy can totally handle my dad! My dad is a horrible person. But Sandy is scary bad when he wants to be. My dad doesn't stand a chance."

"You know, that's exactly what I was thinking. But I didn't think it would make you so happy."

"Are you kidding? It's like a wedding present." Greta started laughing harder.

Then, Daphne started to see the humor too. Stiff, socially horrid Jim Donovan. Sandy, who owned half of Los Angeles and loved Greta like a daughter. A showdown to end all showdowns. It was glorious.

"Apparently you're to be shielded by Timmy's family— and of course Timmy—at all times." Daphne explained the plan as they prepared to leave the room.

"Yes, yes of course. I'm sure I'll need shielding. It's not like I don't still despise him."

Daphne was pleased to see Greta still had laughter around her eyes.

"You know," Daphne said. "I don't actually think he came here to ruin your wedding."

"Probably not. He just ruins things by accident."

But not this, Daphne thought as she led Greta out of the bedroom and into the living room. *We won't let it happen. We won't.*

"I half-expected your father to be standing right here,

thinking he was going to escort you or something," Daphne said.

Greta snorted.

All the guests stood out on the deck, waiting for the bride. Daphne led the way.

They walked as slowly as they could—and again Daphne had to keep from laughing, realizing how such a slow pace was completely unnatural for both of them. Greta followed Daphne's lead out onto the deck. An opening through the group of people allowed her and Greta to pass to the center of the gathering to the arbor. Timmy stood under it, his eyes locked on Greta like a man waking from a dream. Daphne stopped to the side of the arbor as Greta joined Timmy underneath.

Sandy stood on the other side, a small book in his hands, and he began the ceremony. Daphne started to cry then, just a little.

A warm hand encircled her waist, and above the jasmine she smelled a familiar scent of mineral spirits, olive oil and him.

"Hey," Marlon whispered in her ear as he pulled her close. "I just love weddings."

"Me too," she said, leaning against him.

Fourteen

Sandy said some words to conclude the ceremony, and Timmy and Greta leaned in for a kiss. Marlon had held Daphne's hand tucked inside of his while they'd been standing on the deck. He liked having her hand there. Once the ceremony ended, she pulled free to applaud. It took conscious effort on his part not to snatch her hand back again.

He laughed at himself. He had it bad for her, and he didn't mind one bit.

"I have to check on Greta's dad," Daphne told him. "And on some other awkward guest situations."

"I'm staying with you," he said. "I'll be your backup."

"You know anything about Greta's dad?"

"A little." He knew what most people in their small circle knew—that Greta didn't like him. That Greta hadn't spoken to him in five years. That he had hurt her badly enough to be unforgiven.

She nodded. "It'll be nice to have you with me."

He followed her through the crowd to a group that was currently congratulating the bride and groom. Two older men who looked like brothers, if not twins, each hugged Greta and Timmy. Timmy's father and uncle Brian, Marlon guessed. There was another man standing off from the group, stiff-backed, uncomfortable and aloof. He was good-looking and very tall, and he wore a nicely cut suit. He had to be Greta's dad, Jim Donovan.

"Why's he here?" Marlon asked Daphne in a low voice.

"We called him this morning to let him know. You know, a courtesy call. Somehow he made it here in time."

"How'd he know where to go?"

"I might have rubbed in his face where the ceremony was being held." Daphne made a sour face.

Marlon chuckled. "That still doesn't explain how he found Sandy's address. It's not exactly listed."

"You're kidding, right?" She laughed. Her laugh was, as usual, incredibly sexy.

"What do you mean?"

"Give me fifteen minutes and an Internet connection, and I could find Sandy's address. These days, tax records, real estate holdings, gossip websites, everything—it's all online."

"You think he knows how to do that?"

"I think he knows how to pay someone to do that." She paused. "God, I hate him."

"Come on." He took her hand to reassure her. "Let's go see why he's here."

He led her around the crowd of Timmy's family to where Jim Donovan stood. Close up, the man seemed even taller—he had at least two inches on Marlon, and Marlon was well over six feet. Greta looked so much like him it was eerie.

"Hello, Dr. Donovan," Daphne said to him, keeping her tone as formal as Marlon had ever heard her speak. She placed a hand on her chest. "Daphne Saito."

"I remember you, of course," he said. "Thank you for calling me this morning. Although an invitation somewhat prior to the wedding day would have been vastly more polite."

"To be fair," Marlon interjected, feeling Daphne's hand tense, "the wedding was very last minute."

"Is Greta pregnant?"

Daphne coughed to cover her shock and, Marlon thought, her laughter.

"No," Marlon answered because Daphne seemed unable to.

"Who are you?" Jim Donovan asked Marlon.

"I'm Marlon." He held out his hand.

"Jim Donovan." Jim shook his hand. "What is your relationship to this affair?"

"I'm Sandy's handyman."

Daphne coughed again, and this time Marlon was certain she was covering laughter.

"His handyman?"

"Yep."

"Then why are you here?"

Daphne turned her back to Jim Donovan, her shoulders shaking. She glanced up at Marlon. She had tears in her eyes from holding back laughter.

"I guess I was invited," Marlon said. "How about you?"

Daphne lost it. She guffawed. She grabbed hold of Marlon's elbow to keep herself upright. He glanced over at Greta, who stood a few feet away surrounded by Timmy's family. She and Daphne had locked eyes. Greta was smiling.

"Honestly, Daphne. What is the matter with you?" Jim Donovan said.

Marlon had a feeling this was a man who was unaccustomed to being laughed at.

Daphne ran her fingers under her eyes to capture her tears and shook her hands to toss them off. She rolled her shoulders, seeming to get herself together. She turned to face Jim Donovan once more.

"You weren't invited!" She barked at him. "You show up to Sandy's house uninvited and insult Sandy's friend." With these words, she looped her arm through Marlon's. "You are an unbelievable ass."

Jim Donovan straightened his already straight tie.

Daphne giggled again, then worked to straighten her face. "What are you doing here, Jim?"

To his credit, Jim let her berate him with a stoic expression.

"I'm here because my only child is getting married."

"Ah. So you haven't managed to father another one with—what was her name again? Ana something? She was certainly young enough to give you a brood."

Marlon wasn't sure who this Ana person was, but Daphne

didn't seem to like her.

"Don't be crass," Jim said.

"Why the hell not?"

"Because I'm here to ask forgiveness."

"Dad." Greta interrupted. She stood on the other side of Daphne, and next to Greta stood Timmy.

"Congratulations to you both," Jim said, his voice and posture growing even more stiff than before.

"So you aren't here to cause trouble?" asked Greta.

"I just wanted to be here for you," said Jim.

Marlon didn't know Jim Donovan at all, but he spent a lot of time watching people. He believed Jim's words.

"I understand." Greta stepped forward and hugged her father, then stepped back. "It's probably too late for us to have much of a relationship, but I understand."

"I'm Timmy Eisenhart." Timmy reached to shake his father-in-law's hand.

"You probably have a lot of questions," Greta said to her father, still supremely calm. "And I'll answer them. But I won't do it today." Then she took Timmy's hand, and she led her husband away. Greta stopped and greeted her other guests, smiled and hugged them, showed a joy at their presence that she hadn't shown to her own father.

Daphne remained with Jim, and Marlon remained just behind her. Marlon might believe Jim didn't intend to cause trouble, but that didn't mean he was taking any chances with his girl.

"Greta might forgive you some day." Daphne was suddenly fierce. "But I won't."

Jim Donovan, the giant of a man, took a step back from her.

She looked up at Marlon then, tugging on his hand. "Come on, handyman. Let's get something to drink."

He followed Daphne, leaving Jim Donovan alone on the deck, the deck that Marlon himself had built with Sandy over a decade ago, back when Marlon had been in need of a father. Back when Sandy, in a way, had been in need of a son.

He followed Daphne to the closer of the two beverage stations—the one set up in the kitchen—and they each ordered a beer.

"Cheers," he said to her. After they each took a sip, he said, "You worked him over pretty good."

She frowned. "He deserved worse." Then she smiled at him, a smile that tore at his gut in the most pleasant of ways. "You, sir, were amazing."

"Just following your lead."

"I'm not so sure about that. But in any case, thank you. You were excellent backup."

He dipped his head and kissed her. He couldn't help himself. She placed her hand on his chest, and he could feel her fingertips through the fabric of his shirt, through his undershirt, all the way to the skin of his chest, and she burned him raw.

He was not going to make it through the reception. Maybe he could convince her to sneak away with him to his apartment for a short break. That was an excellent idea.

He was about to suggest it when they were interrupted.

"Hey, cuties," said a familiar voice.

He turned to look. It was Miranda, Daphne's friend from college. The tornado on two legs. Her date stood next to her, looking uncomfortable.

Earlier in the evening, Marlon hadn't had much to do except watch Daphne. So he'd stood in a corner and watched Daphne greet guests as they'd arrived. When Miranda and her date had walked in, he could tell something was off, and the off-ness seemed to have something to do with the guy.

The guy seemed harmless enough, though, and he also seemed attentive to Miranda. Marlon couldn't get a read on why Daphne seemed nervous. He just knew he didn't like it.

"Miranda." Daphne's voice was cold. "Are you enjoying the reception?"

"Sure. The food is excellent, and the drinks are excellent and free. The company is," at this point, she looked around, "better than the self-entitled pricks I was expecting."

Marlon winced at her sharp language. He had a feeling it was directed, in part, at Daphne.

Stepping in, he extended his hand to Miranda's date. "I'm Marlon."

"John."

Marlon couldn't swear to it, but he thought John was having trouble meeting his eyes.

"Did you two know each other before Miranda arrived on Monday?" Marlon asked him.

"No, actually." John spoke, it seemed, with both humor and sadness. "Our meeting was just a happy coincidence."

Miranda made a grumpy noise.

John glanced at Miranda with simple longing in his eyes. Marlon wanted to tell the guy this was a fight he wouldn't be winning any time soon. Miranda seemed dead-set on alienating everyone who cared for her: Daphne, John—it didn't matter.

"We'll leave you lovebirds alone," Miranda sneered.

"Fine." Daphne dropped all pretense of being polite.

John reached for Miranda's hand, but she pulled it free as they disappeared into the crowd.

"Happy couple, those two," Marlon said.

Daphne looked grim.

"You know him?" Marlon asked.

Daphne looked startled by his question. "No. I don't know him at all." She pulled away from him. "I have to go talk to Olivia."

She rushed from him, and he watched her go, wondering how Miranda had managed to get under her skin so badly.

And then he saw where Daphne was heading or rather toward whom. She wasn't heading toward Olivia at all. She was heading toward Dan.

While Marlon had been watching the guests arrive, he'd seen Dan come in with Carrie. He'd been pissed off, sure, but then he'd realized he was probably overreacting, like Carrie had said. Carrie and Dan were here, after all, at Sandy's house. What was going to happen? Plus, Dan was a known entity, not some stranger. If Carrie was going to learn about Hollywood dirtbags, Marlon would rather she learn about one whose home address was in Rivet's Rolodex.

Marlon sipped his beer and watched Daphne confront Dan. She spoke quietly but intensely. She was angry with him, that much was obvious. Dan grabbed her hand, and she yanked it away.

Marlon was making his way across the room before he even knew his feet were moving.

"You're acting like a jealous ex, Daph. Classic," Dan said as Marlon walked up. Dan looked at Marlon then, sizing him up. "You clean up nicely," Dan said.

"Thanks," Marlon said.

"Does Sandy buy you dress clothes to wear around the guests?"

"No, he does not," Marlon said.

"Dan, shut it," Daphne said.

"No, Daphne. You do not get to cheat on me and then tell me what to do."

"Why can't you just leave Carrie alone?"

"Carrie doesn't want to be left alone," Dan said. "Ask her."

"I did, actually. Just this morning," Marlon said.

Dan looked at Marlon, suspicious. "Why did you see Carrie this morning?"

"You don't know?" Daphne said. Daphne was certain Dan would have figured out Carrie's connection to Marlon. "Marlon is Carrie's big brother."

"I didn't take biology in college, but even I know that's a little iffy."

"You write for a living. Surely you have an imagination," Daphne said.

"Our moms are sisters. I grew up in her house," Marlon said. "We're blood cousins and adoptive siblings."

"Ah," Dan said. "Kinda like the Brady Bunch."

"Kinda like," Marlon said.

"That makes this even better," Dan said.

"What are you talking about?" Daphne asked.

"You cheat on me with this jerk the night before we break up, and now I'm going out with his sister. Fantastic!"

Marlon watched as Daphne shrunk small. For some reason, Dan's words weren't drawing out her fire but extinguishing it instead. Watching her get hurt pissed him off. He pulled her to him and spoke in her ear. "Why don't you go grab us another round. I'll handle this."

She stared at him with eyes that seemed to swallow her

entire face. She nodded and left.

As soon as Daphne was out of earshot, Dan spoke. "She'll just burn you like she did me. You should get out while you can."

Marlon laughed. "Now your jealousy is showing."

"You can laugh now. But remember what I said. She'll screw you over without a second thought. She's heartless."

"I'm not sure whom you were dating, but that woman is the opposite of heartless."

"It's just a matter of time, man. I'm telling you."

"If you hate her so much, then why are you here?" Marlon asked, genuinely curious.

"You know what? I have no fucking clue."

Dan headed toward the front door, then handed his ticket to the valet. Once Marlon was certain Dan was gone for good, he went to tell Daphne the good news.

Only one thing stuck with Marlon. Daphne hadn't cheated on Dan with Marlon. Either Dan had his days mixed up, or there was more going on than Daphne was telling him.

After fifteen minutes, the valet finally returned with Dan's keys. Dan couldn't believe Daphne would invite him to this event and then rub her new boyfriend in his face like that. She truly was heartless. After all he'd done for her over the years. If it weren't for him, she'd still be schlepping coffees at Sony. There was an ache in his gut where Daphne used to be. He wanted to go home and have a scotch.

"Dan?" Carrie trotted up to him. "Are you leaving?"

Dan looked the girl over. She was a fox, no doubt. But she was also trouble. Marlon's little sister? How was he supposed to know that?

"Yeah, your brother decided it was time for me to leave."

"Marlon kicked you out?"

"Let's just say he made me feel distinctly unwelcome."

"Argh! He told me to stay away from you this morning."

"Did he now?" Dan jingled his keys in his hand.

The way Dan saw it, he had two choices. He could royally

piss off Marlon, Daphne and perhaps even Sandy, and bring this girl with him. Along with their anger, however, he would get a small bit of sweet, sweet revenge. Or, he could leave her here and not put his career in the slightest bit of jeopardy.

Dan wasn't one to resist an opportunity for revenge.

"Wanna come to a real Hollywood party, babe? It'll blow your mind."

"Sure I do," she said with her flashy smile.

They hopped into his MG Midget convertible and headed up into the hills.

Fifteen

Dan loved his MG. The car was a nicely rebuilt model from the late 1960s in a classic British green. The Midget was a tiny thing, but he wasn't a very tall guy, and chicks loved it. He glanced at Carrie next to him, her hair flying behind her in the night, her smile lighting everything up. Her dress had ridden up a bit, revealing her perfectly toned thighs. After downshifting to climb a steep hill, he let his hand drift over to land on her knee. When she seemed OK with that, he slid it up a little higher and left it there.

He turned left off Sandy's street and wove deeper into Laurel Canyon. He was headed toward a house that belonged to his friend Jamison. He'd heard about the party earlier that day, and it had always been his backup plan in case the wedding thing went sideways. He hadn't expected to be able to bring a date with him, especially one that seemed as receptive as Carrie seemed at the moment.

She tilted her head back to stare up at the sky. He looked up too. This high in the hills, you could almost make out the stars.

He jerked the wheel quickly to get the car back into its lane. He'd drifted across the center line while distracted by the stars. Luckily, no one had been coming from the other direction.

Up ahead he could make out cars parked along the street. They'd arrived. He pulled off the road behind the first car they came to and parked.

"We're here." He explained to Carrie whose house it was. Jamison was an independent film producer whom he didn't expect her to know of.

"I love Jamison's work!" she said. "I studied him in film school. Wow. I can't believe I'm at his house."

"He's hardly Sandy."

"Well, duh." She suddenly sounded very young to his ears. "No one is as big as Sandy. He's kind of an exception."

Dan felt miffed for a minute, wanting Carrie to be more impressed with his friend. But then he thought about it—her brother worked for Sandy. It's possible Sandy felt like old news to her.

Plus, Dan was positive she'd never seen a party like this one before.

"Come on." He took her hand. "Let's get groovy."

The front door was wide open, and even from the driveway, Dan could see that the party was already swinging. Like Sandy's house, Jamison's was a midcentury ranch—just much smaller in scale, more like five thousand square feet than twelve or whatever. The view from the front door revealed a spacious sunken living room. When they stepped in the foyer, he felt Carrie's hand tighten in his. Her face, for an instant, looked frightened.

Music blasted from the wall-mounted stereo. Six or seven people sat around the coffee table, chatting over a tall mound of cocaine. One couple stood near the entrance to the kitchen making out. Men and women gathered to watch a young female stripper dance against the black baby grand piano. The dancer gyrated in a G-string and nothing else. On a leather couch in the back corner of the room, a woman had her skirt pulled to her waist. A man knelt on the floor in front of her, his face between her legs. From the woman's facial expression, she was enjoying herself.

"I don't think I belong here." Carrie refused to walk any farther.

"Nonsense," Dan whispered in her ear. "Just have

confidence. Let's see what's going on in the kitchen and grab some drinks. If you want to leave after that, we will. OK?"

"OK." She sounded nervous but brave.

In the kitchen, Dan and Carrie found Jamison. Jamison wore his shoulder-length blond hair in a ponytail. He had on a black suit jacket over a black T-shirt and dark blue jeans. Jamison always was a handsome fuck, Dan thought, annoyed.

"Dan Morello!" Jamison said. "And guest." He swept his eyes over Carrie.

"Hey, Jamison," Dan said. "This is Carrie—" Dan paused, realizing he never did learn how to pronounce her last name properly. "Carrie A."

"Is the A for Aphrodite?" Jamison asked.

Carrie seemed to take the compliment well, giving a mock curtsy.

"Anything to drink around here?" Dan asked.

"Yeah. Bar's set up over there." Jamison pointed to the table tucked in a far corner of the kitchen. It was covered with liquor bottles and glasses. "I'll be in the living room getting busy."

"Come on, babe," Dan said to Carrie. "Let's get something to drink."

When Carrie Ademola had agreed to leave Greta's wedding with Dan, she'd thought she'd been asserting herself against her overbearing brother. She'd thought she was going to get the chance to make some useful industry connections. She'd thought she would have a light-hearted adventure.

When she'd ridden in Dan's adorable car around Laurel Canyon, staring at the gorgeous night sky, she'd felt free and full of life. She'd wanted to put her arms over her head but felt that would have been just a little too much. Besides, doing so would have pulled her dress up even farther, and she hadn't wanted to encourage Dan's wandering hand.

But now they were here at this horrible party. And now she knew she had made a mistake. She couldn't get the stripper's bored facial expression out of her head. Or the people having sex in public. Or the drugs—the enormous pile of drugs. This was not who she was. She didn't belong here with any of these people. She did not belong with Dan or Jamison. Her idols from college had turned out to be broken.

Mostly, she was scared.

"I need to go to the bathroom." She handed her drink to Dan.

"Sure thing, babe. It's this way."

Dan led her through the awful living room and down a short hallway. She entered the narrow bathroom and locked the door behind her. She opened her purse and pulled out her phone. She dialed Marlon's number. She almost hit the button to place the call. She almost did and then decided not to.

Carrie stared at the phone in her hand. She couldn't call him. That would be admitting her mistake. She'd created this problem herself, and she needed to solve this problem herself.

She would just ask Dan to drive her back down to Sandy's house and drop her off. She could sneak back into the wedding reception, and no one would even know she'd been gone.

Decision made, she unlocked the door, then took an immediate step backwards. Jamison was standing there.

"Oh, hi," Carrie said. "Are you waiting for the bathroom?"

"I didn't realize Dan had a new chick," Jamison said.

Carrie's instincts told her she probably shouldn't correct Jamison by telling him she wasn't Dan's new chick.

Jamison continued. "He and that Daphne girl had been together a long time."

"Dan was dating Daphne?" Carrie asked, surprised. She hadn't known that.

"You know Daphne?" Jamison took a step closer to Carrie. She stepped back once more. Jamison was blocking the bathroom doorway now.

Now Carrie's heart was racing.

"Daphne and I are friends I guess."

"She's a fox," Jamison said. "Not as foxy as you are, though." He raked his eyes over her body, lingering on her breasts, on her legs bared by the short skirt of her dress.

"I'm done in here now. Bathroom's all yours." She made to brush past him through the door, and he blocked her way with his shoulder.

"I think I'd like to get to know you a little better," he said. "Besides, Dan's busy in the living room."

Jamison wrapped his hand around her upper arm and pushed her back into the bathroom, past the vanity, and up against the wall opposite the toilet. He closed the door behind him, turning the lock.

She screamed.

He slapped his hand over her mouth, fumbling for the hem of her dress as she tried to fight him off. One of the straps of her dress snapped and fell, baring one of her breasts. He pinned her with one arm, holding her against the wall while she struggled. He lifted his hand from her mouth to touch her bare breast, and she screamed again. She screamed and screamed, begging to God to be heard over the blasting music, knowing she wouldn't be heard, knowing that even if she were heard, no one in this house would come to help her—maybe not even Dan.

After all, he'd brought her here.

She pushed back against the feeling of helplessness that tried to overwhelm her.

She needed to escape. Jamison was touching her bare skin, pinning her neck to the wall with his elbow, but he was distracted by her body. Now. She had to act now. She lifted her knee as high as she could and ground the heel of her shoe into the top of his foot, putting all of her weight behind it.

"Fucking shit!" Jamison yelled, falling back against the toilet, holding his hurt leg in the air.

Carrie grabbed her purse and ran from the bathroom. Holding up the strap of her dress, she ran down the hall and through the living room, vaguely hearing voices calling behind her. But those voices only made her run faster. She ran through the open front door and up the driveway. Once she hit the street, she removed her high heels so she could run faster. She turned down the hill and in short order passed Dan's parked car. She kept running. She would run all the way back to Sandy's, one hand holding her shoes and purse, the other holding her dress.

Minutes later—or more, she couldn't tell—she slowed to a walk. She pulled out her phone. She should call Marlon now, she decided. He would come to her, of course he would. And she needed his help. It was time to swallow her pride.

Just as she was about to dial, headlights turned the corner behind her. She stepped off the street and into the dirt for safety. The car slowed to a stop. It was Dan.

"Carrie! What are you doing out here?"

"Jamison attacked me." She realized she was shaking.

"I'm sorry that happened, babe. Why don't you get in the car?"

Carrie stayed on the side of the road, unsure whether to trust him.

"Don't be silly, Carrie. Let me drive you back to Sandy's house. You can't walk all the way there." His voice was persuasive, sensible. "It isn't safe."

"That party wasn't safe!" she yelled. "Your friend tried to rape me in the bathroom!" Her voice rose at the end as the panic she'd felt in the bathroom threatened to overtake her again.

"Jamison gets a little confused when he's high," Dan said, his voice soothing. "He's mostly harmless."

"He's not harmless!" Carrie screamed at him again, her panic morphing into furious anger. "He attacked me! He's a monster!"

"OK, OK." Dan's tone grew even more soothing. "I get it. Let me take you back to Sandy's where you'll be safe."

Carrie ran through her options, still panicked. Dan could get her to Sandy's house quickly. She wouldn't have to wait for Marlon to find her. She realized then that she didn't know where she was—she couldn't even give Marlon directions. It might take an hour for him to find her out here.

Once she got to Sandy's, she could find Daphne, and Daphne would help her. Daphne would have safety pins stashed someplace and would repair her dress. Marlon would never know about Carrie's stupidity.

She opened the door to Dan's car.

"Atta girl," Dan said. "We'll be there in ten minutes,

tops."

Carrie buckled her seatbelt. She slid her hand into her purse and grasped her cell phone. She pressed the buttons for 911. Then she rested her thumb on the button to initiate the call.

Just in case.

After a few minutes of riding in the car with Dan, Carrie could tell that the ride down the hill was different from the ride up the hill. Dan was driving much more slowly. He was intoxicated, driving deliberately to make up for his lack of reflexes. A couple of times, he drifted across the center line, but then realized what he was doing and jerked the wheel to swerve back into the proper lane.

Suddenly, to Carrie, Dan's adorable convertible felt incredibly small and unsafe.

Up ahead, the road curved sharply downhill and to the right, but Dan seemed not to notice. He kept going straight. Carrie screamed at him to turn, and then everything went black.

❧

Carrie awoke in semidarkness. The setting sun through the trees provided some light to see by. Next to her, still in the driver's seat, Dan was unconscious, blood covering his face. His side of the car was folded around a tree. Her side seemed to be miraculously unscathed. She unbuckled her seatbelt, opened her door and fell from the car. She was too woozy to stand. She crawled instead, dragging her purse behind her. She lay down in the dirt on the side of the road and hit the button to call the number already dialed on her phone.

The 911 operator answered.

"A car wreck," Carrie said. "Can you track my location? I don't know where we are. And my friend, he's bloody and unconscious. He wasn't wearing a seatbelt."

"Tracking your location now. Please stay on the line."

"I have to hang up soon. I have to call my brother."

"Please stay on the line."

"Wait. I know what street we're on." She told the operator

the name of the street. "Just turn left off of Laurel Canyon, and you'll find us."

"Miss, please stay on the line."

"Please find us, OK? I'll call you right back."

She hung up. She dialed Marlon.

❧

Marlon was standing next to Daphne when his phone rang. He hadn't left her side the entire evening after watching Dan hand his ticket to valet. He wanted to meet all of her friends. He wanted to get to know Timmy and Greta better. He knew them pretty well, but not as well as Daphne did. He wanted to be a part of every part of her life. He just wanted in.

He pulled his phone from his pocket. It was Carrie. Strange. Why would she be calling him from the same party? Worry kicked into high gear before he even answered the phone. He stepped out onto the deck for some privacy.

"Carrie?" He answered the call.

"Marlon." She sounded like she was barely awake. "I need your help."

Suddenly Marlon was no longer standing in the middle of a wedding reception. He was alone in a bleak room, and the silence of that room was deafening. "Carrie. I can barely hear you. Where are you? What happened?"

"Car wreck. I'm by the side of the road. Dan's still in the car. He's not OK." She was crying. "I don't know where I am exactly. Not far from Sandy's." She told him the road she was on, where she thought she might be. "I called 911 and told them where I was, but I wanted to call you too."

"I'm coming right now. Hang up and call 911 back." He was frantic. "I'll be there."

"OK. I'm pretty sleepy though. I might be sleeping on the side of the road."

"Carrie?" He shouted into the phone. "Don't fall asleep!"

"What? OK."

"Call 911. And stay awake."

Marlon stopped feeling anything. Even panic had fled. He stepped back into house. He scanned the room. He spied

Sandy. He made his way through the crowd, vaguely noticing that he bumped a few shoulders along the way. He didn't care.

Sandy saw him coming and excused himself from a conversation. "What is it?"

"It's Carrie. She's up in the canyon somewhere. A car accident. I need to borrow your car."

"Yes, of course. But Marlon," Sandy said, "my car is in the garage. It'll take thirty minutes to get it out."

At Sandy's words, Marlon let out a frustrated roar.

∽⚘⚭

Daphne heard Marlon yell. Everyone heard him yell. She dashed across the room to where he was talking with Sandy.

"What's happened?"

Marlon turned his gray eyes on her, and she didn't recognize him at all. "This is all your fucking fault," he said to her in a low voice, turning his back.

"Sandy?" She was shocked by Marlon's anger at her and by the fear that she could see driving his anger.

"Carrie's been in a car accident," Sandy explained. "We don't know where she is. Dan was driving."

Daphne thought of Dan's stupid MG, thought of him driving it too fast in the dark hills, and she went cold.

"Marlon needs to get to her," Sandy said. "But my car's blocked in."

"I'm not," Daphne said. "I parked up the street. Marlon," she called to him. "Marlon, listen to me. My car is out on the street. We can leave right this second."

She touched his arm, and he jerked away from her like she was a viper.

"Please, Marlon," she begged. "Let me take you to her."

He looked past her face, refusing to meet her eyes. "OK. Let's go."

"I just have to grab my keys. Meet me by the door."

Marlon stormed off.

She turned back to Sandy. "Whatever happens, make sure Greta and Timmy don't find out. Protect them. Send them on their honeymoon." She was begging him. "In fact, send them now. Keep them safe from this."

"I'll do what I can."

Daphne ran to the bedroom where she and Greta had dressed and grabbed her purse. She stepped out onto Sandy's front porch to find Marlon there, his eyes cold. She slipped her high heels from her feet. "Come on." She took off running.

They reached her car and hopped in. She started the engine, tossing her shoes into the back seat. She pulled onto the road, heading up into the canyon at a pace she thought Marlon would like.

"Daphne." Marlon's voice was eerily calm. "Drive as fast as you can."

So she did, downshifting to pick up speed, taking corners fast. They turned onto the street Carrie had given Marlon on the phone, a long and winding street, not knowing how far up the hill the wreck would be. She slowed down. Marlon scanned the roadside.

Then they saw it, there in the dark. Dan's crumpled MG roadster was bent around a tree, and Dan still sat behind the wheel, unmoving. There, on the side of the road, Carrie was curled in a little ball, clutching her cell phone in her hand, its screen still lit. Carrie, though, was unconscious.

Daphne parked so her headlights shone on the wreck, and she and Marlon flew from her car. Daphne dialed 911 and gave their precise location, as Marlon ran to Carrie. She was lying in the dirt on the road's narrow shoulder.

Marlon knelt at Carrie's side, draping his suit coat over her seminude body. Daphne hung up with the 911 operator and ran over to Carrie, noticing her torn dress, her bare feet. Marlon ran his hand over Carrie's forehead, calling her name in a quiet voice, and she stirred.

"I'm here, Cee-Cee," he said. "You're safe."

Marlon looked up at Daphne. "This is your fault."

"I know."

Sirens shrieked in the distance.

Daphne stepped over to the car. The tree had stopped the car from tumbling down a steep incline. For that, despite the damage the tree had inflicted on the car, she was grateful. She neared Dan, who looked lifeless. She reached to touch his back and hoped for life. She felt warmth, a beating heart. She exhaled. A death on her hands would be too much to bear.

Daphne noticed objectively that her bare feet were cut from walking across broken glass and other wreckage. She couldn't feel her feet though. She couldn't feel anything.

She could only see. Carrie's still form. Dan's bloody face. The hatred in Marlon's eyes.

Paramedics arrived, and the police. So many men and women wearing different sorts of uniforms, all rushing about, working, doing, saving. They asked Daphne some questions. She answered as best as she could.

She didn't have many answers.

When she saw that Carrie was awake on her stretcher, Daphne walked away from the questioners. Carrie was even smiling at Marlon. Carrie was talking to a police officer. Marlon was scowling. Marlon was scowling at Daphne. But Daphne was standing close to Carrie, and she didn't want to leave Carrie's side.

Then the police officer pointed at Carrie's torn dress. "Did anything else happen tonight?"

"What do you mean?" Carrie asked.

"Are there other injuries we can help you with?" The police officer was a woman, one who seemed kind.

Carrie dropped her head before she spoke. "There was a man at the party. Jamison. It was his house." Carrie paused, as though gathering courage. "He attacked me in the bathroom. He tore my dress." She looked at Daphne then. "It wasn't Dan," Carrie said, emphatically. "Dan came to drive me home."

"All right," said the police officer. "We can talk about that later after you've been patched up."

"How's Dan?" Carrie asked the police officer.

"We can talk about that later too," the police officer said.

And then Carrie was gone in the back of an ambulance, and the ambulance burned Daphne's eyes with its lights and burned her ears with its sirens as it flew around the curve that had destroyed Dan's car.

Dan was being loaded into the back of another

ambulance. But Dan had never woken up, even after the paramedics strapped him to a board and lifted him high. Dan never even stirred. Daphne stood next to his still, bloody form, his nose swollen to twice its normal size, a cut on his forehead still pumping blood.

And then Dan was gone too. More lights, more sirens.

The police officer spoke to Daphne and Marlon, then. "We will stay to assess the scene and handle the wreckage. So long as we have your contact information, you two are free to go."

Free.

"Drive me to the hospital," Marlon snarled in her ear. "Fast."

Sixteen

Daphne pulled into the parking lot at Cedars-Sinai and whipped her car into a parking space. Marlon opened his door before she'd even killed the engine. Together, they ran into the hospital. Only after they'd passed through the sliding glass doors and the metal detectors did Daphne realize she was still barefoot.

Marlon dashed to the information desk to ask where they had taken Carrie.

Daphne looked around her and froze. This was the same room she'd stood in five years before. Five years before, she'd frantically run in, chasing the life of another girl, praying she'd be OK. There was the same long desk. There was the same metal door blocking her way.

Last time, she'd been praying for Greta's life.

This time, she prayed for Carrie and for Dan.

Daphne's world flipped one way, toward the past, and then flipped again, back to the present.

Marlon stalked back to her, anger and fear in his every step. Daphne knew Marlon would never look at her with anything but anger ever again. For a moment, she mourned.

"Carrie's been taken to a room here in the emergency department," he said. "I'm meeting her there."

"I'll come with you," Daphne said.

"No." He held up his hand to stop her. "You won't." He looked at her with such fury that Daphne took a step back. "You put her in danger just by breathing."

Daphne nodded. She couldn't refute him.

"Never come near my family again," he said.

"OK," she said.

He turned to leave her there.

"Did you find out where Dan is?" she asked.

"Upstairs. Surgery," Marlon tossed over his shoulder.

He passed through the big metal door to find his sister, leaving Daphne alone.

She stood in the emergency waiting room, staring at the metal door that led to where Carrie and Marlon would be meeting, a meeting she was barred from, a family she would never be a part of in any fashion no matter what she and Marlon had shared this week. Marlon was gone. Gone.

And Dan might be dying.

Daphne looked upward frantically, searching for the signs that would direct her to the surgical wing. She dashed to an elevator, rode up. She stepped off the elevator, emerging in a sterile hallway. In front of her was a desk. Behind the desk sat a man in scrubs, tapping at a computer.

"I'm looking for a patient," she said, out of breath. "He was just in a car wreck."

"Name?" the man asked.

Daphne told him.

"Are you family?" the man asked her.

"I'm a friend. He doesn't have any family here."

"Wait there," he said, pointing to a gathering of chairs. "I'll let a surgical nurse know you're here."

The man picked up a phone while Daphne found a place to sit. She chose a chair that gave her a view out of the tall windows, of the lights of the city spreading below her. The chair also gave her a view of the two large double doors that led, she presumed, to the operating rooms.

No one else waited in the small seating area. She was alone. She found that odd. No one else's life was at risk tonight, at least not in this wing of the giant hospital.

With a pneumatic whoosh, the two large double doors

opened, and a woman in blue scrubs and a surgical cap emerged. She was pulling a mask from her face.

Daphne surged to her feet, the cold linoleum touching her bare toes causing her to shiver. She squeezed her purse in her hands to force her body to still.

The nurse approached Daphne. When she noticed Daphne's bare feet, she frowned. She called to the man behind the counter. "Can we get her a pair of socks?"

The man nodded and bustled away down a hall.

The surgical nurse turned her attention back to Daphne. "You're here for Mr. Morello?"

"Yes. Dan. I'm here for him."

"Are you family?"

"No."

"Does he have any family here?"

"No one in California. They live far away."

"Are you his girlfriend?"

Daphne considered lying. Considered misrepresenting her relationship with Dan in hopes of getting better information. But she found she couldn't lie when her friends' lives were on the line.

"I was," she said. "Now we're friends." Even that was a small lie. Was she friends with Dan?

Yes, Daphne told herself firmly. They would have figured out a way to become friends again. He'd been angry with her. Hurt. But he wasn't a monster. She knew the difference.

She'd known some real monsters in her life.

Her mind flashed to Carrie's face, when she'd been on the stretcher, looking in her lap, describing an attack in a bathroom.

"He's in surgery," the nurse said.

Daphne's attention jerked back to the present.

"I'll be honest," the nurse said. "It's touch and go right now."

Daphne nodded.

"His car didn't provide much protection, and he wasn't wearing a seatbelt."

"It was an old MG," Daphne said. "A stupid, stupid car." She was angry at Dan's vanity in choosing to drive the old tin can and his stupidity in forgoing his seatbelt.

"There's some spinal cord damage and damage to his skull. Plus, he was severely intoxicated—alcohol and cocaine," the nurse said, her tone perfectly neutral. "The drugs can complicate things."

Daphne nodded and nodded, not wanting to interrupt.

"We're doing everything we can. I'll update you as things progress."

The surgical nurse waved a key card near a scanner on the wall. The big doors opened once again.

"Here," a man said.

Daphne jumped back, startled. The man from behind the counter, a nursing tech she saw from his name tag, was handing her a pair of socks. They were plush, with grippy material on the soles.

"Thank you." She sat to pull on the socks.

"Wait," the tech said. "Your feet are a mess."

"No, they're fine."

"I'm serious. There's blood on the floor. A lot." He took a step toward her. "Let me help you."

She leaned back in her chair, holding out her hands to keep him at bay. "Please. Just let me be."

He nodded. "But I have to clean up the blood. It's a biohazard."

While he scrubbed her blood from the floor, she pulled the socks on her feet. Warmth spread through her body. She looked at her navy blue dress, tattered now, perhaps bloodstained, but she chose not to think about what could be staining her dress. Instead, she stared at the lights blinking on outside the windows and hoped and prayed. She prayed for Dan and for Carrie.

After minutes or hours, Daphne couldn't tell, the surgical nurse emerged from the wide double doors.

Daphne glanced at her watch. That couldn't be right. She had only been waiting thirty minutes. Thirty minutes that had felt eternal, but thirty minutes nonetheless.

Daphne fixed her eyes on the face of the nurse as she reached behind her head to untie her mask. And then another person caught Daphne's attention. Another person passed through the doors, wearing darker scrubs and a floral surgical cap. The way this new woman carried herself, Daphne could tell she was the surgeon.

Daphne could infer what it meant when the surgeon came out after thirty minutes of surgery. Someone had died.

No one else was in the waiting room but Daphne.

They were sorry to inform her. They had done all that they could. The damage was too severe, especially to the cervical spine and skull.

"Do you have information for Mr. Morello's next of kin?" the surgeon asked her.

"Next of kin?" Daphne asked. She couldn't understand what they were asking her. She couldn't make out their words in a world where Dan was dead, and it was her fault he had died.

"We need to notify Mr. Morello's family. We thought you might be able to provide contact information."

"I can't right now," she said. "But I can get it for you. I just have to run home."

"There's no rush," the surgeon said. "If we have to wait till morning to make the call, that's OK. In fact, it's probably better."

Daphne tried to imagine waiting till morning to hear about a loved one who had been dead all night.

Dead, and no one knowing except the woman who had caused it to happen.

"You're just going to let his parents wait all night while their son lies here dead?"

The two women locked eyes for a moment.

"What's your name?" the surgeon asked.

"Daphne. Daphne Saito."

"Daphne. This is how it goes. I'll call his parents in the morning and explain what happened. Then a social worker from the hospital will help them make travel plans to come here or will help them arrange to move the deceased to where they live. But we can't do any of these things at ten o'clock at night."

"OK," Daphne said. "That makes sense." That was all she could think to say.

Daphne didn't know how to take care of dead people.

"Come back in the morning around nine. Bring his family's information to this counter right here. We'll make the calls then."

Daphne nodded.

She fell into a chair.

The surgeon and the nurse turned and passed through the doors once more, gone.

Dan was gone.

Once Daphne was seated, she noticed the red creeping around the edges of her socks. She peered at the bottoms of her feet, where the blood had soaked through the fabric. She must be hurt worse than she'd thought. Suddenly, she could feel the knifing pain in the soles of her feet.

She couldn't walk now if she'd wanted to.

She called out to the tech behind the counter. She was crying, she realized. "Can you help me?" she said, pointing to her bloody feet.

He nodded, picking up a phone.

She, too, picked up the phone. She dialed the only person she knew who'd been in anything like this situation before.

"Daphne?" Miranda said, tentatively.

"I need your help." Daphne tried to even out her voice and failed.

"What and where," Miranda said, leaping into action. She'd always been great in emergencies. Daphne had forgotten that quality of hers.

"Cedars-Sinai Hospital. Come to the emergency entrance. I have my car, but I don't think I can drive."

"I'll be there in twenty." Miranda sounded like she was already in motion. "Just hang on."

"Dan's dead. He died."

Miranda was silent for a moment. "I'm so sorry, Daphne."

Daphne hung up and stared at her bloody socks. After a few minutes, a voice spoke in front of her.

"Are you Daphne?" A doctor stood before her with a wheelchair. Her black hair was pulled back in a tight ponytail. She had brown eyes and pale skin covered in freckles. She seemed about thirty years old.

Daphne nodded.

"Those socks are supposed to be blue," the doctor said. She talked fast.

"I'm so sorry." Daphne was weeping now. "I just didn't notice."

The doctor helped Daphne into the wheelchair, placing her injured feet on the footpads.

"I heard you came in with that big accident tonight." The doctor pushed Daphne toward the elevator. Once inside, she hit the button that would take them down to the emergency level.

"Yeah."

"I heard someone didn't make it."

"No." Daphne cried harder now. "He didn't."

The doctor squeezed Daphne's shoulder. "We've got to fix your feet. You probably didn't feel them because you were thinking about your friend. That sort of thing makes me worried that you're hurt elsewhere too."

Daphne thought of Carrie and Marlon. She was definitely hurt elsewhere.

"No, I'm OK," she said. "I wasn't in the wreck. I just walked around barefoot to help my friends."

"You were wearing high heels, huh?"

Daphne laughed a bit through her tears. "Totally inappropriate footwear for an emergency."

"I'm Dr. Murphy, but you can call me Tory. I'm a resident in emergency medicine. I'll get you cleaned up." She leaned forward and looked at the bloody socks again. "You might need stitches though. Stitches mean crutches."

"I called a friend to come help me."

"Good. Tell me his name, and I'll have the front desk people send him straight back."

"Her name's Miranda."

Tory rolled Daphne into a curtained-off space, then helped her lie down on her stomach. Then she sat on a wheeled stool near Daphne's feet.

Using a pair of blunt-tipped scissors, Tory snipped the socks from Daphne's body, exposing the wounds on the soles of her feet.

"Eek, Daphne. Your feet look terrible."

"What do they look like?"

"You want me to take a picture with your phone?"

Daphne giggled through her tears. "Sure. Here."

She handed Tory her phone. Tory snapped a picture then handed it back.

"Oh. I see." Daphne looked at the picture. "Ground beef. Why didn't you just say so?"

"Employee handbook says to be polite." Tory dug around in some drawers. "I'm going to inject you with some lidocaine to help with the pain. Then I'm going to tweeze out all of the glass and metal and stuff." Once she had her tools set up on a tray, Tory pulled some magnifying goggles over her eyes. "You ready?"

"Go ahead."

She considered rejecting the lidocaine. After all, she deserved to feel the pain.

"My friend Dan," she said to Tory, "he's the one who died. My friend Carrie—she was in the car with him. I don't know how she is."

"She's been admitted for observation, but word is she's fine."

Daphne felt Tory pull a piece of car wreck detritus from her foot. She dropped it in a metal basin. Daphne heard a plinking noise. Another tweeze. Another plink. Tweeze. Plink.

Daphne put her face in her hands and sobbed.

After a while, the tweezing stopped. Daphne felt a cool liquid on her feet.

"No stitches?" she asked, looking over her shoulder at Tory.

"Nope. I used a little glue here and there but you should be fine without stitches if you take it easy. But you do need a tetanus shot. I'm going to let everything dry before I bandage you up. Sit tight."

Daphne nodded.

Tory rolled backwards on her stool until her head poked out of the curtained area. She spoke to someone in a low voice, then rolled back in.

"Where is she?" Daphne heard a familiar voice call out

from beyond the curtain. "Do you know where she is, Tall Person in Scrubs?" The voice was insistent. Demanding. Pushy.

Daphne smiled. "That's my friend," she said to Tory.

Tory rolled out of the curtains again. "Miranda? We're in here."

Daphne heard Miranda's swift footsteps, like a two-legged torpedo coming her way. But Miranda was Daphne's torpedo. Whatever had happened earlier tonight with John, the stakes were higher now. Miranda was someone you wanted on your side when everything was fucked, and Miranda was on Daphne's side.

Miranda slipped through the curtains and took in the scene. She looked at Daphne's feet. "You step on a land mine?"

"Totally looks like it," said Tory. "But apparently these injuries are just a manifestation of her roadside heroism. Let me bandage them up now."

"Of course." Miranda squatted near Daphne's head and took her hand. Miranda was still wearing her dress from the party, although she'd swapped her high heels for flip-flops. "Tell me what happened."

Daphne told Miranda the story of the night after Marlon received the phone call from Carrie. Of waiting for news about Dan in the surgical wing. Of worrying about Carrie but not being able to see her. Of Marlon's harsh words to her, and even of what Marlon was starting to mean to her that week. She was crying again, this time for her heartbreak.

Finally, Daphne said, "Dan is dead, and I'm crying about a boyfriend I didn't even have."

"That's bullshit," said Miranda. "Love doesn't have to take forever. Love can happen in a split second. I saw his goofy ass at your condo yesterday when he brought that portrait of you. He loves you, and you love him."

"He doesn't love me any more."

Miranda waved her hand like she was swatting a fly. "You've never loved anyone before, Daphne," Miranda said. "That's a big fucking deal. And now this asshole that you love just blamed you for his sister's bad judgment and Dan's intoxicated driving?"

"Carrie's just a kid."

"Let me rephrase. He blamed you for Carrie's youthful judgment. Whatever. How is any of this your fault?"

"They would never have met each other if not for me."

"What does them meeting each other have to do with anything?" Miranda's voice rose in exasperation.

"If Carrie and Dan hadn't met, then Dan wouldn't have asked her to Greta's wedding. If they hadn't gone to the wedding together, then they wouldn't have left to go to that party together. If they hadn't gone to the party, then they wouldn't have gotten into the car wreck together. Don't you see? It all starts with me."

"I can't decide if you have a head injury or if you really are this arrogant."

"She doesn't appear to have a head injury," Tory said, drawing the tetanus shot.

"I like you," Miranda said to Tory. Then Miranda leaned in close to Daphne's face. "It's not all about you, Daphne."

"Well!" interrupted Tory, holding up a syringe. "I have your tetanus shot here."

Miranda helped Daphne sit up, then stood back, her arms crossed over her chest, her full lips in a tight frown. Tory rubbed an alcohol swab on Daphne's shoulder before injecting her with the vaccine.

"There. You're all set," Tory said. "Here's a bag of replacement bandages. You should change them morning and night." She cocked her head. "You still don't have shoes to wear, though."

"I brought some." Miranda pulled another pair of flip-flops out of her purse and set them on the floor at Daphne's feet.

"I didn't ask you to bring those," Daphne said. "I didn't even tell you what was wrong with me."

Miranda looked exasperated. "No matter what was going on, I figured you wouldn't want to be wearing high heels."

"Oh, I see," Tory said to Daphne. "She's a mind-reader. She must be great to have around in a crisis."

"Not a mind-reader," said Miranda. "I've just been here

before."

Daphne had a feeling Miranda had seen the inside of more than one emergency room. More than just the one that Daphne knew about, anyway.

Tory said, "The lidocaine I injected should last till you get home. But you shouldn't walk or drive. I've called for a wheelchair to the exit."

To Miranda, Daphne asked, "Can you drive a stick shift?"

Miranda rolled her eyes.

She handed Miranda her keys, and Miranda met her at the entrance with her car. An orderly helped her into the passenger seat.

Once they were on their way, Miranda asked, "Where's Greta? I'm surprised you didn't call her instead of me."

"She's on her honeymoon, I hope. She and Timmy were supposed to go up to this resort in Santa Barbara where Greta went once a long time ago. I told Sandy to make sure they didn't hear about the accident. I didn't want to ruin their wedding too."

"What do you mean, 'too'?"

"I've ruined so much today. At least Greta and Timmy can have something good."

"How many times do I have to say it? Stop being so conceited. It's not all about you."

Miranda drove toward the hospital exit.

"I'm not being conceited."

"Shut up and give me directions back home."

"How did you get to the hospital?"

"John dropped me off."

Daphne had forgotten about John. She'd forgotten about how angry she was at Miranda for showing up at Greta's wedding with him and for deliberately trying to hurt Daphne.

Now that her head was clearer, Daphne wanted to know why Miranda had done such a thing.

"Yeah, I know," Miranda said, preempting Daphne's question. "We can talk about him. But can we wait till we're back at your place?"

"Sure," Daphne said. "Thanks for coming."

Miranda snorted. "Of course I came. Anyone would

have."

Daphne thought back to college, to the one time Miranda had asked Daphne for help, and Daphne had failed her. And Daphne thought that maybe she understood a little bit better why Miranda had brought John to Greta's wedding.

Seventeen

At eleven o'clock Wednesday night, Marlon stood outside of Carrie's hospital room. She was asleep. Her mother, his aunt Donna, was asleep in the recliner next to the bed.

Sandy sat near him in the hallway, in one of the hospital's chairs. And Marlon was royally pissed off at him.

Two hours before, after leaving Daphne at the hospital entrance, he'd found Carrie in a bed, surrounded by doctors. They'd been taking her vitals, checking her for broken bones, shining lights in her eyes. She'd become woozy again during the ambulance ride from the wreck site.

He'd been terrified.

"I'm her brother," he'd yelled over the din. "Tell me what's happening!"

One of the doctors stepped back to speak with him. "It looks like her only injuries are to her shoulder, from the seatbelt, and a concussion. We're going to take her to radiology now. Wait here." The doctor pointed to a chair next to Carrie's bed. "We'll either bring her back here, or we'll send someone to come get you."

So Marlon waited. After a few minutes, he called Sandy.

"How is she?" Sandy asked.

"They're scanning her head and her shoulder. But she's going to be OK, I think."

"Good. How's Dan?"

"I don't fucking care."

Silence.

"Is the party still going?" Marlon asked.

"It's winding down. The newlyweds left shortly after you did."

"You had something to do with that?"

"Before you two left, Daphne asked me to send them off and ensure they have a good honeymoon."

"Don't say her name."

Silence.

"I was so worried about Carrie," Marlon said.

"I know you were."

"I thought she was going to die."

"You did."

"Can you come down here? I don't have a ride."

"Sure thing. Olivia has this place under control. I'll be there soon."

After a while, one of the doctors came back to tell Marlon they were admitting Carrie. He told Marlon where to find her room. Marlon bypassed the elevators and ran up the stairs to Carrie's floor. At the nurses' counter, he demanded to know her room number.

He ran down the hallway until he found her.

She was awake in her bed, talking to a man with a hospital badge and a clipboard. Marlon took a deep breath, then entered.

"Marlon!" she said. To the man with the clipboard she said, "This is my brother, Marlon. Marlon, this person wants money." She giggled.

At the sound of her laugh, Marlon's shoulders released their tension. He pulled a chair up next to her bed, and his legs collapsed.

"Come back later," he said to the man with the clipboard. "I'm calling her mom. You can talk to her about insurance stuff."

Carrie laughed again. "Yeah. You can totally talk to our mom about money. That's super fun."

Carrie's mom hounded after every dollar, bargained over

every purchase and used every coupon, even expired ones somehow. No one, not even banks, liked to talk to Aunt Donna about money.

As the clipboard guy was leaving, a doctor entered. She was tall and slender, and her tag indicated she was from neurology.

"Good news, Carrie," the doctor said. "Your shoulder is only sprained. It hurts, I'm sure, and you'll likely want a sling, but there are no breaks, tears, dislocations or other nasty stuff. More importantly, though, your head scans show a concussion but no other serious injury—no hematoma and no skull fracture."

"Great!" Carrie said, throwing back the blankets. "I can go, then?"

"No way," the doctor said.

"Ugh." Carrie pouted.

Marlon laughed, his relief making him feel faint.

"We need to monitor your concussion for twenty-four hours," the doctor said.

"If you are going to imprison me here," Carrie said, "can I at least go to sleep now? You know sleep deprivation violates the Geneva Conventions."

"Yes, you may sleep now," the doctor said.

"Thank jeebus." Carrie dropped her head back on the pillow and shut her eyes.

Marlon thanked the doctor, who left the room with a smile.

Soon after the doctor's visit, Aunt Donna showed up, worry all over her face. Marlon spoke with her in the hall.

"I'm sure she'll tell you the whole story later, but for now, just know that she's fine."

"But the driver's in surgery? He's really hurt?"

Marlon nodded.

"That's so horrible!" Aunt Donna said.

"Don't feel bad for him. He was intoxicated. He put Carrie in danger."

"What is wrong with you?" Aunt Donna said.

Marlon wasn't sure what was wrong with him, and he didn't want to think about it.

Marlon helped his adoptive mom get comfortable in the recliner in Carrie's room. Then he found a blanket in the closet and tucked it around her shoulders. Soon, both Aunt Donna and Carrie were sleeping soundly.

Then his phone rang. He stepped into the hall to answer it. Sandy was downstairs at the main entrance. He told Sandy where to find him.

When Sandy arrived outside of Carrie's room, his face was grim.

"Do you know where Daphne is?" Sandy asked.

"Why would I know that?"

"Dan is dead."

"Shit."

Cold washed over Marlon, forcing him to think clearly for the first time since he'd received Carrie's call from the side of the road.

He hadn't gotten the full story from Carrie yet, but although Dan had taken her to that awful party, he hadn't let her leave alone after Jamison attacked her. In going after her, he'd been trying to do the right thing.

Now he was dead.

"Where'd you last see her?" Sandy asked.

"At the emergency entrance. That's where we went our separate ways."

Sandy paused, considering. "That's probably a true statement."

Marlon, already stretched thin, snapped at Sandy's mocking tone. "What is that supposed to mean?"

"I get that you're worried about Carrie, and you should be. But Daphne was alone. She'd sent her best friend off on her honeymoon to protect her from this mess." Sandy pinned Marlon with his cinematic blue eyes. "Daphne was all alone. Do you understand what I'm saying?"

Marlon nodded. He did understand. He knew what it was like to be alone and to find out someone important to you was dead.

But he didn't want a lecture from Sandy. He and Daphne were nothing alike. "This whole scene is her fault."

Sandy laughed. He fucking laughed at that. "How do you

figure?"

"Dan and Carrie wouldn't have been together tonight if it weren't for her. Dan would be alive if Daphne hadn't driven Dan to do something stupid."

Suddenly, Sandy's voice got cold and deadly serious. Marlon had apparently touched a nerve. "Women don't make men do stupid things." Sandy's voice was as angry as Marlon had ever heard it. "Men do stupid things, period."

"Leave me alone, old man. You're not my father."

"That is also a true statement." Sandy sat down in a chair next to Carrie's room and crossed his feet in front of him. "Let me know when you're ready to go home."

And now here they were, having their first real fight in the twelve years they'd known each other. Except Sandy didn't look angry at all. He wore that same placid expression on his face that he almost always wore, as though he knew something everyone else didn't. Usually, Marlon thought Sandy's poker face was funny. Right now, when it was directed at him, he didn't like it one bit. Marlon knew what Sandy was hiding behind that poker face.

Judgment.

Miranda neatly pulled into Daphne's parking space and closed the garage door behind them. "Stay there," she said to Daphne. "I'll come around and help you."

Together, they shuffled up the steps and into the house. The lidocaine was beginning to wear off, and Daphne's feet ached.

"Lifeboat," Daphne managed to say, and Miranda helped her to the orange couch. Daphne collapsed.

"You look terrible." Miranda took in Daphne's pitiful form. "Let's get wasted."

Daphne tapped her chin thoughtfully. "I remember a time when you didn't drink at all."

"Me too," Miranda said. "What was I thinking?"

Given Miranda's recent appearance in Los Angeles, and the cause for it, Daphne had a feeling she knew what Miranda had been thinking.

Miranda disappeared into Daphne's kitchen, opening and closing cabinets. She returned with a bottle of vodka, a bottle of grapefruit juice, a lime, a knife, two glasses and a joint.

"That's not TSA-approved," Daphne said, pointing at the weed.

"John got it for me." After a moment, Miranda rolled her eyes. "Yes, we can talk about John."

Miranda made their drinks with a surprising amount of skill for someone who, until recently, had been a teetotaler.

"Alcoholic mom." Miranda nodded at the miniature bar she'd set up on the coffee table. "Just like riding a bike." She handed a glass to Daphne.

"So." Daphne took a sip. "John?"

"We met at Didier's, like I said earlier tonight. He came up to me after you left and asked if you were Akane. I told him no."

"And then you made some deductions."

"And I made some deductions. Want to hear them?"

"No. But also yes."

"You met John out on Saturday night. Then you had a quickie at his place. You lied about your name and number." She paused. "Also, I did some math. You must have been cheating on Dan."

"Nice deductions. I broke up with Dan the next day."

Miranda lit the joint. She took a deep drag and held it, sitting back on the lifeboat. She exhaled. "You might have broken up with Dan on Sunday," she said. "But you were out of that relationship a long time before."

"How can you know that?"

"Because of Marlon."

"What about Marlon?"

"Because you're in love with Marlon, you dodo." Miranda heaved a dramatic sigh. "How did you get through college without higher order processing ability?"

"Don't be a snob."

Miranda laughed. "Too late."

"Back to the topic of why you brought a person to Greta's wedding whom you knew would cause trouble."

"I feel bad about that. I'm sorry."

"Why'd you do it?" Daphne pressed.

"At first I just hung out with John because I could. He seemed interesting, and, well, interested in me. He asked me out, and I said yes. We spent a lot of time together the past two days."

"The wedding?"

"Right, well. Looking back now, perhaps I was still a little angry with you about what happened in college. I just didn't know I felt that way."

"I figured it was something like that," Daphne said.

"You did?"

"I'm not a complete dodo. I've never forgotten what happened in college."

"Yeah, OK," Miranda said. "Me neither."

"But you still came here when your mom died."

"Farthest place I could go without a passport. Mine's out of date."

"Is that the only reason?"

"I don't know." Miranda looked sad for the first time since she'd arrived in Los Angeles.

"Why is it that you are so good at reading other people and terrible at reading yourself?"

Miranda laughed and handed Daphne the joint. "Can you still feel your feet?"

"They really hurt." Daphne took a drag.

"How did you hurt them so badly?"

"I took off my shoes to get to the accident faster. I didn't even notice I was cutting up my feet when I was walking around the wreckage."

"That's what it's like in a crisis," Miranda said. "You don't feel anything. Your focal point narrows to a pinprick."

"That's exactly what it felt like."

"I know."

Daphne had a feeling Miranda did know. She knew a lot more than she was letting on.

"What happened with John tonight? After the unveiling of Daphne?" Daphne asked.

"It's funny. He wasn't mad at me at all."

Daphne smiled.

"After we spoke with you and Marlon, we stayed at the party for a while. Great party, by the way. And then we left around seven I guess. We got coffee at your coffee place. What's it called?"

"Uptown."

"Yeah, that's it. Then I walked back here to go to bed."

"Why'd you walk?"

"I didn't want him to know where you live. I might be spiteful, but I'm not an idiot."

"I don't think you're spiteful."

"Let's review. I dragged your one-night-stand to a party where you'd be surrounded by your new guy and your old guy. I did it because I was mad." Miranda wore an expression of mock concern. "Do you need to borrow a dictionary?"

"I think you were hurt, not spiteful."

"I think I need my weed back," Miranda said.

Daphne handed it to her.

"How'd you get to the hospital?" Daphne asked.

"You called me almost as soon as I got back here. I grabbed a change of shoes for both of us, and then ran back out, dialing John. He was still in the neighborhood. He picked me up at the corner of San Vicente and brought me."

"Did he ask what was going on?"

"Yes. But I didn't have anything to tell him except that you needed me."

"What'd he say then?"

"Actually, he said the strangest thing. He said he'll be seeing me again soon. He said he had a feeling." Miranda rolled her eyes. "Who talks like that? Creeps and weirdos."

"And boys in love."

"Barf."

Daphne started crying again, quietly this time.

"Your feet, or something else?" Miranda asked.

"Something else."

"Yeah." Miranda picked up Daphne's hand. "I know."

Eighteen

Eventually, Marlon had let Sandy drive them home. Eventually, by the time they'd made it to Sandy's, Marlon had apologized for saying hurtful things.

After they'd climbed out of Sandy's car, Sandy had pulled Marlon into a hug. "I'm not your father," Sandy had said to him. "But you're the only kid I've got."

After they'd parted ways to go to bed, Marlon might have cried a little bit as he walked up the steps to his home.

They'd agreed to meet for a quick breakfast the next morning and then head back to the hospital to check on Carrie.

ॐॐ

Around eight o'clock Thursday morning, Marlon let himself into Sandy's house and headed toward the kitchen. Sandy was sitting at the table drinking a cup of coffee. He had another cup for Marlon.

"You sleep all right?" Sandy asked him.

"Not really."

"That's to be expected, I guess."

"I guess."

They ate the bagels Sandy had picked up from the market, then headed to the hospital. Sandy valeted at the main entrance, and they walked inside together. This morning, with the crisis past, Marlon was able to notice the stares Sandy garnered from passers-by. Like usual, Marlon found them funny. Los Angeles was populated with stars. Ordinary people who lived in LA, people like Marlon, became inured to their presence. But there were very few megastars, and it seemed impossible for anyone to become inured to those.

Sandy was a megastar.

They rode the elevator up to Carrie's floor and strolled down the hallway to her room. Aunt Donna was helping the hospital caterer clear Carrie's breakfast tray from the room. Donna came out into the hall when she saw Marlon and gave him a big hug.

She looked up at him, her face so nearly the same as his own mother's. "Marlon, did you sleep at all?"

"Sure I did, Aunt Donna. How about you?"

"Well enough," she said. "Carrie's doing great. They're going to let her go today."

"That's good news. I'm sure she's happy to be sprung from her prison."

Marlon could see Carrie in the room clicking the remote control for the television, frowning at the options on the screen.

"Trying to keep that girl in one room for more than a few hours at a time has been a struggle since she could walk." Aunt Donna laughed, and behind her laugh, Marlon heard a deep sense of relief. "Oh! Sandy," Donna said. "I didn't see you over there."

Indeed, Sandy had been hanging back, letting Marlon speak with his aunt in private.

"Hi, Donna." Sandy kissed her cheek, and Donna blushed a deep red. "It's nice to see you again."

Even his no-nonsense aunt wasn't immune to Sandy.

"Carrie said she wanted to speak with you," Donna said to Marlon. "I'll go downstairs to get some breakfast and leave you two alone."

Sandy sat in the hallway chair he'd occupied the night before. Marlon ducked into Carrie's room and pulled a seat up next to her bed.

"Hey bro," she said. "This place doesn't have cable."

"I hear you're getting out of here today, so you won't have to suffer long."

She looked at him with sad eyes. "Dan died."

"I know."

"He was kind of a jackass, and he was too drunk to drive, but he came to help me." Tears filled her brown eyes.

Marlon took her hand. "He shouldn't have taken you to that party in the first place."

Last night, after she'd been admitted, Carrie had given him some details about Jamison's party. When Marlon thought about that Jamison guy putting his hands on his sister, he could barely control his need for violence.

"I asked Dan to take me, Marlon. He was going to leave Sandy's by himself."

"He still shouldn't have taken you."

"Marlon, are you listening to me? I spoke the words. I asked him to take me." Carrie sounded annoyed.

"Some part of him must have known what he was doing. He knew he was using you to get back at Daphne."

"Wait." Carrie interrupted him. "Where is Daphne? I haven't seen her at all. Is she OK?"

"I don't know." Marlon heard the coldness in his voice.

"You don't know where she is? Or you don't know if she's OK?" Carrie's eyes narrowed. "Oh shit, Marlon. You're mad at Daphne about me?" Carrie started laughing. "You're a dummy."

"She's the reason you're here," he said.

"Oh jeez." Carrie rolled her eyes.

"She's the reason you almost died," Marlon insisted.

"No, Marlon," Carrie said. "None of this has anything to do with Daphne. How can you be so dumb? And you are obviously ruining all of my hard matchmaking work."

"You can forget about that," he snapped.

"Why can't you let this be my mistake?" She gestured at herself lying in the hospital bed. "I screwed up! I begged Dan—a guy I barely knew—to take me to a party at a place I didn't know, and, to top it off, I didn't tell anyone I was leaving! It was all so stupid."

Marlon just shook his head.

"And Jamison, he can take some of the blame." Carrie looked sad, even spooked for a moment. "And Dan shouldn't have driven drunk."

"He was high too."

"But if you don't let this be my mistake, I can't learn from it." Marlon tried to speak, but Carrie held up her hand. "If it is my mistake, big brother, I won't make the same mistake again."

Her last words clicked into place for Marlon. He felt his resolve begin to weaken.

"You won't make this mistake again." He repeated her words back to her.

She nodded. "And if it's my mistake? Then it can't be Daphne's."

He frowned, unwilling to let go of his anger toward Daphne. Even though, he now realized, he really wanted to.

"Are you ruining everything with her because I was an idiot?" Carrie asked.

"Dan was intoxicated. He shouldn't have been driving."

"Sure, OK. Both Dan and I were idiots," she said. "But perhaps Dan has been punished enough," she said, her voice quiet.

Marlon leaned back in his chair, covering his face with his hands.

"You don't have much to say, big brother."

"I do not."

"I think it is possible that you have fucked up."

"It's possible."

"Her ex just died. She's emotionally wrecked. She probably needs someone, don't you think? And what did you do, you stupid stubborn male person?"

"I sent her off alone."

"You are ridiculous." She wrinkled her nose, as though he smelled bad. "Go away. I don't want to talk to you until you tell her you're sorry."

Marlon stood, smiling down at Carrie. "I'm glad to see your smart-ass skills haven't been harmed in any way."

She didn't answer him, just waved him away while

pressing buttons on the remote control.

Marlon left the room, closing the door behind him. Sandy stood, raising his eyebrows.

"Good news, then?" Sandy asked.

"She seems completely fine," Marlon said. "Also she dressed me down a bit."

"I heard some of it."

"Naturally." Marlon was accustomed to Sandy's shameless eavesdropping.

They headed toward the elevators.

"Any thoughts about what I should do?" Marlon asked.

"What do you think you should do?"

"I should probably start by apologizing to her."

"Probably."

"Do you think it's possible for her to forgive me?"

"It's likely she's not even mad at you, you fuckwit," Sandy said, exasperated. "The question is whether it's possible for her to forgive herself. Especially after what you said to her."

Marlon stopped short and pulled his phone from his pocket. He dialed Daphne's number. The call went to voicemail. He hung up and sent a text message. "Please call me." He called again, and again got her voicemail. This time, he left a message. "Daphne. It's Marlon. OK. Listen, I'm sorry. I was completely wrong. I need to talk to you. Please call me."

After hanging up, he asked Sandy, "Is she ignoring me?"

"Maybe," Sandy said. "Maybe she's just busy."

∽∾

Daphne pulled into the hospital parking lot with Miranda in the passenger seat. They were both hung over, but Miranda more so. Daphne had told her she didn't have to come this morning, but Miranda had just said some colorful words about the bullshit of Daphne's self-sacrifice and trudged out the door by her side.

Daphne had put Dan's parents' contact information in her bag. His parents lived in Tempe, Arizona. Daphne's soul ached thinking about the news they were about to receive.

Dan was their only child.

As she and Miranda passed through the glass doors of the hospital's main entrance, her phone rang. She pulled it out of her bag and frowned.

"It's Marlon," she said to Miranda.

"Cocksucker," Miranda said.

"I wonder what he's going to yell at me about now." Daphne silenced the phone.

They headed to the elevators. Daphne's phone beeped that she'd received a text message.

"It's a text from Marlon. He's asking me to call him."

"Did he say please?"

"Actually, yes," Daphne said. "I hope Carrie is OK."

"You're really worried about her."

"I am."

"And you haven't seen her since the wreck?" Miranda asked.

"No. Marlon wouldn't let me. Tory told me she was all right—but that was last night. Anything could have happened since."

Daphne's phone rang again. Marlon. "I don't think I can answer this." Daphne started to cry. "You do it."

"If it's important, he'll leave a voicemail," Miranda said. "If he doesn't, we'll text him back."

They waited. Finally, the voicemail signal beeped. They listened to the message together.

"An apology," Miranda said. "Interesting."

"I don't deserve an apology."

"Ugh." Miranda grabbed Daphne's hand and dragged her onto the elevator. "Let's deal with one critical event at a time."

Up on the surgical floor, Daphne told the tech at the desk, a woman this time, why she was there. The tech seemed to know exactly what to do with Daphne's information and with Daphne.

"Could you please wait over there?" the tech said, pointing to the same waiting area where Daphne had waited for Dan to die the night before.

Daphne sat in a chair next to Miranda. She glanced at her bandaged feet.

"The ibuprofen isn't doing much," Daphne said.

"You were supposed to stay off your feet. Yet here you are tromping all over town."

"I was supposed to bring in this information."

"I bet you could have called it in."

"That didn't feel right."

Miranda picked up her hand. "I know."

A woman came out through the large double doors. She, like Daphne, was Japanese, and her hair was cut in a perfect pixie. She wore a white doctor's coat and carried a clipboard. She interviewed Daphne, asking about Dan and his family, and took the notes that Daphne had brought. She told Daphne that the surgeon on Dan's case would be calling Dan's parents that morning to make a formal notification of death.

"Can I call them after that?" Daphne asked.

"Sure. Just wait until after we call them. Noon should be safe. It would be nice for them to hear a familiar voice."

The woman pointed at Daphne's feet. "Are you OK?"

"I'm fine," Daphne said.

Miranda groaned.

"What? I'm fine," Daphne said again.

"You would be finer if you had better pain medicine," Miranda said.

"You were seen last night?" the doctor asked.

"Yes. By Tory Murphy in the emergency room. I hurt my feet at the crash."

"Let me page her. She can probably call in something to the hospital pharmacy for you. Do you have time to wait?"

Daphne nodded.

"Is your mobile number in our system?"

Daphne nodded again.

"OK. You'll get an update from the pharmacy in the next thirty minutes or so."

"Thank you." Daphne felt tears starting to come.

The woman put her hand on Daphne's shoulder. "Sometimes, in crises, we feel like we're supposed to suffer. But we're not."

Daphne looked closer at the woman's ID badge. She was a pathology resident. A doctor familiar with death. She wondered how much this doctor knew about suffering.

"Thank you," Daphne said. When she moved to stand, Miranda helped her to her feet.

The pathologist headed back through the double doors.

Miranda and Daphne took the elevator back to the first floor to find some food and kill time while waiting for the prescription.

At the food court, Miranda left Daphne to rest her feet and stood in line for greasy fast food to cure their hangovers.

Daphne's phone rang again. Marlon. Her concern about Carrie overcame her desire to avoid him. She declined his call but sent him a text message.

"Is Carrie OK?" Daphne wrote.

"Yes. She's still in the hospital but is being released this afternoon. Where are you?" he replied.

She didn't respond. She wanted to see Carrie, to apologize to her. How could she find her?

She called Sandy.

"Daphne," Sandy said. "It's great to hear your voice. I'm so sorry to hear about Dan."

"Thank you," she said with a small sob. "Thank you for caring about what happened to him."

"Oh Daphne," Sandy said. "You cared about him, and I care about you. It's simple math." The warmth of his voice transmitted through the phone, bringing more tears to her eyes.

"I'm back at the hospital," she said.

"Why? What's going on?"

"I'm helping the hospital notify Dan's family. They didn't know how to reach his parents."

"Are you alone?"

"Miranda came with me."

"Ah." He sounded pleased. "Did you need something?"

"Yes. But it's all right if you want to say no." She took a deep breath. "I'd like to visit Carrie."

"That sounds like a great idea."

"It does?"

"Of course. She's already asked about you."

Carrie had asked about her? Carrie wasn't angry with her?

How was that possible?

"I don't know what room she's in," Daphne said. "Will you tell me?"

"Sure. I forgot the room number, though. Let me ask the nurse real quick."

Sandy was here at the hospital too? Why?

She waited, hearing only hushed voices on the other end of the line, then Sandy came back and told her the room number.

"Thanks, Sandy."

"You do know this wasn't your fault."

"Smoke. Fire. You've been around long enough to know how that works."

"I have definitely been around. And I know this wasn't your fault."

"Sandy, you have always been a great friend to me. Thank you for that."

༄

Sandy and Marlon stood in the atrium entrance to the hospital. Marlon paced while Sandy finished his call to Daphne.

"She's speaking to me in the past tense. That's not a good sign."

"What does that mean?" Marlon asked, coming to a stop in front of Sandy.

"When a person starts thanking you for your friendship as though it were about to end, it usually means that person is about to do something stupid."

"Daphne is too sensible to do something stupid," Marlon said.

"She's not too stupid to disappear. And she could. She could send in her scripts to her agent from anywhere on Earth. We'd never see her again."

"She wouldn't disappear on Greta."

"She would if she thought it was the best thing for Greta."

"This is crazy!" Marlon said, pacing again. He thought of the girl who'd slept in his bed that first night, who'd awoken in the early morning hours and told him she was a terrible bet. She really believed that about herself. And he had only confirmed it for her with his horrible words to her last night: *You put her in danger just by breathing.*

And then he'd made her sit alone while her friend died. Dan hadn't been perfect, but he'd been in her life. She'd been alone, and she'd been alone because of Marlon.

"Tell me what to do," he said to Sandy.

"If I were you? I'd go wait outside of Carrie's room and catch her on her way out. If she tells you to stay away from her, I'd do what she says. But I wouldn't let her go, man." Sandy shook his head. "This right here is one of those moments of truth that you hear about."

ॐ☙

Daphne knocked on Carrie's door. Miranda sat down to wait in a chair just outside of the room, sipping a huge cup of coffee.

"Come in!" Carrie called from the other side.

Daphne cracked the door, making sure no one else was in the room. Then she opened the door all the way.

"Daphne!" Carrie squealed. "Come sit. I'm so bored."

"Hey, Carrie."

Daphne sat in a chair next to Carrie's bed, careful not to touch the bed or Carrie. Carrie seemed a priceless artifact that Daphne would damage by accident.

"I'm so sorry about Dan," Carrie said. "It's just horrible that he died."

Daphne started crying despite herself. "Damn it," she said. "I swore I wouldn't cry in here."

"Why not?" Carrie asked. "It's really sad. He was a genius, and he was your friend."

"But he hurt you."

"Not on purpose. Plus, it's my fault too." Carrie tilted her head. "Wait. You're sounding an awful lot like Marlon."

"What do you mean?"

"Are you two determined to not let me take any responsibility for my bad judgment?"

Daphne laughed. "When I was your age, I had essentially no parents and plenty of bad judgment. I would have been mortally offended if someone tried to tell me I wasn't responsible for my own actions."

"Finally, someone understands me!"

"But Carrie, the world is a big place. Things happen around us in ways we can't always see. It's not as simple as flipping a switch and the lights come on."

Carrie looked at Daphne like Daphne had lost her mind. "I have no idea what you are talking about."

"Dan is partly to blame. You are partly to blame. But I'm partly to blame too. I came to apologize to you."

"Are you serious? For what?"

"For ever putting you in Dan's path. I think he used you to get back at me because I hurt him."

"Even if that were true, he made that choice. And I made the choice to get in his car—twice. No, three times. And none of those choices were yours."

"Please accept my apology. It's important to me."

"Daphne, this is ridiculous!"

"You'll understand some day."

"Ooooh! Now you're talking to me like I'm a child. You and Marlon deserve each other." Carrie crossed her arms. "Go away."

Daphne stood, smiling slightly. She loved seeing Carrie so animated, so healthy. Carrie made her happy. But Daphne knew Marlon was lost to her, and rightly so, because she had put another innocent girl in the path of a dangerous man.

"Bye, Carrie."

"Ugh. See you at Rivet."

Daphne didn't reply as she backed into the hallway and closed the door behind her. She smiled to herself, thinking of Carrie's annoyance.

She dropped her smile when she saw the two people facing off in the hall. Miranda stood, arms crossed, blocking Marlon's path. Marlon looked at Daphne over Miranda's shoulder, a beseeching expression on his face.

Daphne turned and shuffled away from them. She wasn't sure where the hallway led. She just needed to escape.

"Daphne, wait!" Marlon called.

"Stop, you imbecile," Miranda said. "She obviously doesn't want to talk to you."

"I just need a minute. Just one minute."

"Pushy men. Why do you always think women owe you their time?"

Daphne paused in her shuffling. She laughed a little at Miranda's exasperated words.

"Fine." Daphne turned. "You can have one minute."

Marlon dashed around Miranda and stopped short in front of Daphne. "What happened to your feet?" he asked, examining her bandages.

"Your minute is passing fast."

"Carrie told me she wouldn't talk to me again until I apologized to you."

"You apologized on your phone message. Problem solved."

Daphne kept her voice cold. She had to be cold because Marlon was saying everything she wanted to hear. She wanted to dive into his arms, let him hold her. But she couldn't let him hold her. He'd been right last night.

She put them all in danger.

"I said horrible things to you," he said. "There's no excuse."

Daphne glanced at her watch.

"God, Daphne! Give me something here."

"OK, Marlon. I have something for you." She put on her most disdainful expression. "I realize Dan is, you know, dead, so he can't confirm this for us. But I want you to think back to the party last night."

"OK." Marlon sounded wary. Good.

"Think back to something he said right before he left. Basically his last words to us. You know, his last words to us, ever."

Marlon winced. Excellent.

"He said I cheated on him with you the night before I broke up with him. He thought it was poetic justice that he was going out with your sister."

Daphne watched as Marlon processed the memory of

Dan's words.

"I didn't understand what he meant at the time," Marlon said, "except that he was using Carrie to piss us off."

"Well, of course he was using Carrie to piss us off. But what you didn't understand was that I did cheat on Dan the night before I broke up with him. I just wasn't with you when I did it."

Realization crossed Marlon's face. "There was another guy."

"There was another guy." Daphne counted with her fingers. "There was another guy, there was Dan, and there was you. All in one week."

Marlon shook his head, as though doubting her words. She was playing on the most basic male insecurity. In her experience, no man wanted to date a promiscuous woman. Ever. Men wanted their virgin fantasies. Their faithful, adoring girlfriends. Thing was, Daphne could never be a virgin fantasy. There was no point in trying.

Daphne dropped the next bomb.

"Move along, Marlon," she said. "We had a nice couple of days. You were an excellent rebound."

He looked at her with open disbelief. "You're lying."

"Miranda!" Daphne called. Miranda stepped over. "Who was your date to Greta's wedding? Be very specific."

Miranda gave her a questioning look. Daphne nodded.

"He was the guy you slept with last Saturday night," Miranda said. "Awkward timing on my part, lady. Sorry about that."

"I'm not lying, Marlon," Daphne said. "I'm glad Carrie's OK. But I don't really see any reason for us to talk any more."

She turned her back to him, and Miranda fell into step beside her.

"I don't believe you," Marlon called out.

"Grow up," Miranda said to him because Daphne couldn't speak through her silent tears. Once they were far enough away that he wouldn't be able to hear them, Miranda said, "Well, that was sufficiently cold. I think he almost bought it. I, for one, am impressed with your acting skills."

"I need him to believe me."

"Why?" Miranda pressed a button on an elevator to take them down to the hospital pharmacy.

"I need them all to stay away from me. It's better for them if I'm not in their lives."

"Are we seriously back to this?"

"Miranda, you didn't see what happened to Greta. This is like a nightmarish instant replay. And this time, someone is dead."

"What happened to you to make you feel like all the terrible things that occur are actually within your control?"

Daphne thought for a moment. "Nothing. And everything."

Miranda put her hands on Daphne's shoulders. "My mom spent the last fifteen years trying to leave this world in one way or another. At first I blamed myself. I thought, if I were just a better daughter, then she'd want to stick around." Miranda laughed, but it wasn't really laughter. "At some point you have to realize you aren't in charge of what other people do to themselves or to other people. You can only stand by and watch."

"That can't be right," Daphne insisted.

"But it is. And it's awful."

Nineteen

Marlon didn't say anything on the drive back home, and Sandy was happy to let him stew. Sandy had figured things wouldn't go well with Daphne at first. After all, Marlon had screwed up pretty badly, and Daphne was a tough one. Marlon would tell him what happened soon enough, and Sandy was a patient man.

Finally, Marlon slammed his fist down on his knee in frustration. "She called me a rebound."

Sandy chuckled.

"Of course you think this is funny."

"Of course. Watching you in love for the first time is more entertaining than I ever imagined it would be."

Marlon was silent for a while.

After Sandy turned left at Chateau Marmont, Marlon spoke again. "She also told me she slept with someone else last weekend, the night before she broke up with Dan. What am I supposed to think of that?"

"That she's a human being? That she was in an unhappy relationship?"

Marlon quieted again.

"But I think you're missing the bigger picture," Sandy said. "What you're really supposed to think is that she's trying to drive you away."

"It's working," Marlon snapped.

"Really?" Sandy said. "Why?"

"I don't want to be a rebound from Dan!"

"Jesus, Marlon." Sandy tried not to laugh again. "Dan is dead. Furthermore, Carrie's survival was a near thing."

"I know that!"

Wow, Daphne had Marlon all twisted up. Marlon needed to see that he'd brought this tongue-lashing on himself.

"And most importantly," Sandy said, "Daphne blames herself for it. Mostly because you told her it was all her fault, and she believed you."

Marlon grumbled.

"You did this. If she's driving you away, it's because she thinks it's what you want. Maybe she thinks it's what you need."

They rode in silence up the canyon. Marlon seemed to consider Sandy's words.

Seeing Marlon like this, so fragile, so immature, reminded him of when he first met the kid, twelve years before. Marlon had been eighteen, a freshman at UCLA. And he'd been lost as hell.

That spring, Sandy had been considering an anonymous donation to the art department there. He was touring the facilities. Marlon was taking a studio art class, Painting the Human Form or some other nonsense. But in Marlon's hands, the course wasn't nonsense. Sandy saw this working-class kid doing something brilliant. More importantly, in the kid, Sandy saw himself.

Sandy had a look around the classroom, striking up conversations with the students. Most of them were star-struck by his presence, but after so many years of these interactions, Sandy was good at putting people at ease. When Sandy spoke with Marlon, the young man wasn't star-struck at all. Marlon gave him a challenging look. He was daring Sandy to say that he didn't belong at this fancy school with these fancy kids.

Sandy's wife had never wanted to have kids. It was one of the reasons they'd split. That, and her serial sleeping with other men. The divorce, only a couple of years old at the time, still stung. Sandy was alone in his mansion.

The guest house was empty too.

"The semester's almost over," Sandy said to Marlon. "You got a summer job?"

"I'll figure something out."

"What are you interested in?"

"Not the movies, that's for sure."

Sandy laughed at Marlon's dig. "You got any superpowers?"

The question caught Marlon's attention. "Yeah," he said. "I can build anything out of wood."

"A carpenter?"

"A cabinet-maker."

Sandy smiled again, this time at the kid's boldness. "I'm interested in building a deck, and I could use some help. It'll likely take all summer." He handed Marlon his card. "Call me if you're interested."

Marlon called two weeks later. At the end of the semester, Marlon moved into the guest house for the summer. But at the end of the summer, Marlon stayed on. He stayed on all through college and then after. For a while, Marlon had been meticulous about earning his own way. He'd kept accounts, deducting rent from his pay. Sandy knew Marlon needed to feel like he wasn't—once again—living off someone else's good graces. Sandy knew Marlon needed to learn that he, himself, was indispensable. That he was special.

Eventually, Marlon figured that out.

And as for his paintings, well. Marlon did have a gift. At first, Sandy hung a few of Marlon's paintings in his house. After a week or two, Sandy's friends started asking about them. Sandy was coy, telling folks that the artist was a recluse, but that Sandy had a connection. Word began to spread about this Barr fellow, and how you had to go through Sandy to get his work. People even speculated that Sandy was the artist.

Now, Marlon could paint on commission and name his price. His paintings hung all over Laurel Canyon and beyond.

There was even a Barr painting hanging in that asshole Jamison's house. Sandy had seen it once when he'd been convinced by a friend to stop by for a party.

Sandy knew exactly what Carrie had seen at Jamison's house.

Sandy knew what Jamison was.

When he pulled into his driveway, instead of parking down in the garage, he left his car up by the front door. He had a feeling they'd be needing the car again sooner rather than later.

Sandy didn't tell Marlon, but he was really worried about Daphne.

☙

Around four o'clock that afternoon, Marlon came into Sandy's house holding his cell phone open in his hand. Sandy saw the urgency on Marlon's face. He rose from the chair where he'd been reading a script.

Marlon spoke into the phone. "I'm going to put you on speaker, OK?" Then he pressed a button and set the phone on the coffee table. He sat near it and motioned for Sandy to do the same.

"Miranda?" Marlon said. "I've got Sandy with me now."

"How'd you get Marlon's number?" Sandy asked Miranda.

"I stole it from Daphne's phone when she was asleep." She sounded impatient. "Stop wasting time with stupid questions. I think you guys need to do something."

"What's happened?" Sandy asked.

"After we got back from the hospital, Daphne and I both went back to sleep because we'd been up all night. But when I woke up, something felt off. I went into Daphne's room, and she was gone. But like, gone-gone. A lot of her clothes were gone, like she'd packed for a trip."

Sandy met Marlon's eyes. Marlon looked desperate.

Miranda continued. "And I found this crazy note on the kitchen counter. Look, can we call Greta now? This feels like DEFCON 1 to me."

"What did the note say?" Sandy asked.

"It said—hang on, I'll just read it to you. 'I have to make this right. If I don't see you again, I'm sorry about what I did to you in college.' Don't worry about that, that's our old business. But, well, it was serious business. Anyway, then she says, 'Tell Marlon I do love him.' Ha. I was totally right about that, by the way. And then she says, 'I just don't want to hurt anyone else.' That part, to me, sounds completely ominous. Also, that's Marlon's fault. Marlon, you are an asshole."

Marlon looked sick. He also made no move to defend himself.

"Can we come over there?" Sandy asked. "Take a look around?"

"I dunno," Miranda said. "Do you think that would help? Marlon made her feel like some kind of Typhoid Mary. Maybe you could leave him behind."

Sandy glanced at Marlon. He looked even more wretched.

"I think we can help, Miranda. I have resources."

"Ugh," she said. "You sound like my dad." After a moment she said, "Fine. But call Greta while you're on your way. She'll want to know that her sister's in trouble."

"I will," Sandy promised.

He headed out the door, and Marlon followed, radiating guilt and helplessness.

After they climbed into the car, Sandy asked him, "Do you want to ruin Greta's honeymoon, or should I?"

"I'll do it," Marlon said. "It's my fault."

"To be fair," Sandy said, "she probably would have felt guilty no matter what. You just pushed her over the edge."

"That doesn't make me feel better," Marlon said.

"Wasn't supposed to."

Marlon picked up his phone and dialed, leaving his phone on speaker.

"Marlon?" Greta said. "What's going on?"

"We have a situation."

"Is it the kind of situation that means I get to come home now?"

"What?" he asked. "Aren't you having fun?"

"I'm not very good at relaxing."

"I guess that's true." Marlon laughed despite the dire situation "Greta, it's Daphne. We're afraid she's in trouble."

"Hang on," Greta said.

Muffled voices spoke on the other end of the line.

"I'm back," she said. "We're packing now. Tell me what's happening."

Sandy listened while Marlon filled in Greta. Sandy sped toward Daphne's condo, realizing that Marlon seemed to be getting over his fear of fast-moving automobiles.

When Marlon finished explaining the situation to Greta, he said, "I told Sandy I didn't think she'd do anything stupid." Greta didn't respond. "Right, Greta? She won't, will she?"

"No, Marlon. You're wrong. Daphne would absolutely sacrifice herself to save someone she loves. She'd do it in a heartbeat. She's done it before."

Marlon looked at Sandy with frantic eyes, and Sandy just nodded, sadly.

Greta said, "We just have to figure out what she's planning on doing and hope we can stop her in time."

Twenty

At five o'clock on Thursday, Daphne sat in a corner booth at Rivet, her back to the room, reducing the chances of her being spotted. She knew that coming to Rivet, a place where she was known, was risky, but Rivet itself was a key part of her plan.

She'd also known that leaving a note at her condo had been risky, but the chances of Miranda acting on the note were slim. Miranda didn't know her way around Los Angeles. She didn't even have a car. She could call John to help her, but he was relatively new in town, and he certainly didn't know the places where Daphne would be. Places like Rivet.

And Daphne had needed to leave a note. She'd needed to let them all know that she loved them, despite the horrible things she'd said.

She hadn't said anything in the note to Greta, though. Greta already knew that Daphne loved her. And Greta would be annoyed that Daphne had left something as silly as a note.

She glanced at her watch. It was time. Daphne dialed Jamison from her cell phone.

"Yeah," he said by way of greeting.

"Is this Jamison?" She added a touch of sadness to her voice.

"Yeah." He sounded even more impatient.

"Jamison." She sniffled. "This is Daphne Saito."

A pause. "Hey," he said. "Rough news."

"The worst. I'm heartbroken. I was hoping…" She paused dramatically. "I was hoping you might have dinner with me tonight. You and I, we were the last of his friends to see him alive."

Jamison paused again, considering. "Where were you thinking of going?"

"How about Rivet?"

Jamison laughed. "Daphne, I can't get into Rivet."

"I can."

"Oh," he said. "That's cool."

He swallowed her lure like she knew he would.

She told Luis to expect Jamison in the next half hour or so, and she told the host to seat him at her table. She ordered herself a soda water with lime, a fake cocktail, because her plan depended on her not getting drunk tonight, and on Jamison getting very drunk.

She wore all black—her black leather pants, her black cashmere sweater and her black booties to hide her bandaged feet. She'd worn the sweater on purpose. It still smelled like Marlon, and thinking of Marlon made her feel brave.

When Jamison arrived, she stood to greet him. She let her real grief over Dan's death show on her face, but she carefully disguised the disgust she felt toward Jamison.

For a split second, Daphne allowed herself to picture Jamison cornering Carrie in the bathroom. Jamison tearing Carrie's dress. Jamison, who deserved everything Daphne was planning for him tonight and more. She kept her face placid while the vicious thoughts churned.

"Daphne." He kissed her cheek. "It's good to see you again, even under these tragic circumstances."

"Thanks for coming," she said. "I just wanted to reminisce, you know?"

"Sure, babe," he said with what could only be described as a leer. "Anything you want."

"Let me order you a drink. You want what I'm having?"

"Vodka tonic?"

"Yeah." She let his presumption form the lie. "Have a

seat. I'll speak to the bartender."

She strolled to the bar, giving Jamison a good view of her legs in her leather pants. Most men found the pants irresistible. She had a feeling Jamison would be like most men.

At the bar, she flagged down Quentin.

"Hey, Daph," he said. "Can I help you with something?"

"My friend wants to get wasted on vodka tonics. I'm driving, so I'll just stick with sodas. But let's keep my booze-free state between us, OK? I don't want him to feel bad."

"Sure thing. I'll let your server know."

She nodded her thanks and headed back to the booth. She slid in next to Jamison, sitting close enough that they could share body heat. It was easy enough for her to hide her revulsion. She worked in Hollywood, after all.

"I can't believe you've never been here before," she said to him.

"It's hard to get in, you know."

"I do know."

"The owners must be pompous pricks, keeping it so exclusive."

"They must be."

Daphne knew Jamison was on Rivet's no-fly list, and she knew Sandy had put him there. And she knew Sandy had put him there because Jamison never went anywhere without his cocaine.

"Well, I'm here now, thanks to you." He wrapped his arm around her shoulder and squeezed. "You're a doll."

Daphne pretended to be delighted to be out to dinner with a man she wanted to dismember. She knew she was a good actress, but this evening's performance was strong even for her.

They ordered dinner and ate slowly. Daphne listened to Jamison tell stories of how he'd first met Dan just after college, how they'd run in the same circles for a while, trying to get their big breaks. How Dan's break had come first. How Dan had introduced Jamison to all the people Dan met, giving Jamison every opportunity Dan could.

That sort of loyalty and generosity sounded just like Dan.

Daphne wondered, if Jamison had made it first, would he

have done the same for Dan? Highly unlikely.

Throughout the meal, Daphne ensured Jamison's cocktail glass was never empty. She listened carefully, growing more and more satisfied as his words began to slur. When he stood to use the restroom and almost stumbled, she smiled to herself.

Around seven o'clock, it was time for the next part of her plan.

They were drinking one more round of drinks. "I have an idea," Daphne said. "Let's drive up on Mulholland. Say goodbye to Dan up there. I think he would have liked that. You know, because it's poetic."

"I don't think I can drive on Mulholland, babe. I need to stick to straighter roads."

That Jamison was considering driving at all made her want to strangle him. But his words were just the excuse she was hoping for. "That's OK," she said. "We'll take my car. Then I'll bring you back here, and you can head home. It's even better this way. We can be together."

When she said they could be together, Jamison's eyes got hot. He was thinking what Daphne wanted him to think. Her lure was set strong.

They waited at the valet stand for Daphne's car, then climbed in together. She silenced her phone and put it in its usual spot in the cup-holder. The screen kept flashing.

"Popular girl." Jamison gestured at her phone.

"I am." She had a feeling that by this point her note had elicited some reactions. She considered turning off the phone entirely but opted against it.

"Why don't you put yours there too," she said. "That way we'll have no distractions."

Jamison fished his cell phone from his pocket and set it next to hers in the cup-holder. Then he placed his hand on her leather-clad thigh. She gritted her teeth and forced a smile at the intimate touch.

She drove up the 405 to Mulholland Drive, then headed east along the ridge. She drove up into the hills just as the sun was setting, glancing to her right for the perfect place to park. When she found it, she pulled the car onto the side of the road and killed the engine.

"Why are we stopping here?" Jamison asked.

"I thought we could look at the view."

"Isn't there an official overlook up ahead?"

There was an official overlook up ahead, but Daphne couldn't execute her plan in a fenced-in public location. And she couldn't risk having witnesses.

"I don't want to be around tourists," she said. "Aren't tourists the worst?"

"Yeah, they're awful." He nodded with her.

"I want to be alone with you when we think about Dan." She gave him her best smile. "Or maybe you could help me forget him." She dipped her chin and looked up at him, giving him her most entrancing look, the one she knew he couldn't resist.

Because no one could.

Jamison hopped out of the car and followed her to the edge of the road. Their feet nudged the steep drop-off. Gravel fell into the shadows below.

"Careful, babe." He wrapped an arm around her waist, nuzzling her neck. She let him hold her for a moment, letting him get his fill.

"I'm chilly," she said. "Wait here. I have a jacket in the car."

She stepped back from him. Time slowed.

He stood at the edge of the cliff, staring at the lights of the city spread below them like fireworks. His stance was wide and unsteady.

Here was the man who'd ripped Carrie's dress from her body. Who'd chased her from his house in the middle of the night. Whom Dan had to rescue Carrie from. And Dan had died for it.

If Daphne were chaos itself, Jamison was the man who triggered these particular tragedies.

And he was standing, drunk and likely high, on the edge of a cliff.

And she was standing right behind him.

☙❧

Around six-thirty, Timmy and Greta had arrived back from the resort in Santa Barbara County. They'd come straight to Daphne's home. According to Sandy, Sandy and Marlon had arrived at Daphne's apartment in record time, because Marlon finally let Sandy drive at a normal speed. Greta would have laughed if she weren't so worried about Daphne.

When they'd first arrived, Greta had read the note Miranda had found.

Now the note lay on the coffee table. Marlon and Miranda sat on the lifeboat. Timmy sat on a kitchen chair pulled up next to the others. Greta stood near the kitchen, listening to them speculate about where Daphne had gone. They were all taking turns calling Daphne and sending her texts, hoping she'd answer or reply. So far, nothing.

Sandy had been on the phone since their arrival, but no one was sure whom he was talking to, and he wouldn't say.

It was now after seven o'clock, and they still knew nothing.

"It's obvious she's taken herself out of the picture." Marlon sounded shattered. "I pushed her away."

"Daphne isn't suicidal," said Timmy. "Even when she hates herself. She lashes outward, not inward. It's super charming."

Greta wanted to laugh at that one.

"The cops are looking for her plates," Sandy said. "And no I won't tell you how I pulled that off." He was looking at Miranda when he said the last part.

"Did anyone think maybe she doesn't want to be found?" said Miranda. "Maybe we should let her go?"

Marlon and Timmy looked at her like she was crazy. Sandy gave her a small smile.

Finally, Greta spoke. "She doesn't want to be found." She nodded at Miranda. "And she does lash outward." She nodded at Timmy. "And you did push her away." She nodded at Marlon. "But if she's lashing outward, and she was pushed away—"

"Shit," said Sandy.

"Call him," Greta said. "Make up some nonsense about a project."

Sandy made a call, then hung up. "Voicemail. I'll try again." He dialed, leaving the room.

"Who's he calling?" Marlon asked.

"Jamison." Timmy spoke this time. "Daphne went after Jamison by herself."

Greta turned to Marlon, and for the first time, he saw no friendliness in her green eyes. He saw no emotion at all. At the moment, her resemblance to her father was uncanny. "If anything happens to her because of you, I will never forgive you."

Sandy reentered the room, hanging up his phone. "I left him a B.S. message about a pilot I'm working on. If he gets the message, he'll call me."

"Thanks, Sandy," Greta said.

Miranda, who had been oddly quiet, spoke up. "Daphne's not exactly going to go over to Jamison's house with a gun. She's not an idiot." She paused, thoughtful. "She'd have to coax him out, convince him to come to her. What does she have that he doesn't have?"

"Real friends," said Greta.

"A career," said Marlon.

"Access," said Sandy. "I banned him from Rivet. And she knows it. We had a long, hilarious chat about 'known cokeheads' one night."

"It's worth a try," Marlon said. "I'll call over there." He dialed and asked to speak with the host. His face brightened during the conversation, then he hung up. "She was there. And she was with a guy no one knew. They left together about twenty minutes ago in her car. The guy left his car there. The valet chief is going to text me when he finds out who the car belongs to." At that moment, Marlon's phone beeped. He held it up for all to see. Jamison's name was on the message.

"My turn," Greta said, picking up her phone to send a message.

≈

It had not been Daphne's plan to push Jamison off the cliff. No. She'd planned to leave him up on Mulholland that night, sans cell phone, to let him know what it felt like to be alone and scared on the side of the road. To feel, in just one small way, some of the terror Carrie had felt. And to hopefully get him in a bit of trouble.

But right then, standing behind him, she pictured her hands on his back, his feet slipping on the sandy ground, his body falling into the darkness.

The plan would work. His intoxication. His history of drug use. The unprotected overlook. It would be so easy to say he simply fell.

She would report the fall to the police. She would be horrified, and she would be sad. It would be a tragedy. Perhaps he was feeling the loss of his best friend, and he was taking unnecessary risks. She'd tried to save him, she would say. The police would believe her. Of course they would.

One push.

One push and there would be no more Carries in the bathroom. No more Carries who hadn't been able to fight Jamison off.

One push and she would report his death. And then, once the furor died down, she would disappear. She would sell her condo and take her savings and disappear forever to a place where she would hurt no one ever again.

But what would one push do to her?

What would it do to Daphne to become one of the monsters?

She took one step back from him. Then another. Then she turned.

She dashed to her car. She jumped in, locking the doors. She grasped the steering wheel with both hands and rested her head there. She wept, then. Suddenly, Jamison was trying to open the passenger door. He was banging on the glass. He was yelling.

"Let me in! What the fuck, Daphne!"

Suddenly, she wasn't weeping any more.

She could speak plainly, without a hitch in her voice.

She cracked the passenger-side window so he could hear her. She held up his cell phone so he could see it, then dropped it on the seat next to her.

"Get back to town on your own, you asshole."

She threw her car into first and sped off, tossing gravel behind her.

Twenty-one

About three miles down the road, Daphne got out of her car. She placed Jamison's cell phone behind the rear wheel of her car, then backed over it. She picked up the crushed device and tossed it from the cliff. Climbing back into her car, she picked up her own phone and dialed 911. The operator answered.

In her very best North Carolina accent, Daphne spoke. "Hi," she said, her tone frightened. "I'm up here with my husband and kids on Mulholland Drive. We were at a scenic overlook and saw a man selling drugs! He had cocaine or heroin—it was some kinda white powder."

"Can you provide a physical description?"

Daphne described Jamison in detail. "When he saw us he started running west." She gave his approximate location. Then she smiled.

After she hung up, she glanced at her phone. It was flashing with unread text messages. She read the most recent one.

It was from Greta.

For an instant Daphne was thrown back to five years ago, to another night, when she stood on another, metaphorical cliff—but no. She was here, in her car, and Greta was trying to reach her.

Greta was trying to save her.

"That was a really stupid note you left," Greta's text message said. Daphne laughed. Of course Greta would find the note stupid.

"Need you to come back now. Going to have brunch with my dad tomorrow. Need you there."

Before she'd left her apartment, Daphne had packed a suitcase full of clothes, her toiletries and her laptop. She had enough of her things that she could disappear for a while if she wanted to. And part of her really wanted to.

And here was Greta, yanking her back.

Daphne felt relief. She dialed Greta.

"You ready to come home now?" Greta asked.

"I almost did something terrible."

"Did you do it?"

Daphne paused. Did she do it? She didn't push him, no. But she'd come so close. What was the difference, in the end?

"I didn't do the thing I wanted to do," Daphne said. "No. I didn't do it."

She heard Greta exhale. "Good. I'm glad. Where can I meet you?"

"I'm up on Mulholland of all places."

"So just come home. We're all at your house."

"Who's there?" Daphne asked, surprised.

"Me and Timmy, Miranda, and Sandy and Marlon."

All five of them, at her house, looking for her? Why? How? For a moment, she felt astonished they'd all come for her.

But why was she astonished? Hadn't she spent all of these years building herself a new family? Why *wouldn't* they come for her?

Wouldn't she do the same for them?

Something broke free in the back of her mind. An idea that perhaps she'd gotten something very, very wrong.

"I, um, can't go back that way."

No, back that way was Jamison and perhaps the police.

"We can all head to Sandy's house," Greta said. "You can take Mulholland to Laurel Canyon and meet us there."

"When I get there, can you and I talk first? Somewhere

alone?"

"I'll make that happen," Greta reassured her. "Head to Sandy's, and I'll meet you outside."

"You're having brunch with your dad tomorrow? Aren't you supposed to be on your honeymoon?"

"Since we came back early, I figured I'd get it over with. Seemed practical."

"Of course." Daphne smiled to herself. Oh, Greta. Always practical.

"You'll come?" Greta sounded almost nervous.

"I'll do anything for you, Greta. You know that."

Daphne drove slowly. She wanted to give her friends a chance to beat her to Sandy's house. She wanted Greta to be waiting outside for her when she arrived.

If Daphne arrived first, she might lose her nerve and consider taking off again.

As she drove, she thought about Jamison. What Jamison had done to Carrie and what he'd tried to do to Carrie were both horrific acts. But what Daphne had considered doing to Jamison was just as horrific.

Tonight, she hadn't plotted a murder. But then she'd stood there behind him, and she'd thought about it. For a minute, or even longer, she'd thought about pushing him to his death.

How could she come back from that?

How could she be loved after that?

She turned down the hill onto Laurel Canyon and rode the curves until she reached the turn onto Sandy's street. His driveway gates were open, and she saw multiple cars in front of his house. Timmy's Audi wagon. Sandy's Aston Martin. And another car she didn't recognize, a Camry, she thought, with someone sitting in the driver's seat talking on the phone.

She pulled into the driveway, but she continued down to the garage. She parked in front of the second bay, blocking in Marlon's car-in-progress. By the time she got out of her car, Greta was strolling up to her.

Daphne threw her arms around Greta, and Greta threw her arms around Daphne, and for a moment, everything felt right.

"Where's Jamison?" Greta asked.

"How did you know?"

"Long story, and I'll tell you later."

"I almost killed him." Reality crashing into her. "He stood on a cliff-side, and I almost pushed him off."

"What do you mean almost?"

"I thought about doing it. I stood behind him and thought about it."

Greta looked at Daphne with consideration. "But that wasn't your plan tonight, was it."

Greta's words weren't a question.

"No," Daphne said. "Pushing him wasn't my plan."

Daphne explained her plan to Greta, every detail, how she'd convinced Jamison to put his phone next to hers in the cup-holder, how she'd left him there on that dark, lonely road. How she'd called the police to come find him and the stash of cocaine she was certain he had, because, according to Sandy, he always had one.

"You should have taken his shoes too," Greta said. "Then it would have been perfect retribution."

"You are not helping." Daphne smiled.

"Where were you going to go, after?"

"I don't know. I brought enough stuff to keep me going for a while without having to spend much money except for food and a place to sleep."

Daphne turned from Greta then, unable to face the friend she'd almost abandoned. She stared at Sandy's small forest.

But Greta knew what Daphne was thinking. Of course she did. Greta always knew. It was why Daphne loved her.

"Why leave, Daphne? I need you."

"I did a cost-benefit analysis. And the costs of having me around just seemed too high."

"Miranda told me how you blamed yourself for the car wreck. I think she called you, let me get this right, an 'arrogant asshole.'"

"Of course I blame myself! Dan only invited Carrie to that party because of me."

"That might be part of the reason, but it wasn't the only reason. She is kind of hot."

"You know what I mean, Greta. You of all people. By introducing Carrie to Dan, I pushed her in front of a moving bus."

"No." Greta sounded annoyed, even angry. "No. You do not understand the basic laws of cause and effect."

"Sure I do."

"And your lack of understanding is making you hurt everyone—and I mean everyone—who cares about you."

Daphne leaned against her car, stifling an eye roll.

Greta glared at her. "You think that you do one small thing, like introduce two humans to each other, and then, because of that one small thing, those humans are doomed. Right? Isn't that what you think?"

"Yes." That was exactly what she thought.

"But there are too many variables. Too much life for that kind of strict determinism."

Daphne chewed her thumbnail. "I see what you're saying. But I'm not sure I believe you."

"This is how chaos works, Daphne. Say you are indeed an initial condition, fine. The effects that come after you can't be linear. Lightning doesn't travel in a straight line."

"No. It just follows me around."

"But it doesn't. You introduced Carrie to Dan, but after that, what happened was out of your hands."

"Bad things keep happening to people I love, Greta. You can't deny that."

"What you're saying is that you deserve to be alone." Greta grabbed hold of Daphne's shoulders and looked her in the eyes. "You're looking for a reason to punish yourself."

Daphne nodded. Greta's words made sense. "I think I am. I drove my family away. I nearly drove you away. I drove Marlon away." She laughed, but even to her own ears the laughter sounded broken. "Every time I slept with another guy, I think I was hoping Dan would find out, and I would drive him away too."

"But why, Daphne? So many people love you. So many people want to love you."

"I told Marlon about what my father did to me."

Greta's mouth rounded into a silent O.

"I think something broke in me when I was a kid that never quite healed."

Daphne had told her childhood secret to Greta back when they were in college, the horrible thing her father had done to her, the no-longer-secret event that had driven her mother and sisters from her.

The event that, perhaps, had damaged Daphne more than she'd thought it had. When a guest at her father's motel had ripped her child's body in half and how her father had let him. Maybe she was still ripped in half.

What was a girl's body worth? Five hundred dollars? A thousand? More? Or was it worth nothing?

Did she deserve to suffer? Perhaps. But Carrie didn't. All of the Carries, the Gretas. They didn't.

Why had Daphne chosen to move to a place and to work in an industry where a woman's body was forever in a transaction? She could never escape. No wonder she was the source of so much chaos. She didn't even realize how much pain she carried in her all the time. How much that pain drove her.

"I can't go in that house," Daphne whispered.

"Why not?" Greta asked. "Everyone is waiting for you. Everyone helped find you. They were worried because they care."

"It's not enough." It wasn't. She was too broken to be in their perfect world. She thought of Greta and Timmy standing under their arbor yesterday, the perfect handmade arbor draped in jasmine. And thinking of the arbor made her think of Marlon and Carrie.

There was no way she was going into the house.

"Fine," Greta said. "It's your call. Can I come visit you on your deserted island?"

"You'll let me go?"

"You're a grown-up. I just want to know if I can visit. Timmy thinks we should have kids, and I thought you might like to see them."

"You want to have kids?" Daphne asked, incredulous.

"Not right now. In a couple of years. Before I'm thirty. I'm reading the science on it."

Of course Greta was reading the science on it. For a split second, thinking of Greta with kids, Daphne felt overjoyed. Daphne would be the perfect aunt.

And then it hit her. "You're tricking me."

"I'm not lying to you."

"But you're throwing in my face what I'll miss if I leave."

"Of course I am. I don't want you to leave. But," Greta said, not allowing Daphne to interrupt, "there's more to it than that. I wanted to show where your conceited idea that you are the source of all the bad things goes awry in yet another way."

"Miranda called me conceited too."

"She's not wrong."

"She was really annoyed with me."

"I like her even more now than I did in college."

"Well, you've both changed a lot."

Greta smiled. "Let's say you do have some super power and can somehow determine the outcome of human relationships. Which you can't. But let's say you can. That means every outcome that occurs based on you setting things in motion is your fault, right? Isn't that what you're saying?"

"Yes? I think?" Greta made it sound so ridiculous.

"Bananas. But we'll go with it. Here's the thing, though. Why are you only taking the blame for the bad things that happen?"

"Because bad things keep happening?" Daphne said, uncertain.

"This is where what you are saying is making me fucking crazy!" Greta poked Daphne in the chest. "You want to have it both ways. The bad things are your fault. The good things just happen for no reason."

Suddenly, Daphne lost her temper. "Where's the good, Greta?"

"I know you're thinking about what happened to me," Greta said. "Don't tell me you're not. But look, even good things came out of that. Lots of good things. Look at where we are right now! We're standing in Sandy's driveway. Who could have predicted that? Timmy and I own Rivet. We're married. He wants to have kids—good lord! So many good things came out of one awful night—things that could never have been predicted, not by anyone."

"But you almost died."

"But I didn't. Also, I think my condition was a little overblown, actually."

"You looked like shit."

"I'm not saying it didn't hurt. But seriously, the concussion wasn't that bad."

"Dan did die," Daphne murmured.

"People die sometimes," Greta said. "Do you want to talk to Miranda about that and see what she has to say?" Greta held out her hand.

"Oh no. Let's not do that right now," Daphne said quickly. Miranda had seen a lot of death for someone her age. Too much.

Daphne stared at Greta's hand. Finally, she took it, and together they began the long climb up the driveway to Sandy's front door.

Greta opened the door, and Jodie and Foster trotted up and licked Daphne's hand. Seeing the dogs' round brown eyes, she almost started crying again.

Then she looked at her friends.

Sandy, Marlon, Timmy and Miranda were sitting around the coffee table. Miranda had a deck of cards in her hand. There was cash on the table.

"Miranda?" Daphne asked, scandalized.

"We're playing spades. None of them knew how. Can you believe it?"

"Seriously?" Daphne said. Behind her, she could hear Greta trying not to laugh.

"Well, we had to do something. They were all making me crazy with their manly pacing," Miranda said. "God. Back and forth. Back and forth."

"I do not pace," said Sandy.

"Correction. Timmy and Marlon were doing manly pacing. Sandy was lurking." Then she mumbled, "Vast improvement, dude."

Daphne saw Sandy smile. It seemed Sandy liked Miranda, sharp tongue and all.

Marlon rose, placing his hands on the back of his chair. He stared at her, hope on his face.

Sandy stood. "I'm exhausted. Lock up when you all leave, OK?" He headed into the kitchen toward the master suite.

"We have an annoying brunch to get ready for, Greta," Timmy said. "We should get home."

"See you in the morning?" Greta asked Daphne.

"I'll be there," Daphne said.

"You should all come," Greta said to Miranda and Marlon. "It'll make my dad extra uncomfortable. Bring Sandy too."

"I'm heading home too," Miranda said. "Well, to your home, Daph." She pocketed her winnings from the table. "John's taking me car shopping tomorrow. I'm going to have one last fling with this credit card."

"How are you getting home?" Daphne asked.

"We can drop you," Greta said.

"John's out in the driveway sitting in his car."

Daphne remembered the car she didn't recognize out in the driveway. She thought of the man waiting in the driver's seat. John seemed more than willing to do what it took to catch Miranda's attention.

"Don't worry," Miranda said to Daphne. "I'll have him drop me at the corner."

"Actually," Daphne said, "I don't mind if he sees you home. It's safer that way."

Miranda smiled then. "Message received."

Timmy and Greta left. Miranda left. And then Daphne was alone in the living room with Marlon. He remained on the far side of his chair, keeping the furniture between them. She felt like a great cat, and he the animal-tamer.

"What happened tonight?" he asked.

"I almost did a terrible thing," she said. "But then I didn't."

"But then you didn't."

"I thought about doing it. Part of me wanted to do it."

She told him about the cliff, and about Jamison, and about how long she stared at his back before running to her car.

"If the cops didn't find him, he's probably still up there."

Marlon smiled. "No one picks up random guys on Mulholland in the middle of the night. I feel super-duper bad for him."

"Poor guy." Daphne smiled too. "His feet are going to be really sore by the time he walks to a pay phone."

That's when Daphne noticed how badly her own feet were aching. She collapsed into a chair and removed her booties. "Oh shit." Spots of blood soaked through her socks.

"Daphne." Marlon rounded the chair. "What happened to you?"

He knelt in front of her, looking at her feet.

"I didn't have shoes on at the wreck. I didn't notice I was hurt, not till after." She looked to the side.

"Not till after what?"

"Not till after Dan died."

Marlon reached out and wrapped his hands around her calves. He was watching her carefully, waiting to see if she would protest, she figured. So she nodded, giving him permission to touch her.

He rolled her socks from her feet, revealing even bloodier bandages. He looked up at her. "Jesus, Daphne."

He scooped her into his arms and carried her down the hall toward the guest rooms. They entered the room where Daphne had dressed with Greta for the wedding just the day before. He set her on the edge of the bed. "Don't move."

He disappeared into the bathroom, and she heard water start running in the tub. Then he came back to her. "I'm getting the first aid kit from the kitchen. Don't move."

"You told me that already!" she yelled after him.

He came back with a large, yellow toolbox and opened it on the bed next to her. He extracted bandages, tape and scissors, placing each on the bed. He also had damp, dark brown towels. Using the scissors, he snipped the bloody bandages from her feet and tossed them in the trash. He blotted her feet with a towel, removing a lot of the caked-on blood.

Then he eyed her tight leather pants.

"I don't suppose you can roll those up," he said.

"Nope."

"We'll have to wrap a towel around your waist. Hang on."

He returned with a plush white bath towel from the bathroom.

"I think I'll need help getting out of these," she said, gesturing at her leather-clad legs. "Usually I use my feet to pull them off."

Marlon swallowed hard. She smiled.

"Here, I'll unzip them." She leaned back on her elbows and unclipped the top of her pants, pulling down the zipper. "Hand me the towel." She took the towel from him, draping it over her waist down to mid-thigh. "Now, you grab each ankle and pull. And don't worry. They're supposed to be tight."

Marlon looked like he'd eaten a lemon. Daphne felt a small bit of delight.

He knelt in front of her, gripping the ankle opening of one leg and slowly tugging the pant leg down. Then he switched legs and did the same. He switched back and forth, moving nearly in slow motion, until he'd worked the pants past her hips and to her knees. Finally, he grabbed the waistband and pulled the pants the rest of the way off. He held them in his hands for a moment before draping them on a chair.

"Thank you," she said. "I wouldn't have been able to do that and stay off my feet."

"Stop talking." Marlon lifted her in his arms again. "I can barely think."

Daphne tucked her face in his neck and laughed.

Instead of setting her on the cold edge of the bathtub like she'd expected him to do, he held her in his lap while she soaked her feet in the warm, soapy water. She leaned against his chest. The water turned pink as the blood rinsed off, and the warmth soothed her. After a few minutes, he set her down on the closed toilet lid and used another one of the brown towels to dry her feet. Then he rewrapped each foot in a bandage. She watched the top of his head as he worked, his brow wrinkled in concentration. She reached out and ran her fingers through his hair.

"Carrie's mad at me too, you know," she said.

"What for?" He came to his feet.

"She said you and I were conspiring not to allow her to

make her own mistakes."

"That sounds about right."

Daphne felt the familiar feelings of guilt well up inside of her. Then she remembered Greta's lecture and shoved the feelings away.

No more.

"You weren't a rebound." She looked up at him from her seat on the closed toilet lid.

"I don't blame you for what happened," he said, kneeling in front of her. "At all."

"I get it," Daphne said. "When your worst nightmare comes true, you need someone to blame it on. You and I both blamed me."

He picked her up in his arms again. This time, he put a small kiss on her lips. Then he reentered the guest room and placed her on the bed. She lay back against the pillows.

He backed away from her, stopping once he reached the closed bedroom door. He leaned against it. "You should stay here tonight. Sandy won't mind of course. In fact, he'd probably prefer it."

"What would you prefer?"

"What would I prefer?" He smiled sadly. "Something I could not possibly ask of you."

"Then I'll have to ask it of you." She held out her hand to him.

"Daphne—after how awful I acted?"

"You were upset. I forgive you."

He crossed the room and sat by her on the bed. He caught the end of her towel skirt with his fingertip.

"We're like the opposite sides of a coin," he said. "You're constantly afraid you'll hurt the people you care about, and I'm constantly afraid the people I care about will be hurt."

"Wise observation."

"What a terrible way to live." He shook his head.

"Also wise."

He lay down behind her on the bed, putting his arm around her, pulling her close. "Do you think we can change?"

"Greta seems to think so," Daphne said. "She wouldn't call it change, so much, as understanding what forces are acting in the background. I think I've figured some things out."

"This car wreck was the first time since my mom died that anyone close to me has been in danger. It was my first test. I think I failed." He rested his chin on her head.

"Really?" Daphne said, placing her hands on his, pulling their bodies even closer together. "We're here, aren't we? I'd say we passed."

She rolled to face him, putting her hand on his cheek.

"Sandy says I'm in love with you." Marlon tugged on her ponytail.

"Miranda says I'm in love with you."

At her words, Marlon's gray eyes darkened. "Miranda's a little scary, but she is very smart."

"She's actually very scary, but you don't know her well yet."

"Yet?"

"I think she's going to move in with me, so you'll being seeing more of her."

"Daphne, you make me want to buy a car."

"Can I come write on your deck?"

She reached for him as he reached for her, their arms moving fast, her towel falling away, their lips meeting hard. She could feel the calluses on his fingertips as his hands reached under her sweater, and she never wanted to be touched by smooth hands again.

Acknowledgements

This book, like any book, could not have been written without the support of many people.

Thank you to my publisher, Velvet Morning Press, who believed enough in my first book, *Entanglement*, to let me write a series.

Thank you to my fellow authors and beta readers who read the drafts of this book: Chris Adigun, Lisa Cooper Ellison, Lauren Faulkenberry, Jordynn Jack and Janet Linger.

Thank you to my supportive writing collective, the Tall Poppy Writers, and our founder, Ann Garvin.

Thank you to the local coffee shops that provide great spaces to write: La Vita Dolce, Market Street Coffee, Jessee's, and lately, Gray Squirrel Coffee Company.

Thank you to my parents, who have embraced my career as a writer with alacrity.

Thank you to my husband, who never acts surprised when my attempts turn into successes. And thank you to my kiddos, who let me read my favorite childhood stories to them every night.

About the Author

Katie enjoys her three professions—novelist, freelance journalist, and lawyer—for one reason: her love of the written word. Fiction or nonfiction, Katie thrives on putting thoughts to paper and sharing them with the world. She lives in Chapel Hill, North Carolina, where the energy of the campus and cafés inspires her to keep writing.

Katie hopes you enjoyed *Chasing Chaos*. If you did, please consider leaving a review on Amazon. Even a few sentences can help future readers decide to pick up the book.

Check out the rest of the Entanglement series:

Entanglement: Greta follows her best friend, Daphne, to LA after college, and the complicated friendship puts Greta in the path of a dangerous man. Can she survive? Forgive?

Love & Entropy: A tension-filled weekend at a lake house will change lives forever in this prequel to *Entanglement*.

For more on Katie, check out KatieRoseGuestPryal.com. Or drop her a line at katie@katieroseguestpryal.com.

Read on for a sneak peek at *Entanglement*…

Go for a ride in this novelette…

Nice Wheels

Barbara, a medical resident, lost her husband when his plane was shot down by enemy fire in Afghanistan. She wonders if she will ever love again, feel warm again. She freezes out Chris, a fellow resident at the hospital who also has a difficult past. But Chris isn't easily deterred. As a second loss tears at Barbara's heart, will Chris be the one to break down the barrier?

Get it for free! Join Katie's new release mailing list and she'll send you a free ecopy of *Nice Wheels*. http://bit.ly/pryalnews.

Entanglement

a novel

KATIE ROSE GUEST PRYAL

One

Los Angeles, December 1999

From her hospital bed, Greta considers the single flickering fluorescent tube behind the translucent ceiling panel. She imagines the electricity coursing through, the mercury atoms generating invisible ultraviolet light. Phosphorescence. Even though she can't see the mercury, she knows it is there, and knowing gives her comfort. At least the elements are still behaving as they should.

Nothing else is. Everything she could count on has been smashed.

Everyone she's counted on has betrayed her.

But she won't cry any more. She did that for a while tonight, but the nurses took turns watching her through the narrow glass of her door, curious and prying. So she stopped crying. She couldn't bear them.

The ICU bustles. The wall clock indicates that the hour is three o'clock, and the darkness outside her window indicates that the time is antemeridian. Next to her, a morphine-derivative drip beeps every sixty seconds. She supposes the doctors selected this particular class of painkiller because it doesn't have blood thinning properties. Properties that would be deadly given the bruising on her brain.

Her father would be happy. She can hear him now: *Never sacrifice your genius for a little pain.*

She blinks once to clear her vision, to refocus.

She knows she probably won't die of her head injury, although she had trouble maintaining consciousness when she first awoke twenty-four hours ago.

A concussion, the doctor said. *You're out of the dark, but this is going to hurt like hell.*

She appreciated his honesty. It seemed to be in short supply in her life.

The hospital reminds Greta of her daily vigils at her dying mother's bedside when she was in high school. She glances at the empty chair next to the bed, grateful no one sits there out of obligation or duty. Marcellus, her landlord, who came with her to the hospital, left soon after the doctors whisked her into radiology. Even Daphne and Timmy have left, sent away by Greta after she woke.

She couldn't stand to see their guilty faces.

೪-ৎৎ

Timmy arrived first, waiting for her when she opened her eyes, his face covered in love and pain.

"Greta," he said. "What happened? Who did this?"

She didn't tell him. She wasn't sure why. She knew who attacked her. After all, she spoke with the man before turning her back on him, before he struck her.

But something in the tone of Timmy's voice made Greta hold back. He looked guilty for some reason, as though he'd been the one holding the weapon.

And her instincts were indeed right. He did feel guilty. Although Greta didn't believe in sixth senses or ESP, she knew that humans—like any animals—could perceive unconsciously more than they could perceive consciously, and that these unconscious perceptions could add up to a split-second conclusion. And the conclusion she drew when she saw Timmy was that he'd done something to hurt her.

Had he ever.

Daphne arrived later, after Greta had sent Timmy away. Daphne, supremely perceptive, knew she was in trouble before Greta had said anything at all. Daphne also knew there was nothing she could do to earn Greta's forgiveness.

Greta had always had a hard time forgiving people.

"I'll go now," Daphne said.

Greta nodded in assent.

"I'll love you forever, Greta." Daphne's voice broke. "You are my family."

Greta turned away. Daphne was her family, too. And now she knew what family meant to Daphne.

ॐ

Greta shuts her eyes and tries to place the events of the past thirty hours in chronological order. Without this deliberate effort, the faces and places merge and swirl, and causation gets lost in the muck of it. It's really important to her that the causes are clear. As clear as the effects.

The effects: lying in a hospital bed in the ICU with a dislocated shoulder, a concussion covered by a sutured scalp, and a large hematoma on her face.

The causes: That's what she's trying to work out. She's always believed that with enough application of concentration, she could solve even the most complicated equations.

She admits to herself that this time she might be stumped.

She thinks of Timmy once more, of the pain on his face while he sat in that plastic chair.

She thinks of Daphne sitting by her side, reaching out for Greta's I.V.-splintered hand while Greta turned away.

Greta wonders if the rest of her might splinter as well, into shards of energy, into the particles that compose her body, until there's nothing left of her on those white sheets.

She'd be free.

She clamps a lid on her wonderings and reaches for her cell phone. She needs a strategy, not a reverie. She needs to make sure she'll be safe: from the police officer sitting outside her door. From Daphne and Timmy. And from the man who might still want to hurt her.

She presses the telephone buttons with one hand. She listens for the ring and then the voice.

Find out what happens next... Buy *Entanglement* today!

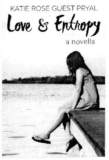

CPSIA information can be obtained at www.ICGtesting.com
Printed in the USA
LVOW08s2206020616

490959LV00007B/710/P